SPIN MOVE

Published by Thomas & Mercer, Seattle

www.apub.com

Amazon, the Amazon logo, and Thomas & Mercer are trademarks of Amazon.com, Inc., or its affiliates.

ISBN-13: 9781477827277
ISBN-10: 1477827277

Cover design by Cyanotype Book Architects

Library of Congress Control Number: 2014948610

Printed in the United States of America

SPIN MOVE

A WHITE COLLAR CRIME THRILLER BY

DAVID
LENDER

THOMAS & MERCER

ALSO BY DAVID LENDER

Sasha Del Mira Thrillers
Trojan Horse
Sasha Returns (A Short Story)
Arab Summer

White Collar Crime Thrillers
Bull Street
Rudiger Stories (A Collection of Short
Stories—Also Available Individually)
Mickey Outside

Other Thrillers
The Gravy Train
Vaccine Nation

ACKNOWLEDGMENTS

Thank you to Cindy Begin and Manette for being my first draft readers and critics, and to Manette for your love and support throughout the process. Thank you to David J. Bikoff, MD, PA, FACS, for your assistance with the medical aspects of the manuscript, and for some great catches in your other comments and critiques.

Thank you to David Downing for proposing the title, and for another great editing job. Your ideas and comments were, again, consistently on point. You're a pleasure to work with.

Thank you to Robin Cruise for your laser-like focus and excellent suggestions in your copyediting.

And thank you again to the team at Amazon Publishing.

For Styles

CHAPTER 1

John Rudiger sat at his usual table in the Beach Grill Restaurant beside the pool at the Blue Moon Hotel in Antigua, his lunch in front of him. He looked off in the distance at his house, three stories of glass, marble and steel that had taken two years and $5 million to build into the rocky hill at the end of Blue Moon Bay. He scanned the curve of the bay, the brilliant blue of the Caribbean, the salt-white sand of the beach. *I never get tired of it,* he thought, and then the moment was shattered as his gaze drifted back to Senior Sgt. Carlen Isaacs of the Royal Police Force of Antigua and Barbuda, seated before him.

"Is John Rudiger's mind wandering?" Isaacs said.

Rudiger took off his sunglasses and leaned forward, staring directly into Isaacs' face. Rudiger said, "No, I was intentionally not paying attention. I figured if I didn't respond you might just get up and leave me in peace with my lunch."

Isaacs said, "This important discussion. To you and Carlen Isaacs."

Rudiger didn't answer. He glanced yet again at the young mother reading on a lounge chair on the pool apron, her toddler son next to her fidgeting, ready to make a break for it.

Isaacs said, "You don't do nothin', and Carlen Isaacs tellin' you, there be trouble. For you. This U.S. Attorney in New York,

Charles Holden, must've closed big case and now has time on his hands. Never seem to forget about you. Every year, two years—"

"I know. He sends his people down here, and they always go home with nothing."

"But you don't do right thing, pretty soon one come down here and he don't go home with nothin'. He go home with John Rudiger. Extradited." Isaacs put his elbows on the table and leaned forward at Rudiger. "And he especially pissed off about this Katie girl he send last time."

Rudiger shrugged. "Nothing I can do about that."

"Maybe not, but Holden, he track her to Cape Verde, see she got big house now, pay lots of money to doctors for her daddy, figure you gave money to her when she come down here and then you two go back to New York and get it where you hid it."

So how much is this going to cost me? Rudiger figured he'd find out soon enough. Isaacs never took too long to get to the punch line. He looked back at the mother and son next to the pool just as the boy scooted out of her grasp toward the pool. Rudiger came half out of his seat, then relaxed as one of the waiters grabbed the child and delivered him into his mother's arms.

Oblivious to the poolside near-drama, Isaacs said, "So you need to protect youself, and only way to do that is for Carlen Isaacs to protect you."

"Why would I need you to do that? I'm an Antiguan citizen with a birth certificate, a public health card and a passport to prove it. John Rudiger. Born and raised here."

Isaacs narrowed his eyes. "New identity Carlen Isaacs arrange for you."

"It was Commissioner Desmond Browne. You just drove me back and forth to get my documents. Remember?"

Isaacs leaned back in his chair. "Even though Commissioner Browne, he retire, he still need money. All he got is pension—"

"I'm his pension," Rudiger said.

"—and Carlen Isaacs got lots of responsibilities, need to take care of family."

Rudiger waited.

Isaacs looked at Rudiger for a long moment, then said, "Commissioner Browne need another $5,000 per month. And for Carlen Isaacs, $2,000 more per month."

"You must have a new mistress or something."

"Carlen Isaacs got lots of responsibilities."

"This is the second time you've hit me up in a year. Don't press your luck."

"You don't pay, Carlen Isaacs get you sent back."

"You get me sent back and who's gonna pay?"

Isaacs didn't respond, so Rudiger said, "And where's the money going? Maybe you take the extra $5,000 in Commissioner Browne's envelope and give him your $2,000."

"You ought to be careful how you talk. Carlen Isaacs Senior Sgt. now, important man with influence. Even if you don't get sent back, bad things could happen to you."

Rudiger shifted his gaze off to his house again. He put his sunglasses on again, then turned to look back at Isaacs. He didn't want to even give him the satisfaction of nodding his agreement. After a moment he said, "It'll be in the drop at the beginning of next month."

Isaacs said, "No. Starting today."

"I said beginning of next month." Rudiger reached forward and unfurled his napkin, placed it in his lap. "Now how about you get out of here so I can eat my lunch?"

Rudiger watched Isaacs get up and saunter away. He now had trouble believing he'd initially felt sorry for Isaacs when Rudiger first arrived in Antigua. Isaacs then a hapless patrolman, a toady who did all Commissioner Browne's dirty jobs. Harried, his superiors always pushing him around, dark semicircles of perspiration under the armpits of his pastel-green uniform. But today Isaacs was almost as insufferably self-important as Browne had been. And harder to deal with. It always amazed Rudiger that Isaacs' lifeless eyes weren't a pretense at trying to play dumber than he really was.

After Isaacs left, Rudiger did the math. Former Royal Police Commissioner Browne, now $17,000 a month. The minister of public health, who'd issued his bogus birth certificate and public health card, $6,000 a month. The superintendent of schools in the Saint George Parish who'd falsified his grammar school records, $3,000 a month. Two low-level clerks at the Department of Motor Vehicles and the public registrar's office who'd falsified his driver's license and passport, $1,000 a month. Current Royal Police Commissioner Benjamin, $12,000 a month. And now Senior Sgt. Isaacs, $7,000 a month. When he first came here 11 years ago, his all-in cost was $50,000 a year. Now it was over $500,000 and it only promised to get worse. Whatever happened to the good old days when a fugitive financier could bribe a bunch of local officials with one-time payments?

A year ago he'd already been thinking of moving someplace that didn't have an extradition treaty with the U.S. The Cape Verde Islands, another paradise off the coast of Africa. Perfect weather, 70s to 80s all year. Beautiful beaches. And Charlie Holden couldn't touch him. In fact, he was the one who mentioned Cape Verde to Katie during their business deal-turned-tryst in New York.

Just thinking about Katie made him smile. The strawberry blonde, petite, with the body as tight as a drum in the navy-blue bathing suit and the flush on her chest. She'd pitched him within a minute of meeting him at the very table where he now sat. She'd admitted that she worked for Charlie Holden in the U.S. Attorney's Office in New York. He'd sent her down there to finally get enough to prove Rudiger was really Walter Conklin and extradite him to the U.S. to stand trial for embezzling half a billion dollars from his hedge fund.

What a joke. *Half a billion dollars, my ass.*

Over $400 million of that had been market losses after he'd fled New York and left his fund unmanaged while the markets were in free fall. Fled because his CFO, who he learned too late had been cooking his fund's books, had panicked, run to the Feds and blamed it all on Rudiger. Rudiger had taken $40 million with him, first heading to Brazil for weight loss and plastic surgery, then ultimately to get lost here in Antigua. Before he ran he hadn't had time to retrieve $50 million in bearer bonds he'd stashed in a safe deposit box in a JPMorgan Chase bank branch on Pine Street in downtown New York.

That was Katie's pitch. She'd said everyone in Holden's office knew about the box, but because they'd uncovered its whereabouts in an improper search, no judge would give them a warrant to open it themselves. Katie had proposed she act as Rudiger's ex-wife, the only other person with signature authority and a key to the box. She said if he tried to go in himself, Charlie's guys would pounce on him. So she'd go in disguised as Angela Conklin and get the bonds for a $10 million cut. They'd rehearsed it, done a dry run, and then Katie walked into the bank branch to close the deal. But he'd never seen her come out again. After waiting around for three or four days, he'd finally flown back to Antigua.

A week later a DHL package from a hotel in Cape Verde arrived with a note saying *Thanks, partner. Good luck.* Inside the envelope were $10 million in bearer bonds.

That made him smile again. He remembered telling her that he'd burned through all but $2 million of his $40 million. That if he had it to do over again, he'd figure out a way to make it work over the long haul on only $10 million. She'd taken him at his word.

But no matter how he looked at it, or how fond he was of her, Katie owed him $30 million. And an apology. The image of her in her navy-blue bathing suit came back to him. And then the image of her taking off that navy-blue bathing suit and showing him how energetic a 30-something Irish girl from Brooklyn could be in the sack.

Thinking about Katie, and with the way things were going around here, maybe it was time to start thinking about Cape Verde again.

———

Katie Dolan walked down the stairs to the first floor of her house on the island of Boa Vista in Cape Verde, her suitcase in hand. It was ten minutes before her car to Rabil Airport was scheduled to arrive; she wanted to check in on Daddy before she left.

As she reached the end of the stairwell, she could see the lights dancing from the television, hear the sound turned down low. Daddy had obviously fallen asleep in front of it again. She entered the first-floor great room, the floor-to-ceiling sliding doors open to the cool air and sound of the surf on Chaves Beach. She now saw Daddy asleep in his Barcalounger in front of the Vizio LCD. She'd had the 70-inch screen mounted on the wall on the other side of the room to keep from obstructing his view of the ocean in the rare moments his eyes weren't glued to it.

She approached him. His deep breathing almost masked the hum of the top-of-the-line DeVilbiss 525DS oxygen concentrator on the floor beside him. Standing over him, she heard the hiss of the oxygen coming out of the prongs hooked under his nostrils. She kissed him on the forehead, then muted the TV sound.

He didn't wake up.

She started across the floor toward the sliding door to the carport, then heard Styles' tail thumping on the sofa. She walked over and stroked the pitbull's head and the thumping accelerated.

"Go back to sleep, little man," she whispered.

Katie rubbed his belly for a moment, then leaned over and kissed one of his ears.

She walked out the door and waited in the breeze off the ocean, the smell of salt in the air, daylight just beginning to show on the horizon. Xavier pulled up in his Range Rover a few minutes later. Katie hurried toward the SUV so he wouldn't honk and wake up Daddy.

"Morning, Miss Katie," Xavier said when she got in.

"Morning, Xavier." She felt tense about leaving Daddy, even though she knew Flora would arrive in the next hour after finishing her shift at the ClubHotel Riu Karamboa a few miles up Chaves Beach. Katie would be gone for close to a week, and Dr. Dewanji had said that Daddy's emphysema could cause him to deteriorate quickly, even in a dry climate like the Cape Verde Islands. Usually patients with emphysema would weaken progressively, lingering on for months, their lung function diminishing until they literally suffocated. But Dr. Dewanji said Daddy's heart, liver and kidneys were also failing, so it was possible, without warning, he just wouldn't wake up one morning.

She looked back to see the flickering light of the TV in the house. "Okay, let's go," she said, setting her jaw.

———

Charlie Holden, U.S. Attorney for the Southern District of New York, sat at his desk at 1 St. Andrew's Plaza in downtown New York City. He checked his watch.

11:56 a.m.

He slouched in his chair, waiting, then got a glimpse of his mid-50ish protruding belly, sucked it in and sat up straight. He burped, getting a repeat taste of the hot dog he'd wolfed down on the street in order to be on time for his noon conference call with Antigua's Minister of National Security, Dr. Winston James.

He glanced at the file on James in front of him. *Political appointee with higher ambitions, three months on the job. Not much to go on,* he thought.

At noon the second line on his phone lit up, Stephanie dialing out to James' office.

At 12:10 he got up and walked out to Stephanie.

"What's going on?"

She was holding the phone to her ear. "What's it look like? I'm on hold."

Holden shook his head and walked back into his office, sat down. He glanced at the file again. Pissant little country of 171 square miles. *The little bureaucrat's got less cops and defense forces reporting to him than the New York police commissioner, and he's got me holding like he's the ruler of the British Empire.*

A moment later Stephanie buzzed him on the intercom and Holden picked up the handset. "Minister James, thank you so much for taking my call."

"My apologies for my tardiness, Mr. Holden. An unfolding crisis of major proportions. Unavoidable."

"No problem, I know how it can be. You prefer Doctor or Minister?"

"Whatever you please, sir. I am as proud of achieving my doctorate as I am of my recent appointment as Minister of National Security of Antigua and Barbuda." The guy talked in a grandiose version of that clipped Caribbean speech Holden heard in Canarsie.

"Very well, Minister. I called to ask your help in capturing a felon wanted in the U.S. for a $500 million securities fraud on his hedge fund investors. His name is Walter Conklin and we believe he is living in Antigua under the alias of John Rudiger."

"My word," James said.

"Yes. And I've had multiple conversations over the years, first with former Royal Police Commissioner Browne, more recently with Commissioner Benjamin—"

"Commissioner Browne? When did this man flee the U.S.?"

"Eleven years ago."

"Mr. Holden, sir, this is rather surprising that you would call me about this now. In light of the fact that you've had conversations for over a decade with Commissioners Browne and Benjamin."

What the—?

Holden sat up straight in his chair, clutched the phone handset tighter. "Minister, I think it's surprising, too. I've been pursuing this matter on and off for, as you say, over a decade and gotten stonewalled at every turn."

"Stonewalled?"

"Yes, to the point that I'm convinced that some of your people, maybe an entire group, are covering up for this man, probably because he's paying them off."

Holden waited for that to sink in.

James said, "Mr. Holden, those are serious accusations. Do you have any evidence of this?"

"Only that we were able to track Conklin, then traveling under his own passport, to Brazil immediately after he left New York. Then he disappeared. But in Brazil we were able to find a plastic surgeon who operated on him to change his appearance, and another surgeon who performed gastric bypass on him. A year later a Mr. John Rudiger surfaced in Antigua with no known prior background, and began building a $5 million house on Blue Moon Bay. We got a tip from one of Walter Conklin's former investors who overheard John Rudiger talking at the Blue Moon Hotel, and swore it was the voice of Walter Conklin." He paused to see if James would have any response. He didn't. "That was when I started sending members of my staff to Antigua to check out this John Rudiger. Searches in the hall of records showed no microfiche of a birth certificate or any other documentation of his identity. Commissioner Browne was very cooperative and sympathetic. He had his men interview Rudiger, who professed to have been born and educated there. My people checked records in the public schools of Antigua for evidence of Rudiger. Nothing. Then, surprisingly, hard copies of records started popping up in the files. Birth certificate, grammar school registration and attendance records, a public health card, and even an Antiguan passport, supposedly issued five years earlier."

"That certainly doesn't sound like a situation, Mr. Holden, that gives your suspicions any credence, now does it?"

Holden clenched his jaw.

"It sounds to me, Minister James, like Antiguan public officials have reverse engineered the alias of a fugitive financier who has very cleverly scattered his money around into the right hands. As a recently appointed senior official in the government of Antigua and Barbuda, you must know that any public scandal involving a host of your officials would be embarrassing to your administration, and a stake in your own political heart. If I have to keep burrowing into this, who knows what corruption inside your government I might turn up? But the arrest and extradition to the U.S. of a long-wanted felon would be a public relations coup for you. I'm certain it would elicit the loudly proclaimed gratitude of the U.S. Justice Department. So, Dr. Minister, can I tell my boss, the U.S. Attorney General in Washington, that I am receiving the full support of the government of Antigua and Barbuda in a matter of significant interest to the United States Justice Department?"

Holden waited. No response, and then he heard a long exhale at the other end of the line.

"Mr. Holden," James said, "I can assure you that the government of Antigua and Barbuda has always spared no expense or resources in cooperating with the United States of America, most particularly your Justice Department. I will give this matter my immediate attention and revert to you with my findings, posthaste. Now I wish you good day, sir," and the line cut off.

Holden pulled the handset away from his ear, sneered at it, then slammed it onto the phone.

———

Ten hours later Katie landed in Geneva after transfers through Lisbon and Munich. She checked into the Hotel du Rhone, exhausted, and went directly to bed.

The next morning she slept late, ate a light breakfast and jumped into a cab to the offices of Banque d'affaires Ducasse. She stepped out of the cab on Rue Beauregard not knowing what to expect, but now realized the setting was appropriate for a private Swiss financial advisory firm dating back hundreds of years. Number 4 was a four-story, 17th-century town house with a limestone facade, with a simple oak door with a glass panel in it. Neither the door nor the facade bore the name of the Ducasse firm. The door was recessed into a carved limestone archway and topped by a cast-iron lantern that extended over the sidewalk. The narrow street housed a row of similarly anonymous buildings.

She tried the door; it was unlocked and she entered into a vestibule. She announced herself to a receptionist sitting behind an antique desk and moments later was led up to a third-floor reception area where she sank into the leather cushions of a Chesterfield sofa that felt like down pillows. The floor was covered with Oriental rugs that overlapped each other. After a few minutes she decided they were arranged that way to prevent the distraction of clacking heels on the oak floors as 20- and 30-something professionals glided past without a sound. They wore blue or gray suits adorned with pocket squares and shirts with white collars and cuffs, and had the air of intensity she'd cultivated as a young lawyer. The walls were paneled mahogany, covered with oil paintings of old people and rising 15 feet to plaster moldings that curved into a gilded ceiling. The chairs were leather and tapestry, worn to an aged patina but not to the point of shabbiness. The place smelled of leather, oiled wood and money. Katie took it all in.

After about ten minutes she stood and looked out the windows at a magnificent park surrounded by granite buildings that appeared to be museums. She was still admiring the scene when she heard someone come through the door on the far wall. She turned. A trim man in his 40s walked directly to her, stopped in front of her and inclined his head.

"It's quite a different view on this side of the building out over Place des Casemates, don't you agree?"

"Yes."

"Father's office is on this side, overlooking the park, Promenade du Pin, but I prefer to face the serenity of quiet little Rue Beauregard."

He wore a form-fitting suit, a lavender shirt and a flowered lavender tie with a rose in his lapel.

Quite the dandy. She figured he set the tone for the nattily clad young professionals.

The man said, "Mrs. Conklin, it's a pleasure." His accent was international-school English, with a slight British intonation and perfect diction.

"Angela, please." Katie shook his hand.

"I am Philippe Ducasse. Thank you for coming." He turned and motioned toward the door he'd come through. "Shall we begin?"

Ducasse walked Katie through the door into a room that was an over-the-top version of the reception area. Rugs were piled upon rugs, mahogany wainscoting running to chair-rail height on the walls with burgundy faux finish on the plaster above it, more paintings of old men, furniture jammed in as if Ralph Lauren and Federico Fellini had competed with each other over decorating it. Every square inch was crammed with leather and wood, every horizontal surface covered with *objets d'art* and scores of picture frames featuring Ducasse smiling out of them with beautiful people Katie didn't recognize.

Ducasse said with obvious pride, "My office."

He pointed to the pediment-topped bookshelves behind his oversize walnut desk. "The books are organized into biographies, decorating and fashion." He flicked a hand around the rest of the office. "Out here we wanted more of a Madeleine Castaing look."

Katie's face went blank. *What?*

"A French decorator famous for mixing French, British, Russian and discarded junk pieces."

Katie didn't respond.

"Very French *Vogue*," he said. "I find it a refreshing contrast to the designer's approach in the reception area—too elder traditionalist in my view." He paused as if for a reaction, and when he didn't get one he then pointed to a chair for Katie and took his seat behind his desk. He settled in and smiled for the first time. "Thank you for coming, Angela. As you'll see, we at Banque d'affaires Ducasse take a very personal approach with each of our clients. We'd like to count you among them."

Katie had started to relax in the reception area, but was beginning to find Ducasse a little off-putting, this pasty-faced man who walked like he had a stick up his ass, now talking to her like maybe, just maybe, he'd one day grow into his inflated demeanor.

Then Ducasse folded his hands and leaned forward with his arms on his desk and said, "Now, let me take you through our presentation." He made a display of pushing a button beneath his desk. A panel on the wall to his right slid back and an LCD screen behind it lit up.

"Banque d'affaires Ducasse is a family-owned Swiss firm dating back five generations, counting among our peers the esteemed private investment banking houses of the Rothschild family and Lazard Frères."

Ducasse clicked through a number of slides showing photographs of the paintings of some of the old men she recognized from the walls of the reception area, various Ducasses, all stalwart Swiss entrepreneurs, he assured her, committed to the financial advancement of their clients.

"As a *banque d'affaires*, we do not accept deposits or make loans. We function as a private investment bank to elite clients who seek our services in mergers and acquisitions, structured private financings and other specialized finance negotiations. Our client list is completely confidential—we never publicize our transactions or advisory assignments, regardless of how groundbreaking—and we select only clients whose wealth and stature in the world will assure the continued discreet profile of our firm."

Ducasse looked from the screen to Katie. She nodded. He clicked to the next slide.

"Ten years ago we embarked on a new venture with the creation of our first private equity fund, Ducasse PE Fund I. With this we've quietly become a major factor in investing in uniquely profitable special situations, agnostic as to nationality or structure of the transaction."

She'd read most of this on their website and had been briefed on it by Mr. Bemelman, her private banker at Amalgamated Swiss Bank, where her money was stashed in a private account. Bemelman had recently recommended Ducasse as someone who could help her meet her private investment needs.

Ducasse then ran through slides showcasing the various home-run investments of Ducasse PE Funds I through IV— homebuilding sites in South Carolina that paid out 4 to 1 after the housing market in the U.S. recovered from the financial crisis;

a vacation time-share business that paid out 10 to 1 after they bought it out of bankruptcy and teamed up with the founder to rejuvenate it; an island off the coast of Dubai that Rod Stewart abandoned as a money sinkhole after Dubai collapsed and which Ducasse Fund III repurposed into an adult amusement park.

Ducasse sent Katie's eyelids fluttering for the following 45 minutes by pushing the button under his desk to change slides, none of which interested her. Every so often he would throw a glance at her that she thought was intended to be provocative, like she was supposed to be impressed. Katie was starting to wonder if the man had ever gotten laid, because half his gestures looked like they were more designed to attract similarly pasty-faced Swiss bankers than athletic former lawyers for the U.S. Attorney's Office who had in fact gotten laid more than once or twice, although not enough lately, thank you very much, and, incidentally, owned a house on five acres of beachfront on Boa Vista, Cape Verde, and wasn't at all impressed with his French *Vogue*–style office.

When Ducasse got to the slides on rates of return for their previous four private equity funds, Katie woke up. *Wow!* She sat up straight.

Ducasse said, "Yes, I see a reaction. Internal rates of return on each of our four existing private equity funds of 32%, 37%, 41% and 29% net to our investors, after our 20% carried interest. While the private placement language says, 'Past performance is no indication of future performance,' we believe we can do better still. Our first fund was $100 million, the second $250 million, the third $500 million, the fourth $1 billion, and our objective for our current, fifth, fund is $2 billion." Again he leaned forward and rested his forearms on his desk and made solid eye contact with Katie.

"We think you are exactly the profile of our core investor. Young, wealthy, with adequate discretionary income to allow us to hold a significant portion of your assets and grow them meaningfully over the next 5 to 7 years." He clicked to another slide showing a series of bar graphs, each substantially bigger than the last. "You've indicated an interest in investing $15 to $20 million in our Fund V. The attached chart assumes a $20 million investment, and shows its growth in value over each of the next seven years, based on past performance."

Katie sat up and squinted at the screen.

"As you'll see," Ducasse said, "your $20 million investment, based upon the weighted-average rate of return of 33.49% of our first four funds, would grow to $151 million by year seven, roughly 7.5 times your initial investment." He leaned back in his chair as if waiting for a reaction.

Katie just looked at him.

Ducasse said, "That is assuming you accept payouts from the existing fund without investing in our subsequent funds." He clicked up a new slide and looked at the screen. "This slide depicts what your return would have been had you invested in fund number one and continued to invest in each of our subsequent three funds by rolling over your distributions from the first fund into the second, then the distributions from the second into the third, and so on. As of today, your initial $20 million investment would have grown to $247 million, or 12.3 times your initial capital over seven years." Ducasse leaned back in his chair again. "Mrs. Conklin, our firm offers the most discreet seclusion of your investor participation in our funds from any outside prying eyes. We are keenly aware of who your ex-husband is and know that his notoriety might foreclose you from similar investment opportunities. As such, we believe Banque d'affaires Ducasse presents you with one of the most unique investment opportunities in the world."

Katie didn't like him threatening that nobody else might take her tainted money, but smiled anyhow.

Ducasse said, "Let me be abundantly clear. That means that as traditional Swiss bankers, we don't care where your money comes from, including if it was from your ex-husband's ill-gotten gains."

The presentation went on for another half hour, most of which seemed to Katie like boilerplate they could've done without, but she figured their lawyers had insisted upon it. After Ducasse turned off the screen and closed the panel on his office wall again, he said, "Can I answer any questions?"

"I need to digest this," Katie said. "But you should know I'm interested, still at the $15 to $20 million level."

Ducasse leaned toward her and said in a lowered voice, "You should be aware that we are offering our initial investors in Ducasse Fund V an unusual opportunity." He paused, as if Katie would be sitting on the edge of her chair to hear this. She realized this was the final pitch and decided not to show any reaction. Ducasse went on. "Our first ten investors will be afforded the opportunity to invest alongside Banque d'affaires Ducasse as partners. Normally we ask our investors to commit to an investment amount, which we then draw down with capital calls as we fund our investments. However, if you would step up to the level of $30 million and fund it immediately, we would offer you the opportunity to share in our profits as sponsors of the fund."

Katie leaned forward, now interested.

"If you were to deposit the full $30 million in funds with us today, we would offer you a three percentage-point share in our 20% carried interest in sponsoring the fund. What this means is that you would receive 3% of any profits of the fund, and reduce our share of profits to 17%. So if you were to have done so from our first fund, your net returns as an investor over the last four funds would have been increased to 35%, 40%, 44% and 32%. Going forward, that would mean your $30 million investment over a seven-year time horizon would grow to $265 million." Ducasse paused.

Katie felt a tremble someplace in her body, not sure where it was, but realized this was an opportunity that she might not see again.

Ducasse said, "As I said, we are a private, family-owned firm. We pride ourselves on affording our clients both complete discretion and unique opportunities to profit from the relationships we've developed over five generations. We hope that you will join us as a member of our invitation-only private club, and become part of our lucrative family of investors who will continue to profit from the investments we continue to see around the world."

Ducasse stopped and looked at Katie, once again as if for a reaction.

At that moment someone knocked on the door. "That must be Father," Ducasse said.

A man in his 80s with a full head of white hair stepped through the door, wearing a tailored double-breasted suit and a pin-dot tie against a white shirt with a spread collar. Ducasse stood up. "Father, glad you could make it. This is the potential investor I told you about. Please meet Angela Conklin."

The man crossed the room with the stride of one in his 50s as Katie stood to meet him. "A pleasure, Mrs. Conklin." The elder Ducasse never made a move to sit down, so they all stood and talked for a minute or two, and then the man excused himself and left.

Ducasse said, "Hopefully you'll get to know him better. He's still active in the business on a daily basis." When they sat back down, he said, "I gather you're not flying home until tomorrow. May I suggest I buy you a casual dinner tonight, allow you to ask me any questions you might have? Or not. Either way, will you allow me to show you some of the more quaint aspects of our beautiful city?"

Katie felt warm for the first time since arriving in Geneva. Maybe the man wouldn't be such bad company for the evening. "That would be nice. Thank you."

———

At 7:00 p.m. the bellman called upstairs to let Katie know her car had arrived. She checked herself one last time in the mirror: a simple but elegant black dress, not too much makeup, a gold chain with a solitaire diamond around her neck and diamond earrings. *Okay, ready.*

When she emerged from the revolving doors of the Hotel du Rhone, a chauffeur held open the rear door of an antique Bentley. He drove them out of the main commercial section of Geneva, through winding streets and up the hill into Old Town. He stopped the car in front of a house on a cobblestoned street of three- and four-story town houses. The driver had obviously called ahead, because when Katie climbed the limestone steps, Ducasse was waiting for her with the door open. He was smiling, looking much less formal than in the office, wearing a tan peaked-lapel suit, again with a rose in his lapel, and a magenta-and-lilac tie over a lilac-and-purple-checked shirt.

"Thank you so much for coming," he said and leaned forward to kiss her on each cheek. "Please, this way." He led her into an intimate sitting room off the main hall, with lilac-painted walls and minimalist furniture. They sat in upholstered chairs adjacent to each other by a coffee table on which hors d'ouevres were arranged around a silver champagne bucket and glasses.

"That's a beautiful suit," Katie said, meaning it.

"Thank you. The suit is Dries Van Noten, the shirt and tie Charvet." He waved a hand at the room. "And as you can see, lilac is my color." He leaned forward and grabbed the bottle of champagne, poured. "Champagne is a perfect way to get to know each other better, don't you think? I've made a reservation at 8:30 p.m. at one of my favorite restaurants here in Old Town, so we've plenty of time to get acquainted before dinner."

He handed her a glass of champagne and held his up. "A toast to what hopefully will be a long and mutually profitable relationship."

Katie clinked his glass, sipped, then looked around the room. The furnishings were simple but elegant, with no bookshelves and few horizontal surfaces to cover with the myriad *objets d'art* and photographs as in his office. The walls served for that instead, sporting photographs of elegant women in vintage dresses, vintage cars and what appeared to be politicians of yesteryear. She recognized Winston Churchill among them, sitting at his desk with a cigar. She said, "I'm surprised at how different your home is from your office."

"My decorator was a protégé of the Italian design master Lorenzo Mongiardino. I asked him for a much more relaxed ambience, and I'm very pleased with what he accomplished. Many of the photographs are Cecil Beaton's, including the famous one of Churchill at his desk at 10 Downing Street. I bought that at auction recently. Some of the others are of women Beaton photographed in vintage dresses I own in my collection."

"You collect vintage dresses?"

"An indulgence. I've one of the largest vintage dress collections in Europe. I had to lease warehouse space to contain it, in fact. I also collect vintage automobiles. The 1962 Bentley S2 Cloud that Franz picked you up in is one of mine. An extravagance I sometimes wish I'd never yielded to, but there's nothing better than motoring around town in a 1936 Bentley Drophead Coupe with the top down and a beautiful woman at my side."

His comment surprised Katie, since she'd gradually begun to think Ducasse was gay. And yet there was something in the way he looked at her now that showed his interest went beyond cultivating their business relationship.

They had just finished the bottle of champagne when Ducasse got to his feet. "I'd love to show you my most recent acquisition, one of Cecil Beaton's early designs for the Liza Doolittle character in *My Fair Lady*. In fact I'd love to dress you for the evening. You have amazing shoulders, and you're not afraid to stand erect to show them off. You'd look stunning in this dress, complemented by a string of pearls. It's very unusual, with balloon sleeves, similar to what Karl Lagerfeld created for his 1985 collection."

Katie said, "Oh!" and looked down at her simple black dress.

"Don't misunderstand me, please, you look terrific. I was only suggesting a little diversion as part of the evening fun."

Katie agreed. Fifteen minutes later they descended his front steps into Ducasse's Bentley, Katie in Beaton's cream-colored silk creation, adorned with an opera-length strand of pearls.

The nature of Ducasse's interest in her was constantly on her mind throughout the quiet dinner they shared at a small restaurant in Old Town. The waitstaff obviously knew Ducasse, and left Katie and him to themselves in the corner of a private room off the main dining room, as if they knew his modus operandi. She half expected him to be more overt about making a pass at her, realizing she was a little disappointed as they got up to leave when he hadn't.

In the car on the way back from dinner, Ducasse began asking Katie about her background and she immediately raised her guard; she didn't know enough about Angela Conklin to be confident she wouldn't say something that would give herself away. She offered merely, "I married Walter when I was very young. That all fell apart with his scandal and flight from the country."

It only took one question from her about his education to send him off on a ten-minute tear talking about himself, which she'd begun to realize was one of his favorite subjects. He related his miserable boarding school years in Switzerland, then his matriculation to St. John's College, Cambridge, where he was gleefully happy reading for a History of Art Tripos. He was fortunate enough to have been chosen to sing in the famous Choir and never missed a May Ball. He leaned over and confessed in a conspiratorial whisper that he had, unfortunately, never eaten a swan or seen a ghost. Katie had no idea what he was talking about but laughed as if he was as funny as he seemed to think he was. Then he told her of his efforts after graduation from St. John's to work in the art world and the subsequent tension with Father, who wanted to draw him into the family business; the French woman he'd been engaged to when he was 22 who broke it off once she saw that Father was dead set against the marriage; and then his subsequent apprenticeship at Banque d'affaires Ducasse, leading to his discovery that he not only enjoyed the business but was good at it. And then his rise to his current position of managing the firm on a day-to-day basis. By that time Katie was convinced he had no romantic interest in her. But when his driver pulled the

Bentley up to the front of the Hotel du Rhone, he leaned over and she didn't resist as he kissed her on the lips.

"It was special to spend time with you," he said. "I hope our business relationship flourishes, and who knows what else?"

Katie was surprised that she felt a slight thrill, and a tickle of anticipation.

"Yes," she said. "Thank you for a wonderful evening."

"My pleasure. And please, keep the dress. No one else could do it justice, and I can't imagine leaving it orphaned on a hanger in a warehouse. If you wouldn't mind, you can leave the pearls with the concierge. He knows me."

"Here, I'll give them to you now."

"Don't. It would spoil the image."

Katie climbed out of the Bentley and started toward the door, thinking, *The man's a mystery. One minute he's a bore, the next he's charming.*

———

The next morning Ducasse sat at his desk, his face buried in the first draft of the firm's annual financial statements. The outside auditors would descend on them in 30 days. He wanted to make sure he was current with the state of the firm's finances, and could anticipate any of the auditors' due diligence questions. He'd just finished reading the chief financial officer's report when he heard a knock.

Father.

The door opened and the man entered.

Ducasse pushed his chair back to stand.

"Don't get up," Father said. "I just wanted to know how it went with Mrs. Conklin last night."

"She's no movie star, but she's an attractive, stylish and fascinating young woman."

"That isn't what I meant."

"I didn't press her over hors d'oeuvres or dinner. I felt it was better to use a soft sell. You know the old saying, 'You can catch more with honey than vinegar.'"

"I always found the direct approach worked better for me."

"I find that modern women need more cultivation." Ducasse leaned back in his chair. "I'm doing a methodical job of developing her."

Father said, "Not the way it was in my day. If you see it's there, close the deal. How much is she thinking of committing to?"

"She's still at $15 to $20 million, but I think I can talk her up to $30 million."

"But isn't she flying home today?"

"She's stopping for a few days in Paris first. She needs time to think about it."

"You'll lose her if—"

"Father, I know what I'm doing. Leave Mrs. Conklin to me."

Father continued to stand in front of the door. Ducasse said, "Anything else?"

"Yes. What about Mrs. Stoltz?"

"Hesitating."

"I thought she was almost there for $25 million."

"She was, but now she's having second thoughts."

"But didn't we finally hire her niece as an intern?"

"Yes, but it hasn't seemed to quite turn the trick."

Father raised his eyebrows. "Do you want me to—"

"No, Father."

"You haven't even let me finish my question."

"I know what you're thinking. You're a bit, shall we say, 'mature' for Mrs. Stoltz. Please let me handle it. Besides, we've a young man here in accounting who I understand has already cozied up to the niece. Perhaps he can give us some insight into what the niece knows of Mrs. Stoltz's thinking."

CHAPTER 2

Rudiger was in the living room on the lower level of his house, seated in front of the coffee table with the *Wall Street Journal* spread out on top of it. A cup of tea sat on the end table next to him, an envelope with a pile of $20 Eastern Caribbean bills sitting next to the teacup. He'd just buzzed Charisse on the intercom and was waiting for her to arrive. He looked up at the Caribbean, a sight he never tired of, particularly from this room, three walls of glass suspended from the cliff that made it seem like there was nothing between him and the sea. He could hear the waves lapping on the rocks beneath him, frigate birds calling out as they circled the water for fish and young turtles. The air smelled like the morning rainstorm that had blown in, then out, about ten minutes earlier.

He heard Charisse enter. He picked up the envelope and stood as she approached. "I understand you're going to your sister's again this weekend and I wanted to give you a little something for her kids."

Charisse said, "Oh no, Mr. John, you don't have to."

"Come on. I insist." He handed her the envelope. It was their little routine, Charisse always affecting reluctance, Rudiger insisting, and finally Charisse showing her gratitude. It had been going on for about five years, after he learned that Charisse was giving

EC $100 a month to help out her older sister, Marjorie, who now had five children.

"How are the kids doing?"

Charisse's face lit up. "Oh, marvelous. And the new baby, he's a fat one." Her smile broadened.

Rudiger knew a fat baby was a status symbol on the island, where most children were underfed. He also knew it was a great source of pride to Charisse. Without children of her own, Marjorie's kids took up a big space in her life.

Charisse thanked Rudiger three or four more times and went back upstairs.

In a way, she was the only family he had down here. He remembered how she'd shown up at the Blue Moon Hotel almost nine years ago, when the builders were just finishing construction on his house. He'd been sitting at his table at the Beach Grill Restaurant when he looked up to see a bone-thin island girl of maybe 17 walk across the patio with confident strides, her chin high. She stopped in front of his table.

"Are you Mr. John? Mr. John Rudiger?"

He smiled. "Yes, can I help you?"

She glanced over to the end of the bay at his house, then back at him. "I see you are almost finished building your house. I am Charisse Jamison. I have come to apply for a position as housekeeper. I'm a good worker, and educated. I just finished high school in Saint John's Parish in the advanced students' program with almost all top marks." While she spoke she reached into her purse and pulled out a paper. "This is my high school diploma." She placed it on the table facing him. "I am trained in housekeeping and I'm a good cook. I raised my three younger sisters while my momma and my older sister worked. I cooked for the family, cleaned the house, things I know well and could do for you. I'm a good girl. I don't use tobacco or alcohol and I would not presume to bring boys to your household. I would respect your privacy because I know you have many women friends—"

Rudiger started laughing. "Please, sit down, you're making me uncomfortable."

Charisse pulled the chair out and sat down but kept right on talking "—I could live at your house all week, take the bus home to my momma's house for weekends and be back in time to prepare your breakfast on Monday mornings."

Rudiger held up his hand to stop her. "What did you say your name is?"

"Charisse Jamison, seventh-generation Antiguan."

But despite anything Rudiger tried to do to stop her, she kept on talking. He finally landed on the strategy of insisting she have lunch with him, figuring that putting food in her mouth would shut her up. It didn't work. After lunch he hired her to start two weeks later and she'd been with him ever since.

He smiled, thinking about her, then went back to his *Wall Street Journal*.

By 12:30 p.m. he was sitting at his table at the Beach Grill Restaurant, eating his usual lunch, local seafood over salad greens, watching the activity in and around the pool. Four women he didn't know were sitting on chaise lounges. One was a petite blonde who was a possibility. She had a sharp tongue that kept her friends laughing. Her attitude reminded him of Katie's.

That threw him into a whole series of other thoughts. Katie had crept into his mind a lot lately, since he'd started thinking about Cape Verde again, his $30 million and her.

He kept seeing her in that blue bathing suit, her smart-ass smirk. Katie sitting across from him when they first met, coming straight at him, even pushing her chest out. In that moment he realized that he really didn't have anybody here, and the person he was closest to was his housekeeper. *Pathetic.* The constant stream of flight attendants was something most men would kill for, both an opportunity and a challenge. Sometimes it was as easy as shooting fish in a barrel, sometimes the thrill of a tense race against time because of deadlines imposed by flights back to wherever. Then there were the regulars, too. Those he'd known for years.

But it was getting old after more than a decade, and what stood out most in his mind now was that leaving Antigua wouldn't be so bad, and maybe, just maybe he'd see Katie again.

Rudiger looked up from his lunch to see Senior Sgt. Carlen Isaacs coming toward him across the pool apron, walking fast.

Just what I needed.

When Isaacs was within earshot, Rudiger said, "One of the drawbacks of being a creature of habit is that people know where to find you."

"'Creature of habit.' You Americans and you funny expressions."

When Isaacs sat down across from him, Rudiger said, "This better be important."

Isaacs stared back at him with those dead eyes. "A problem. We need to talk."

"What?"

"It's you friend, Charles Holden, U.S. Attorney from New York again."

"We already took care of that."

Isaacs shook his head. "Now Holden, he tired of getting no place with Commissioner Benjamin. Now he call Minister of National Security Dr. Winston James."

Rudiger felt a jolt but forced himself not to show any reaction. *Not on the payroll.*

"So?" Rudiger said.

"So Commissioner Benjamin, he get call from Minister James and I get call from Commissioner Benjamin. Minister James very upset. Commissioner Benjamin even more upset."

"I don't see what the big deal is. It's no different than any other time. I have all my documents in place and if Minister James wants to get really curious, he can investigate and he'll find everything in order. Plus, I'm paying all of you to make sure it goes that way. Now are we finished here?"

Isaacs leaned forward, put his elbows on the table, his tough-guy move.

Here we go.

Isaacs said, his voice low and menacing, "You need to do something big, and fast, or this all come down. And not just on you."

"So what are we talking about? Do I need to get to this Minister James?"

"You don't understand. Minister James, he crusader. And politician. He love to work with big shot like Charles Holden, bring in big fish, advance his own career, help him run for higher office, maybe."

"So how much for Minister James?"

Isaacs let out a sigh, shook his head and sat back in his chair. "Maybe you not just playing dumb. Maybe you dumb. Maybe Carlen Isaacs got to draw you map, like you Americans say. Minister James not for sale. And so all of us you paying, particularly Carlen Isaacs, we exposed now."

There's always a price tag.

"You rich man, and you got reasons to stay here, so you got to share some of those riches."

"What do you think I'm doing now?"

"Carlen Isaacs not talking about monthly payments. Carlen Isaacs taking heat. You in Carlen Isaacs' jurisdiction. Carlen Isaacs need good-bye money in case he gotta run from Antigua, from Minister James. Run from mess John Rudiger make." Isaacs had a wild look in his eyes Rudiger had never seen before.

Rudiger didn't respond, waiting, his forearms tense.

"Carlen Isaacs need $2 million."

Rudiger couldn't restrain a laugh. "That's absurd. I don't have that kind of money."

"How many millions you leave New York with? How many more you get with this Katie girl? How many millions you make investing that money? You got plenty."

"In the first place, you guys have been bleeding me dry for 11 years. The annual payments are north of $500,000 now. My house cost 5 million bucks to build, and the insurance on it alone is over 100 grand a year. And despite what you might have heard, over a decade ago I didn't leave New York with very much money. And my recent trip up there with Katie? She scammed me. Yeah, we got some money, but she took it all. So now I'm down here trying to live my life and you guys are getting rich off me." Now it was Rudiger's turn to lean forward on the table. "I'm running on fumes, you hear me?"

Isaacs' face curled up in confusion. "What?"

"I thought you were big on American expressions. 'Running on fumes.' It means I'm out of gas. Going broke."

Isaacs looked perplexed for the first time. He glanced to the side. He apparently hadn't figured on this. After a few moments he turned his head to look at Rudiger's house. He said, "You say insurance. You say you built you house for $5 million. How much it worth now?"

Rudiger knew where he was going. He didn't answer.

Isaacs turned back to him. "How much?"

"I couldn't sell it if I tried," he said, playing dumb.

"Not thinking about selling. Thinking about burning it down."

Rudiger felt perspiration on his upper lip, resisted the urge to wipe it off. He hoped Isaacs hadn't noticed it. He said, "Glass, steel and marble don't burn so well. Besides, I won't do it."

"Carlen Isaacs could."

Rudiger swallowed hard, noticed that his throat was dry. He looked into Isaacs' eyes and now realized what he saw in them: fear. *And desperate people do desperate things.*

———

Rudiger's hands and arms were trembling as he drove back to his house. He couldn't tell whether it was because he was angry, rattled to his bones, or both.

Enough of this, he kept saying to himself over and over. *Enough, I'm done.*

As he walked in the door, Charisse took one look at him and said, "What's wrong, Mr. John?"

"Nothing I can't handle."

He forced himself to smile and walked downstairs to his office. He pulled out his file cabinet and fished around for a copy of his insurance policy. It was an extended replacement cost policy, which called for repair or replacement of the house using like kind and quality materials, not limited to the company's required insured value. He flipped a few more pages. In the past year the company had upped the required insured value to $12,287,560 based upon its estimate of the replacement cost.

Rudiger eased out a breath.

He put the policy back and pulled out his iPhone, scrolled through his contacts to his friend in Hollywood, a producer who vacationed here eight years ago and hit it off with Rudiger. Rudiger had introduced him to a number of the British Airways flight attendants who came in for two or three days at a time. The man had been grateful, and Rudiger had called in a few favors over the years.

Rudiger dialed. He got the man's voicemail. "Jack, it's John Rudiger down here in Antigua. I've got a little job I could use some help with. Give me a call when you get a chance to see if you can hook me up with somebody." By 5:00 p.m. that day, Jack had called back and put him in touch with a colleague who did special effects for his movies. They agreed on a price of $50,000, 25 in advance and 25 upon completion. The man agreed to get on a plane the next day.

Rudiger drove out to the airport to pick him up the following afternoon.

"Hi, Steve Trilling," the man said as he climbed into the front seat. "You work fast. I called my bank when my plane landed and your first wire transfer arrived."

"A deal's a deal." Forty-five minutes later Rudiger parked at the Blue Moon so Trilling could check in. He drove home, then dropped Charisse off at the bus stop shortly after 5:00 p.m. to go visit her mother for the night. Rudiger ate dinner alone at the Blue Moon. After it was dark he called Trilling. They drove to Rudiger's house and he brought Trilling downstairs. He walked him through the equipment room, past the air conditioners and then out the door to the enclosed cubicle that housed the generator.

"Wow, that's a big sucker," Trilling said.

"Twenty thousand kilowatts," Rudiger said.

Trilling walked over and knelt in front of the generator. He placed his hand on the 2-inch natural gas line and whistled. "Enough pressure to run a 400,000 BTU pool heater." He pointed to where the 2-inch gas line stepped down into a ½-inch line that fed into the generator. "See this? The big line feeds into the smaller line, which if I set it up right, will do the trick for you."

Trilling opened the generator cover and started tinkering. He then pulled a side panel off. He shut off the valve feeding the gas, then pulled out some tools and started taking something apart.

Rudiger said, "So what's the procedure?"

Trilling didn't look up from his work. "The generator is set up to turn on automatically when the power goes off. A sensor detects the power outage, starts the gas feed and then fires a battery-operated spark to start the engine. All I really need to do is take this little sucker out, and the fireworks will start." He turned around and held up a brass nozzle. "Removing this orifice will turn your ½-inch gas line into a high-pressure, 400,000 BTU flamethrower. You leave this outer door to the generator cubicle and the interior door to the equipment room open and the flames will shoot into the house. From there they'll blast three stories up your central stairwell like a volcano." He looked back down as he continued his work. "How far away is the nearest fire department?"

"It's probably a couple of miles. But let me put it this way, the English Harbour police station closes around 12:00 p.m. and doesn't open again until 6:00 a.m. the following morning. It's only got one telephone line that doesn't allow anybody to leave a message. I've never called the fire department, but I can't imagine it's much better."

Trilling looked up. "Well, whether they get here or not, it should all be over in about 10 or 15 minutes."

Trilling continued to work for another five minutes, then reattached the side panel and closed the top of the generator. He stood up.

"That's it," he said. He motioned for Rudiger to come over. "See this valve? I've got it straight up, which means the gas is shut off. Whatever you do, don't turn it back on until you're ready to go live. How often does the power go off around here?"

"Every other day or so, usually at night when everyone's home from work running their air conditioners."

Trilling grinned. "It's gonna be quite a show. Just like in the movies."

————

The next morning Charisse arrived back at the house in time to make Rudiger's breakfast. After she'd cleared it from the table, Rudiger went back downstairs to his bedroom. He closed the door so that Charisse couldn't see and packed two bags. The first was his suitcase, the second a smaller overnight bag. He kept it simple: four each of his standard uniform of Tommy Bahama shirts and Bermuda shorts. Sandals and shoes, three pairs of jeans and two sports jackets, plus his workout gear. Miscellaneous T-shirts, socks and underwear, and his toiletries. Finally, he made sure he pulled all his documents, including the other aliases he'd had prepared over the years, from his safe and put them in the false bottom of his overnight bag. He stashed the bags in his closet, then went downstairs to the living room to read his newspapers and drink his tea in front of the Caribbean. He dozed on the sofa until Charisse buzzed him on the intercom.

"Mr. John, it's 11:30. You want a gin and tonic?"

"Yes, that would be nice. I'll be right up." By the time he got up to the first floor Charisse was finishing mixing his drink. He said, "I won't need you anymore today. You can get over to Marjorie's a little early. I'll be heading over to the Blue Moon for lunch. Then some of the ladies I know from Lufthansa are coming in this afternoon, so I'll stay over there for dinner. Pack up your things and after I finish my drink I'll drive you to the bus stop when I head over to the Blue Moon."

"Thank you, Mr. John," she said.

A half hour later Rudiger drove past the Blue Moon, dropped Charisse at the bus stop, and then turned around and drove back to his house. He walked downstairs, opened the door to the equipment room, passed through to the generator cubicle and reached down and turned the gas lever on. He entered the equipment room and changed out the alarm backup battery, substituting a dead one he hadn't discarded yet for the good one so the alarm wouldn't come on with the power off. He walked back into the house, leaving both doors open as Trilling had advised him to do, then picked up his bags from the bedroom and put them in the back of his SUV.

He pulled into the Blue Moon and waved Jimmy, one of the bellmen, over to check his bags and valet park his SUV. He headed straight for his table at the Beach Grill Restaurant.

Three new women lounged by the pool. They must have been the flight attendants from American Airlines that Anton at the front desk had told him about. He made a point of removing his sunglasses so that the slim brunette who kept diving into the pool and then going back to her lounge chair, each time glancing over at Rudiger, would see that he was checking her out. Her glances his way meant she had potential, although he was a little uncertain about how to play it given that Katrina would be arriving on her Lufthansa flight later that afternoon. She'd be expecting him to be looking forward to the fact that she would make herself available to him. Katrina, now in her late 40s, still full figured but a little thicker around the middle, with two children at home and a husband named Rolf who was a car mechanic, and who he really didn't want to know any more about than that. He decided that if for some reason Katrina didn't show, the brunette might be a good backup. But no matter what happened, he'd need someone to vouch for his whereabouts. Because if the expected Friday night drain on the power grid caused a blackout, then the 400,000 BTU fireworks on the cliff would erupt and he'd want to make sure he had an alibi.

A few minutes later the brunette took another dive into the pool. This time when she climbed out she caught his eye and smiled at him.

Rudiger smiled back. He raised his glass, pointed at it and opened his arms as if to say, "Will you join me?" He pointed to the chair in front of him. She averted her eyes and lay back down on her chaise lounge.

Rudiger shrugged. He finished his lunch and Tammy cleared it. He turned in his chair to look at his house on the cliff at the end of the bay and felt a pang, unsure if it was regret or nostalgia. A sound to his right made him turn back to see the brunette now stood beside him wrapped in a towel.

"You must be new here," she said.

"No, in fact I'm not."

"Yes, you must be. Because you're in my seat."

"This is my seat."

The brunette just stared at him. She looked barely 30, tall and thin, not much going on upstairs in that one-piece, but long legs all the way down to the ground. She wore a grin on her face and had the longest eyelashes he'd ever seen.

"Are you gonna get up out of my seat or not?"

Rudiger smiled. He stood up.

"I'm John Rudiger."

"Kelly Baldwin."

"How long are you here for?"

"I fly for American. We're in for the night, then we fly out tomorrow in the early afternoon."

What the hell. Katrina can wait until tomorrow.

———

Rudiger took Kelly to Cedric's, an authentic local restaurant about a mile from the Blue Moon. The place had about eight tables arranged in a circle around a fire pit out back behind a shack that served as the prep kitchen. Cedric would stoke the pit in the late afternoon so that by 6:30 or 7:00 the coals were red-hot. Cedric's specialized in the local fish, whatever the catch that day, and a few specialty pork and lamb dishes. Rudiger always enjoyed sitting around watching Cedric and his chefs cook, hearing them razzing and laughing with each other. The smell of seafood and meat on the wood fire, the sounds of grease spattering onto the flames and sizzling up.

Kelly was much better looking dressed for dinner, her hair set in a wave and just enough eye makeup to lend real drama to those long lashes.

After they ordered their meals, Kelly said, "I'm not as easy as I came off back at the hotel. I was kidding around, mostly. A friend of mine flies for American, too, and she met you down here six months ago. Linda Wilson." She looked up at Rudiger for a reaction.

He raised his eyebrows.

"She said you were a fun guy and that if I was in Antigua for a night or two I should look you up."

"I hope I'm not disappointing you."

She reached across the table and squeezed his hand. "I'm sure you won't."

So much for not being easy.

Later, Kelly said, "Linda also said you've got quite a house above the bay. I hope I get a chance to see it tonight."

Maybe the whole west side of the island will.

Kelly was naturally chatty after two piña coladas, easy to be with, and dinner flew by. Rudiger decided she wasn't what she held herself out to be; she was a nice girl who'd probably never gotten wild at a Club Med, or any other place in her life, and he was gonna make sure it stayed that way. It was about 9:30 as Rudiger paid the check.

When they got back into his SUV, he said, "How about a nightcap out by the pool?"

"Sounds great."

They'd been seated at a cocktail table near the pool at the Blue Moon for about ten minutes, Rudiger sipping a gin and tonic, Kelly a piña colada, when Kelly said, "What's wrong?"

Rudiger realized his gaze was following a set of headlights inching up the road toward the cliff at the end of the bay. It was clear the car was beyond the turnoff to the road that wound over the hill and that it was heading toward his house. He remembered the valve on the gas line he'd turned back on. He looked back at Kelly.

"I'm sure it's nothing. But excuse me for a minute. I need to make a phone call."

The only person he could think of who would be driving up to his house at this hour was Charisse. Once or twice in the past she'd forgotten something for the weekend and come back to retrieve it. He thought about it. Neither Charisse nor her sister owned a car, but maybe a neighbor was driving her back. He felt a flash of alarm and his heart rate increased.

He walked to the front of the hotel, scrolled to Charisse's cell phone number in his iPhone and dialed. She must've had it turned off because his call went directly to voicemail. He scrolled down to find Marjorie's phone number at her house. He called and it rang ten times but no one answered. He tried Charisse's cell phone number again with the same result.

Now he could feel his heart starting to pound. He thought of running back to the table to excuse himself with Kelly, then decided he didn't have time. Just then the hotel went dark, the power out. He saw his SUV still in the circular drive; the valet hadn't parked it yet. Feeling a rush of adrenaline, he climbed in and stomped on the gas.

Oh no. No, no, no.

As his SUV fishtailed out of the Blue Moon's driveway onto the road he could already see the glow of flames through the windows of his house. He pushed down harder on the accelerator, gripped the steering wheel tighter. He reached the turnoff for the road to his house, his SUV swerving on a patch of gravel. He clenched his teeth as he got the car back on track, afraid to take his eyes off the road in front of him, but aware of the orange glow increasing in intensity on top of the hill.

Another quarter mile.

At that moment a huge fireball erupted into the night sky as if a bomb had gone off. He felt it like someone slammed him in the chest, gasped and stomped the accelerator to the floor. As he got to the top of the hill he saw an SUV sitting in his driveway framed against the flames that were shooting everyplace out of his house. As he approached he realized it was a Jeep, and as he got closer, saw police markings. His pulse rammed in his ears.

He screeched his SUV to a stop and got out, ran as close as he could toward the heat of the flames, then saw the car number 27 on the side of the Jeep. He felt a flush of relief and crashed to his knees.

It was Isaacs' Jeep.

He stood up and looked closer. Isaacs was nowhere to be seen, but he could see a 5-gallon metal gasoline container in the back of the Jeep. So the man really was gonna burn down his house, and must've been caught inside when the natural gas fire from the generator blasted the place.

Serves you right, you dumb son of a bitch.

Rudiger decided he'd better get out of there, so he climbed back into his SUV and drove back toward the hotel. When he was halfway there his cell phone rang. It was Charisse.

"Mr. John, I'm sorry I was away from the phone. I saw you called. Everything okay?"

He decided he'd break the news to her another time. "Yes, everything's fine. I was just looking for something, but I found it. Have a nice weekend."

Rudiger left his SUV in the circular drive of the Blue Moon and walked toward the pool. Everyone, including all the staff, was standing out by the pool and on the beach watching his house burn. He stood and watched. "Look at it." "Wow, you see that?" "Amazing," hotel guests were pointing and saying. About 15 minutes later he heard sirens and saw headlights heading up the hill toward his house. He walked toward the pool, realizing he'd forgotten all about Kelly. She was standing near the table where they had been seated, her back to him, watching the flames.

Rudiger walked up behind her, placed his hand on her shoulder and said, "Guess you won't get a chance to see my house tonight."

———

It had taken the fire department half an hour to turn off the gas main so they could get close enough to Rudiger's house to start dousing the flames. By then there wasn't much left inside it to burn; the place was a total loss. Rudiger spent most of the next morning, Saturday, at the site with the police and fire departments. He watched from a distance for a while. After he identified himself, they finally let him through the yellow police tape to approach the house. As they brought out a body bag on a stretcher, Rudiger walked up to the fireman who seemed the dumbest, the one everyone else either bossed around or ignored, and said, "What's the status?"

The man said, "Still investigating, but look like foul play."

Rudiger felt tension in his scalp. "What do you mean?"

"We see. May take time to identify body. Maybe Senior Sgt. Isaacs caught in his own ruse, maybe not."

Rudiger waited for the man to go on. When he didn't, Rudiger said, "Anything else?"

"Generator gas line may been tampered with. Our men working on that now."

Rudiger's face felt like it flushed with heat. He saw the man look at one of the senior firemen observing them. The man walked away from him.

Not good. Now his scalp was tingling and his head felt light. He watched as two policemen stood by Isaacs' Jeep, talking to each other and taking notes as they looked at the gas can in the back of it. After that, Rudiger called the insurance company to report the loss. The insurance company had an adjuster based in Barbados and would send him later that day. They told Rudiger that since there was a fatality, they would need to wait for the police report before paying the claim. That gave Rudiger a wrench in the gut.

He talked to the cop who looked like the lead investigator to register his shock that Isaacs was apparently there to burn his house down. He made sure the cop knew he'd be staying at the Blue Moon and wanted to see a copy of the police report as soon as it was available.

By midday Rudiger decided there was nothing more he could learn or accomplish there, so he went back to the Blue Moon, ate lunch, went upstairs to make plane reservations, then decided against it. Next he got ready to call Charisse, then decided he'd wait until Sunday evening, not ruin her weekend.

He asked a couple of the staff to put a chaise lounge and a side table on the beach for him. He bought a weekend *Wall Street Journal* and the *New York Times* and sat down on the chaise lounge to read his papers. He had Tammy bring him gin and tonics.

After two hours he put the papers down and stared out at the Caribbean, turning things over in his mind. If the police or fire department started an investigation about tampering with the generator, who knew where that might lead or how long it might take, and when, if ever, he might get paid by the insurance company? Or be brought in by the police as a suspect? And what about the whole thing with Charlie Holden going to Minister James? With Isaacs gone, would it blow over? Not likely, but at least probably nothing would happen for a few days, so he had time to wait and see, think it over. At a minimum, the guys he was paying off would need to find a new bagman and reorganize. But one way or another, eventually he needed to get the hell out of Antigua.

He fell asleep on the chaise lounge.

On Sunday morning he did the same, reading his Sunday *Times* on the beach with his tea. Just before lunchtime he decided he couldn't wait any longer to phone Charisse.

"Oh, Mr. John, I'm so sorry," she said when he told her about the house. "Are you okay?"

"Yes, I'm fine. And I don't want you to worry. I'll continue your salary until you find another job, and of course I'll write you a recommendation letter. I'm sure you'll find something else soon, and if the pay isn't the same I'll supplement it."

"Thank you, Mr. John . . ." she said. Her voice trailed off and she went silent.

"Charisse, it's going to be okay."

After a moment she said, "I'm not worried about me, Mr. John. You need someone to take care of you. What will you do?"

"I think it's time for me to move on, maybe try someplace new."

"Yes, maybe that's a good thing, Mr. John."

On Monday morning, while he was reading his newspapers on the beach, he heard footsteps in the sand behind him, saw two shadows cross his range of vision and then looked up to see two officers from the Royal Police Force of Antigua and Barbuda standing over him in their pastel-green uniforms, hats in place.

It didn't seem like a casual visit. Rudiger felt a spasm of dread.

"Mr. John Rudiger?" the tall one said.

"Yes. Is this about the police report on my house?"

The tall one shook his head. The short one said, "Minister of National Security Dr. Winston James want to see you."

"About what?"

The short one said, "He discuss that with you."

"When?"

"Now. He in his car up at the hotel."

Uh-oh. Rudiger remembered what Isaacs had said about Minister James: a crusader, and not for sale. He put down his newspaper, slid into his sandals and started walking back to the hotel, the two men flanking him. A black Mercedes was parked in the circular drive. The men walked him around to one of the rear doors and opened it.

The man inside said, "Mr. Rudiger, please sit down."

Rudiger got in and the door was closed behind him. The car was running with the air conditioning on, but he felt uncomfortably warm.

"I am Minister of National Security Dr. Winston James. I thought we could have a little chat. I won't take much of your time."

Minister James was a dark-skinned black from the islands, well dressed in a suit and tie with a white shirt. He smelled of a subtle cologne. His speech said he'd been schooled in one of the wealthier parishes of the island in the private schools the British set up for their children hundreds of years ago when they colonized Antigua.

Rudiger said, "Okay." He had an ominous feeling that this was it. And yet somehow he felt relieved.

"First, I'm sorry for the recent loss of your home. Unfortunate."

Rudiger hesitated, wondering if Minister James was just warming up with some small talk.

"As you may know, the 600 members of the Royal Police Force of Antigua and Barbuda and the 220-strong Antigua and Barbuda Defence Force, including the Coast Guard—both the active and retired professionals—all fall under my jurisdiction. We have had certain unsavory elements in these departments in the past, but I can assure you I'm doing everything in my power to weed out the criminal element to remedy that situation."

Rudiger now froze. *Here we go.*

"I regret your recent difficulties with Senior Sgt. Isaacs, who appears to have met his end burning down your house. I recently became aware he was a blackmailer, a thug and one of the criminal elements I'm committed to eradicating from our departments. I'm also aware that he was extorting money from you based upon the threat to have you extradited as a man who is a fugitive from the United States, living under an alias in Antigua." Minister James paused and looked Rudiger in the eye.

Rudiger thought about it, then nodded.

"Mr. Rudiger, we are a quiet island country and we don't like scandals. And I'm particularly committed to avoiding any such unpleasantness on my watch as minister. Senior Sgt. Isaacs' behavior will be publicly exposed as an example of my campaign to excise the cancer from our departments. The police and fire department reports on the fire in your home will note the presence of an empty gasoline can next to Senior Sgt. Isaacs' body on the second floor, and another full can in the back of his Jeep. The reports will conclude that in addition to using gasoline as an accelerant that Senior Sgt. Isaacs tampered with the gas feed to your generator, and was probably the victim of his own sabotage. You will be absolved from any responsibility for the fire."

Rudiger had to fight to keep from grinning.

"The reports of our police and fire departments reflecting those facts will be filed later this morning. I will make a statement to the press outlining our findings shortly afterward. I'm certain under those circumstances your insurance company will pay your claim promptly and that you will be free to do whatever, and go wherever you choose."

Rudiger cleared his throat and said, "Thank you."

"I expect that you will leave Antigua promptly, never to return, and that I will be able to inform U.S. Attorney Charles Holden in New York City that John Rudiger is, by all my investigations, a citizen of Antigua in good standing, with no outstanding warrants, no police record, has all his residency documents in order, and that I have no reason to believe otherwise. But in addition, he has apparently left the country for parts unknown." He reached into his jacket pocket and held out an airline ticket folder to Rudiger. "Havana is a short flight away, and has a vibrant community of expatriate Antiguans embraced by the Cuban government." He looked Rudiger in the eye, held it. "However, if you choose not to leave voluntarily and without any scandal or embarrassment to my ministry, I will use my powers to assure that you *do* leave, nonetheless."

Rudiger said, "Actually, Minister, I'm booked on a flight tomorrow morning to São Paulo."

The minister smiled and put the ticket folder back in his breast pocket. "Excellent. As a public servant, I am always happy to save the Antiguan taxpayers money. Good day, sir."

CHAPTER 3

Once Rudiger reached the Cape Verde Islands two days later, Katie's house wasn't that hard to find. Dawn was just streaking on the horizon when a taxi dropped him under the carport next to a spanking new Range Rover. The two-story house went on forever, must have been 6,000 square feet. It was tan granite, steel and glass, very modern. The first floor had a 20-foot ceiling, looked like a great room taking up most of it, and the second floor rose to one side, a balcony all around it.

He left his bags under the carport next to a high-end off-road bike and walked around to the side of the house facing the beach, stepped up onto the teak deck. The sliding doors were open and he could see flickering light from a TV inside. He approached the doorway. A dog walked out, looked like a pitbull.

Rudiger froze. *Uh-oh.*

A moment later, the dog walked back inside. Rudiger took a few steps back, trying to decide what to do. "Can I help you?" a voice said from inside the house. Rudiger stepped toward the doorway, saw a man in a wheelchair with an oxygen tube under his nostrils, craggy face, white hair, big mitts for hands, looked to be about 60.

"You must be Katie's father. Frank, right?"

"Yeah. And you?"

"John Rudiger." He walked inside and shook Frank's hand.

"Well I'll be damned. The man himself."

"Sounds like I've got a reputation."

"At least every couple of days, when Katie and I are sipping our first drink, she raises her glass and toasts, 'To John Rudiger. The man who made it all possible.'"

The dog walked up to Rudiger again, a ball in its mouth, wagging its tail and its ears pinned back. It circled him, now wagging the entire rear half of its body. Rudiger stepped back onto the deck, reached down to pet it, and the dog rolled on its back. "You're a tough guy, aren't you, boy?" The dog grunted and stuck his paws in the air. Rudiger knelt and rubbed its belly. "What a great watchdog."

"Come on in," Frank said. "You're welcome here anytime."

"Thanks. Is Katie up yet?"

"She's in Europe. Geneva. Working on some investment deal."

Rudiger looked around. "Nice place." He glanced back through the doors to the ocean. "And some location."

"Yeah, Katie bought it about a year ago from the bank that foreclosed on the mortgage. Some Italian industrialist got it mostly built, then went bust. Katie put a little more money in to finish it. She said it reminded her of your place in Antigua."

"A little."

Frank said, "You hungry?"

"Starving. Feels like all I've had to eat is airline peanuts for two days."

"Come on."

Frank led Rudiger across the floor, unplugged himself from his oxygen concentrator and opened a door into an elevator. Frank rolled himself in and the dog followed, his ball in his mouth. Rudiger stepped in. When they got upstairs, Frank hooked himself up to another oxygen concentrator. He wheeled himself down a hallway and into the kitchen. The dog settled on a mat next to the stove with a grunt.

While he cooked eggs for Rudiger, Frank said, "So what brings you to Cape Verde?"

"It was time to leave Antigua, and I figured I'd look up Katie, see what she's up to."

"She'll be surprised, and pleased."

"When's she coming home?"

"Three or four days."

They ate, after which Frank put both their plates on the floor for the dog to lick them. Frank had cooked an extra egg for him, too.

Rudiger looked closer at the pitbull. He was solid muscle, with a barrel chest, a trim rear end and a brindle coat with white front paws. Rudiger said, "He's a beautiful dog."

"And a good boy. The best, in fact," Frank said. "He's about 18 months old. We got him about a year ago. A young couple from Connecticut abandoned him in their room at the hotel up the beach, the place we stayed until Katie bought the house. The staff let Styles hang around the hotel for a month or so, until he kind of adopted us, so Katie adopted him."

"Unusual name."

Frank shrugged. "It was on the tag on his collar. Katie wouldn't hear of changing it."

Afterward they went downstairs again. Frank slipped his oxygen hose under his nostrils and wheeled himself out onto the deck.

He picked up an orange plastic Chuckit! ball launcher. He pressed the cupped end of the launcher onto one of Styles' balls, then reached back and hurled it about 50 feet onto the beach. Styles tore after it, grabbed it in his mouth and trotted back. He dropped the ball on the deck next to Frank, then sat in a crouch with his head lowered, his nose close to the deck.

Frank handed Rudiger the launcher and said, "You try. Standing up you can throw it much farther."

Rudiger took the launcher, wound up and threw the ball as far as he could toward the ocean. It landed on the damp sand from the high tide about 150 feet away, then bounced up into the air. Styles was under it in a flash, leaped and caught it on the first hop, his body extended like a wide receiver catching a pass in the end zone.

"Wow!" Rudiger said.

Rudiger threw another ball. While Styles ran after it, he turned to Frank and said, "You guys like it here, huh?"

"What's not to like? The temperature almost never goes above 80 or below 70. It rains enough to keep all the scruffy vegetation alive, but never those driving rainstorms I remember slogging through on the streets of Brooklyn. The weather's perfect for my emphysema, dry heat."

Rudiger remembered Katie telling him that her cut from helping him retrieve the bonds would make whatever time her dad had left less painful, more enjoyable. Looks like she'd accomplished at least one of her goals.

"A year ago my doctors in the States gave me about a year to live. I'm still here, and I feel better than I have in a couple years. And Katie's been able to fly some really good doctors in here for me from Europe. But my best guy, Dr. Dewanji, he's here full-time." He looked over at Rudiger and smiled. "So I'll raise a toast to you tonight. Thanks. You made this all possible."

———

They were all taking a late-morning nap, Frank in his Barcalounger, Rudiger and Styles on the sofa. Rudiger awakened to the sound of a car pulling up outside. Styles got up, found a ball and trotted outside through the open sliding doors. Rudiger followed him out onto the deck to see a woman, skinny and short, climb out of an old Ford Bronco and walk toward him. She wore a yellow uniform and soft-soled shoes, like a nurse's.

"Oh," she said. "Company?"

"Hi, I'm John Rudiger, a friend of Katie's."

"I'm Flora. I take care of Mr. Dolan, do housekeeping. I work at the ClubHotel Riu Karamboa, come here when my shift ends. Mr. Dolan okay?"

"Yes. But he's sleeping." The woman nodded and walked past Rudiger into the house.

She bent over to look at Frank, checked the oxygen concentrator, then walked upstairs.

Rudiger stood around for a few minutes, then climbed the stairs. He found Flora in the kitchen preparing a vegetable that looked like kale, a skillet heating on the stovetop. Flora turned as Rudiger entered, said, "Mr. Dolan need his fresh vegetables according to the doctors. Nothing artificial, no pesticides or chemical fertilizers. Ms. Katie have them fly in from Africa every week." She turned back to her prep work. "Special grass-fed beef, too," and she pointed with the knife to two hand-formed frozen hamburger patties sitting on the counter next to a pile of more vegetables. "No hormones or antibiotics. Ms. Katie very strict."

"I see."

Flora turned around and smiled. "I can cook hamburgers on the stove, but Mr. Dolan like them better on the grill outside. I no good at it. You know how?"

Rudiger smiled back. "Sure. I'll take care of it." He grabbed the burgers, put them on a plate, walked downstairs out to the deck and turned on the grill.

When he came back in, Frank asked, "Is that Flora?"

"Yeah." Rudiger paused. "You have any gin?"

"A little early in the day, isn't it?"

"Not for me." Rudiger checked his watch. "In fact, it's about 45 minutes past my time."

Frank pointed to a bar across the room. "No gin. I'm a Jameson's man and Katie drinks dark rum."

"With club soda and lime. I remember. That'll do for me. You?"

Frank said, "You twisted my arm. On the rocks."

Rudiger walked over and fixed their drinks. After lunch at the table out on the deck, Flora cleared their plates, then came back down and said, "Mr. Dolan, time for your walk. Here's your iGo." She put a machine about the size of a small airline carry-on bag on the deck.

"It's a portable, battery-powered oxygen concentrator," Frank said. "The doctors want me to walk for between a half mile and a mile a day. Makes me stronger. Katie has marks on the roadside from here to the highway every quarter mile."

Rudiger picked up the iGo and said, "How about we walk along the beach?"

"Much better," Frank said, once Rudiger helped him through the soft sand until they reached the shore where the wet sand was firmer under their feet. "I don't know why I didn't think of walking along the beach a long time ago." Rudiger had brought the launcher, and began throwing the ball ahead for Styles.

They were walking south. Rudiger looked ahead at the curve of the beach. Nothing visible as far as he could see, perfect white sand, rocky hills rising inland off in the distance. He turned to look back in the other direction. As far north as he could see there was nothing, either, even though he knew that's where the big hotels were. It made him feel calm, peaceful. He turned around again, said, "I could get used to this."

Frank said, "Yeah, but there's not a lot to do here. If this was gonna go on forever, I'd worry about Katie. Not much of a life for her." He looked over at Rudiger, his face pensive. "But I'm not gonna last forever, and afterward she'll have a chance at a real life again."

Rudiger wasn't sure what to say, so he didn't say anything. After a moment he asked, "You want to keep going or turn around?"

"No, I'm good."

They walked in silence, Rudiger throwing the ball for Styles.

"Although I do worry about Katie a little," Frank said after a while. "When I'm gone she'll be all alone. She's been taking care of me in one way or another since her mom died."

"That was a long time ago, wasn't it?"

"Sixteen years. A car wreck. Katie was devastated, but after the funeral she kinda pushed her tears and grief down deep someplace. She said it was because she needed to take her mom's role around the house. And she did. After school she shopped, cooked, cleaned, did the laundry, everything that Sarah did. So when I'm gone she won't have anyone to take care of." He looked over at Rudiger again. "I'm afraid all that stuff she buried down so deep is gonna come back up and clobber her."

———

Late that afternoon Rudiger said, "I guess I should head up the road to one of those hotels."

Frank said, "I won't hear of it. I told you, you're welcome here anytime, as long as you want to stay. Katie would say the same thing."

It was settled.

They ate their dinner in front of the 70-inch Vizio on folding tray tables Rudiger found in a closet. Rudiger commandeered an upholstered chair from the upstairs living room, forced it into the elevator, then pulled it up next to Frank's Barcalounger. Flora had thawed two rib eye steaks. She couldn't refer to any of the beef without calling it "hormone and antibiotic free, grass fed," and had a similar comment about any of the vegetables: "nice leftover kale, organic—no pesticides or fertilizers—you can reheat it for dinner, Mr. Rudiger." Rudiger grilled the steaks outside and Frank was in his glory, taking his rib eye rare.

The "Oscar's Birthday" episode of *The Odd Couple* had just ended. Frank was still laughing about it.

Rudiger enjoyed Frank's reaction to the show as much as the show itself. He asked him, "You want another Jameson's?"

"Why not? The only time I get to drink too much is when Katie's not around. She keeps me on a pretty short leash."

While Rudiger was fixing the drinks, Frank scrolled through the program guide. He said, "Not much on for another half hour. Then it's *Hawaii Five-0*."

"Works for me." Rudiger handed Frank his Jameson and sat back down. Rudiger said, "You'd think with hundreds of channels that Dish Network would have more of the old stuff like we did back in New York. You're, what, about ten years older than me? You remember channels 5, 9 and 11? Always something on. Mostly reruns, but those were some great old shows."

"You grew up in New York?"

"Yeah. Hell's Kitchen, 44th and 10th Avenue."

They killed the next half hour talking and laughing about old TV shows. *Gunsmoke* was Frank's favorite, *The Rockford Files* was Rudiger's.

Frank said, "James Garner was perfect for the role of Rockford. A real average schlub as PI. You remember that stunt he would pull in the Firebird? When he was getting away from the bad guys where he'd stop, shift the Firebird into reverse, drive back in a straight line and yank the wheel around so the car would do a 180-degree spin, then shift into drive and speed off."

Rudiger said, "Sure. It was his trademark move."

"Yeah. The Secret Service calls it a 'Rockford' and they teach it to their agents as an evasive maneuver, even when driving for the president."

"No shit?"

"No shit." They both laughed. They sipped their drinks and watched the episode of *Hawaii Five-0*. When it ended Frank stood up and said, "I gotta take a leak."

While Frank was in the bathroom, Rudiger scrolled around the program guide. When he got back, Rudiger said, "Frank, look at this." He scrolled down to one station, then across to all the shows, called them out: "*Maverick, My Three Sons, Gilligan's Island, Gunsmoke, Leave It to Beaver, Kojak, All in the Family.*"

Then he scrolled down to the station below it, then across again, calling out the old shows, then down to the next, then across, calling those out, finishing with, "And look, *The Rockford Files*. It's a bonanza."

"I never even saw those stations," Frank said.

"I checked, but you don't get any of them."

Frank said, "Not yet."

––––

Rudiger and Frank spent the next two days the same way. Walking on the beach on the third day, Frank said, "It's so beautiful here." He looked at Rudiger with a wistful smile. "I only wish my son Mike could have had the benefit of this."

"Katie told me about him. He died, what, four years ago?"

"Almost. She took that hard. It really changed her."

"She told me she never felt like anybody ever did anything for Mike, or for you, after you both got sick."

"Yeah. It's different now, because the 9/11 first responders are finally getting the medical care they deserve. But back in the day when Mike got sick . . ." He shook his head. "Nothing. And yeah, Katie's still bitter about that."

"The way she talks about him, she really looked up to him."

"Oh, man, growing up she idolized him. He was five years older, like a god to her. She was quite the tomboy. Mike never excluded her from anything. Back in the neighborhood, Cobble Hill in Brooklyn, he had to argue with the guys about putting her in stickball games on the street." He looked over at Rudiger. "That is, until they saw her play. She was a great athlete, and competitive as hell. One time Mike brought her home with her whole leg and backside scraped up because she slid into home plate on the pavement. I asked her, 'Why'd you do it?' and she looked at me like I'd lost my mind and said, 'Daddy, it was the winning run.' She was feisty, could take care of herself. But most times she didn't need to, because big brother Mike was around the neighborhood to make sure nobody messed with her. He even supported Katie when she busted her way onto the track team in high school."

"Busted her way?"

"Yeah. They didn't have a girls' track team, so in her freshman year she just showed up the first day of practice. The coach said it was only for boys. Mike brought her to the principal and she argued her way to the school board. It took a year, but by the time she was a sophomore she was the only girl on the team. Ran the half-mile."

"Man, that's a tough race. The worst."

"You ran track?"

"No, football, in college, defensive end."

Frank looked over at him. "You must've been bigger then. You any good?"

"Yeah," Rudiger said in almost a whisper. "All-American, two years."

Frank shot him a glance. "Who'd you play for?"

"Harvard."

"All-American. Jeez. Those guys usually turn pro. What happened? You get hurt?"

"No. It just wasn't in the plan. I was a walk-on at Hofstra my sophomore year. Turns out I was good at defensive end. They say football's a team sport, but for linemen that's bull." He looked over at Frank. "We linemen call our domain 'the pit.' Man against man, one-on-one. Brute force, smash-face, and"—he smiled—"a spin move like Lawrence Taylor and some brains don't hurt, either. So Harvard recruited me with a full scholarship. It was never about the football, but that's what got me to Harvard. Harvard undergrad got me into Harvard Business School. For me, that's what it was about." Rudiger looked off at the ocean.

Frank seemed to sense he didn't want to talk any more about it, let it drop. After a moment Frank said, "So Katie's coach said she had ability, but she won races on pure heart. Always ran from the front the whole race. Ferocious. By her junior year nobody could kick past her at the finish. Mike saw most of her meets until her senior year when he started working full-time. But he took off from work to see her win the state sectionals that year. He's most of the reason she went to law school."

"Wasn't he a fireman?"

"Yeah, after. But when Katie was in college, Mike was a paralegal, working for one of the big Wall Street law firms. He was doing great, working his way up, a career in front of him. Then he broke his ankle playing basketball and the docs put him on painkillers. I never learned about it until afterward, but Katie knew he got hooked on them. After Mike's prescription ran out, the street cost was about twice the price of getting high on heroin. So he switched. I knew something was wrong but not what it was. Katie covered for him. She tried pretty much everything to get him straight, even paying for a couple of rehabs, flew with him to one in Florida."

"So he beat it?"

Frank shook his head. "Even Katie thought Mike was fine when he came back the second time. But he was still using, and even figured out a way to steal from the law firm, from the runners taking cash and checks to the bank. Mike estimated he was into them for over 100 grand when they finally caught him."

"Did they send him to jail?"

"Katie stepped in and talked to one of the partners, a woman who had always supported Mike, brought him along. She got the partner to agree that if Mike signed himself into a rehab and stayed clean a year, she'd keep it quiet and make sure the firm didn't press charges."

"Wow. What a break."

"Yeah, and he took it to heart. He was never that religious, but he called it 'a gift of grace from God.' He got clean, joined a church where they shout 'Praise the Lord' all the time. A year later he came and asked me to help him get a job with the fire department. They called him 'The Preacher' at the station house."

Rudiger motioned for Frank to go on.

"We were from different engine companies, but we worked on the same team for three months at the Trade Center after 9/11. I was never so proud of him. None of us knew what breathing in all that gunk down there would do to us."

"When did he get sick?"

"About four years later."

Frank looked over at Rudiger for a long moment.

Rudiger was ready for another throw—Styles in his position, staring at the ball, waiting—but he saw Frank's eyes and dropped the Chuckit! launcher to his side.

Frank said, "By then Katie was out of law school, working for the Manhattan DA's Office. She worked really long hours, but she'd come home to Cobble Hill to check in on Mike almost every night. If she had to work really late, some nights she'd stop home, have dinner with us and then go back to the office. Sometimes she'd stay over, sleep on the sofa in the living room. Many of those nights I could hear her crying in there when she thought I was asleep."

Rudiger felt a lump in his throat.

Frank said, "Those were bad times. It took Mike two years to kinda shrivel into nothing. Hard to watch. Heartbreaking to watch Katie watch it."

Rudiger now felt his throat thick with emotion. He had to cough to clear it before saying, "Katie told me she felt like Mike and you were owed."

"Yeah. I guess that's why it doesn't bother me she's hiding out here on some island in the middle of nowhere where they can't extradite her."

"So it's a good life here?"

"It's quiet, that's all. I watch a lotta TV."

———

Katie was seated in a conference room on the second floor of Banque d'affaires Ducasse. More wood, leather and oil paintings of old people. Ducasse and two of his young associates were seated across from her. Her banker from Amalgamated Swiss Bank, Mr. Bemelman, and a lawyer Bemelman had hired to advise Katie on her potential Ducasse investment flanked her. Ducasse had just finished answering a question of Katie's, and now she glanced to her right to see if Dolger, the lawyer, had anything to say. Katie shook her head. *Incredible.*

She'd had two conference calls with Ducasse from Paris with the participation of Bemelman and Dolger. The previous afternoon she'd flown back to Geneva for a preparatory meeting with Bemelman and Dolger in ASB's office. In all that time Dolger had hardly uttered a word other than, "Everything seems to be in order." After that Bemelman would usually remind Katie that ASB had been doing business with Banque d'affaires Ducasse for hundreds of years.

Katie now looked across the table at Ducasse. He smiled at her, not his business smile, but the same smile as over dinner last night and as he'd kissed her good night in the backseat of his Bentley. *What's up with that?* If he was going to make a move on her, get it over with. Two dinners and two good night kisses and that's it? She was beginning to think she was right about him in the beginning: he was gay. *Maybe he's bi.* Either way it creeped her out. And now that she thought about it, his kiss did, too. It reminded her of when she and Marco Rosetti, who lived next door in Cobble Hill when she was about seven, talked about seeing their parents kissing on the lips. They both wondered what it felt like and agreed to try it. After they did, each of them pulled away, wiped their mouths and said, "Eeww!"

But she wasn't considering investing in Ducasse himself, just his fund, and the investment results for Funds I through IV spoke for themselves. As did the Private Placement Memorandum and the Subscription Agreement, which she'd read with a skilled and critical eye. She'd dissected hundreds of similar documents when working for the U.S. Attorney's Office, and seen all sorts of securities frauds. She knew Swiss securities laws were slightly looser than those of the U.S., so she'd read the documents applying the standards from the U.S. They seemed airtight and on the up-and-up.

Katie was pretty sure she was leaning toward the right decision. She learned in her teens that she had trouble making decisions as easily as big brother Mike. She once talked to Mike about it. Mike had said, "Girls don't make decisions like guys. Girls research everything, consider all the angles until they're all twisted up. Even if guys are gonna do the same research, they pick a finite period of time and just say to themselves, 'Okay, time to make up your mind.' If it's hard to decide between the options, you're probably not making a mistake whatever you decide. If you get stuck, just go with your gut."

That's how Katie had made some major decisions in her life: going to law school; handing over prosecution of her biggest case at the Manhattan DA's Office to a colleague so she could meet with the partner at Mike's law firm when they caught him stealing; and deciding to drop Rich Stevens after her first year of law school. All the right choices. She'd basically made up her mind about Ducasse Fund V when she'd boarded the flight to Geneva from Cape Verde. Still, she wished she had someone who knew finance better than she did to lean on. Somebody like Rudiger. She realized the reason he now came to mind wasn't just for his advice, but also because she was thinking about that kiss from Ducasse. Not at all like Rudiger's. No question about it—when a real man kissed you, it could make your toes curl.

Katie looked to her left at Bemelman and said, "Any more questions for Philippe?" She didn't bother to look at Dolger.

"No."

Katie looked at Ducasse and said, "Okay, we're done. I just need a little time to reflect."

Everyone got up and shook hands. Ducasse showed Bemelman and Dolger out, and his associates trailed behind. Ducasse said, "When you're ready, you can reach me on extension 101," and left.

Twenty minutes later the phone in the conference room rang. It was Ducasse. "I was just wondering about your timetable. It's getting near lunchtime and I can offer to buy you lunch if you like. Otherwise I can have something sent in for you."

"Actually, I was just getting ready to call you. Can you come down?"

Ducasse hesitated before responding, as if he thought she'd be delivering bad news, then said, "I'll be right down."

A minute later Ducasse walked in. Katie was still seated. He stepped to the chair at the head of the table and rested his hands on the back of it. He smiled, but she detected he was tense. He appeared poised to say something.

She waited, not to torment him, just to see what he had to say.

He said, "Before you respond, I thought I'd offer an additional tidbit of information that might interest you."

Katie waited.

"We're close to fleshing out enough commitments, approximately $200 million, to do a first close before the end of September It would be a real boon to our fund-raising efforts to accomplish that. Other prospective investors would then have an opportunity to see we're up and running before the critical fourth quarter. Most of our investors, primarily wealthy individuals and families, commit funds to new ventures only at the end of the year."

Katie sat back in her chair. "Okay."

"You may recall I mentioned in your last visit that were you to fund $30 million up front, we would offer you three percentage points of our firm's carried interest in the fund. If you'd be willing to fund the $30 million today, we would offer you an additional two percentage points, for a total of 5% of our 20% carried interest. If you're agreeable I can have one of my associates bring the papers and we can execute them right now."

Katie said, "I didn't see anything about that in the Private Placement Memorandum."

"It's disclosed in general, I believe under subsection 10.2 regarding preferred rates of return, but we memorialize the details in a side letter between us."

It seemed odd to Katie, but she remembered that there were some differences between Swiss and U.S. law.

Katie said, "Okay. You bring the papers and I'll call Mr. Bemelman to have him wire the funds once we sign."

Ducasse smiled, looking relieved. "Excellent."

Katie decided not to tell him she'd already decided to go ahead even before he'd offered the extra 2%.

———

Charlie Holden stood outside his office beside Stephanie's desk, reading a draft of a brief she had just finished printing for him. Two of his staff members walked up and stopped in front of him. Shepherds and the new guy, Johnson or something.

"Go on in, fellas. I'll be right there."

A minute later he handed the brief back to Stephanie and said, "Fine. Send it off to Attorney General Martin with just the message in the email: 'I think we've got a live one.'" He walked into his office and sat behind his desk. He looked from Shepherds to the new guy. "Well, I heard back from this guy James from Antigua. Same BS as usual. He swears John Rudiger is a citizen in good standing, all his papers in order, but that he's left the country."

Shepherds said, "What happened? I thought James was going to play ball."

Holden shrugged. "Seems like he swept it under the rug, didn't want a big scandal if he could hang everything on just one of his guys, which he did. Some Senior Sgt. Isaacs of their police force, who apparently burned himself to a crisp while torching Rudiger's house. James said Isaacs started blackmailing Rudiger years ago once he found out we were looking into him, insisted he'd have him extradited as Walter Conklin if Rudiger didn't pay off. Found a fat bank account in Isaacs' name, too."

Shepherds said, "Probably the fat bank account because he was one of a group of guys Conklin was paying off."

The new guy cleared his throat.

"Something to say, Johnson?"

"Sir, it's Johnston, with a *T*."

Holden just looked at him.

The new guy said, "I don't understand why this Minister James would expose only one of his own people as opposed to bringing down an entire network that was shielding Conklin."

"I guess because he had a handy set of facts. Isaacs' situation would've come out anyway. Kind of hard to explain a toasted corpse with an empty 5-gallon gas can next to him in Rudiger's house any other way. Too many people would've been aware of it—firemen, cops, locals—to make it go away. And exposing one bad apple was a way to spin it as a minor coup."

The new guy said, "Yes, but bringing in Conklin could've been a major coup."

"Yeah, but maybe James decided exposing everybody else would've made him look like a fool. Corruption throughout his little empire, even though he just inherited it. My bet is a bunch of Antiguan officials will soon quietly retire. This guy James doesn't seem like a dummy."

Shepherds said, "So do you think Conklin's really gone?"

"James said that John Rudiger flew out of Antigua for São Paulo, Brazil. He sent us the records of his passport scan exiting Antigua."

The new guy asked, "Any other trail?"

Holden said, "No, but my bet is he'll find his way to Cape Verde."

"Why?"

"A year ago I sent a lawyer on our staff named Katie Dolan to Antigua to try to prove Rudiger was Conklin. She came back to the States with him and we're certain, posing as Conklin's ex-wife, took whatever was in Conklin's safe deposit box in downtown New York and fled the country. To Cape Verde. We tracked her there on a phony passport in Angela Conklin's name."

The new guy nodded.

"Johnson, I brought you into this case for a reason."

"Sir, it's Johnston."

Holden waved his hand at him. "Right. Your file says you served for two years in the CIA, right?"

"Correct, sir. Covert operations. Then law school, then here."

Holden looked at him. He still looked like he was only 18 years old. "Good. That's why I want you backing up Shepherds on this one. Your CIA background in dirty tricks may be helpful. My hunch is, you'll find Conklin with Katie."

"But, sir, we have no extradition treaty with Cape Verde."

"Just find them both, then we'll talk."

———

Rudiger had gone to bed in the spare bedroom on the second floor adjacent to Katie's, and woke up with the sun. He put on his workout clothes and running shoes, went downstairs and saw Frank still asleep in his Barcalounger with the television on. Rudiger felt warm inside. He really liked the guy. No pretense, no bull. Just a big easygoing Irishman. He turned off the TV and went for a run on the beach. After he got back and showered, he saw Frank was awake.

"How about a walk on the beach after breakfast?" Rudiger said.

"Sure."

Later they walked on the beach, Styles at their side, Rudiger carrying Frank's iGo on his back in a knapsack. Frank said, "So why did you do it?"

"Do what?"

"Take the money and run."

Rudiger said, "Seemed like the only option at the time."

"Whattaya mean?"

"I had a billion-dollar hedge fund and—"

"A billion, how'd you manage that?"

"It was the late 90s, and I'd been working at another hedge fund. I was a wunderkind in technology stocks. This was when the NASDAQ went from 1,200 to 5,000 over a three-year period. Three years running my portfolio was up 100, 150, 200% a year. So I was able to leave the fund and set up my own firm, raised $500 million. I stuck to what I knew, tech stocks. I was on a roll. So yeah, in two years I was managing $1 billion."

Rudiger let out a sigh. He went on. "Then, in early 2000, the tech stock bubble popped and the NASDAQ started to crash. My CFO came to me in a cold sweat and confessed he'd falsified our year-end 1999 returns. We'd done great, up 68%, but he fudged it to say we were up 100%."

"Why the hell'd he do that?"

"Because I was stupid enough to bring him in for a piece of the firm. He got greedy, wanted to suck in more investors, get rich."

"So what'd you do?"

"I decided if I turned him in, my fund would blow up and my life's work would be ruined. So I insisted he keep cooking the books until I could manage my way back to his inflated returns."

"But you couldn't?"

"Of course not. That's always the story when you get stuck in a downdraft in the market. The NASDAQ kept getting spanked. And when my CFO saw that, he panicked, turned state's evidence, copped a plea with the Feds and blamed everything on me. When I found out about it, I only had a day to get out of Dodge."

"That's when you went to Antigua?"

"No. First I went to Brazil, figuring I needed to do something about my appearance. At that time, believe it or not, I weighed about 350 pounds. I had that bypass stomach surgery, then plastic surgery on my face to change my looks as much as I could. I stayed down there for a year, had to stay out of the sun for the entire time while the scars matured."

"So what did you used to look like? How much of that"—he pointed at Rudiger's face—"is you?"

"I traded my lineman's mug for a quarterback's."

Frank laughed. "Yeah?"

"I'm exaggerating. They can't make you look totally different. But losing about 175 pounds, getting a new nose, chin and a different slant to the eyes does a lot. For the first few years if I got up in the middle of the night to use the bathroom, I'd see myself in the mirror and think a burglar was in my house. Still, if you saw a picture of me when I started college, before they beefed me up to 270 pounds for football at Harvard, you'd probably recognize me."

Frank nodded. He said, "So how much money did you take with you?"

"Just over $40 million. And I left $50 million in bearer bonds in the safe deposit box in New York City that Katie and I went to get a year ago."

"Katie said you took it from one of your investors, right?"

"Yeah. Myron Brownstein, a great guy, eccentric as hell. He'd gotten rich by inventing that little plastic C-shaped closure they use to seal the plastic bags on loaves of bread. His wife had passed away, he had no kids, no will and no person or place he wanted to leave his estate to. He had all his money in offshore accounts in the Cayman Islands, gave me investment discretion over them. He had $40 million in my hedge fund and gave me another

$50 million in bearer bonds to invest wherever and whenever I thought was appropriate."

"You kidding me?"

"No. And then just as everything hit the fan with my fund, Myron up and died. My wife, Angela, by then was freaking out, because I told her what was happening right after my CFO copped a plea. Bad move. She was ready to go to the Feds herself. So I said to myself: 'Who's gonna miss Myron's money?' I skipped with the $40 million from his estate and left the other $50 million in bearer bonds hidden in the safe deposit box in New York."

Rudiger paused a moment, thought back to Angela. A year after he ran he'd apologized to her for the mess he'd left her with. She'd apologized to him for the affair she'd carried on for over a year with his best friend, Jerome, the idiot, who'd unceremoniously dumped her after the scandal of Rudiger's hedge fund melting down. On reflection it was hard to blame Angela for her affair, given that he'd let himself balloon up to Mr. Bubba. They'd talked it all through, made their peace. After their divorce was final he'd even sent her money to get her started again, since the Feds stripped her of all their joint assets. He turned to Frank and said, "I'm not proud of what I did, but I can't change it now."

"This was ages ago, though. Hasn't the statute of limitations run out?"

"There's no statute of limitations on fraud. Sometimes when you do things, you're stuck with them, no second chance. But . . ."

"But?" Frank said.

"But if I had it to do over again, I'd have just admitted to my investors my CFO cooked the books, taken my lumps and moved on." Rudiger looked over at Frank and smiled. "I don't think I'd be that bad at selling cars."

"I'd buy one from you. But that doesn't strike me as your lifestyle."

"Didn't strike me that way, either. I was used to the high life in New York. Couldn't imagine eating macaroni and cheese the rest of my life. That's why I did what I did." He shrugged, got a twist of regret in his guts. "I was younger then."

CHAPTER 4

Katie's head bobbed as Xavier's Range Rover bounced over the last few turns in the long driveway from the highway to her house. She was beat from the ten-hour trip from Geneva, but she was almost home and the air smelled great, even the dust the Range Rover kicked up. She couldn't wait for a shower, to see Daddy, curl up on the sofa with Styles.

They crested the last hill, started down, just past dusk, and she got a rise of excitement as she saw the house all lit up.

What the—

There was a giant satellite dish on the roof—it had to be at least eight feet across—where the old two-footer had been. *What's Daddy doing?*

Xavier pulled under the carport and stopped next to Flora's Bronco. *She's here late.* Katie had Xavier drop her bags on the deck and paid him. She stepped inside and stopped cold.

She felt a flush of blood to her head, then a wave of heat down to her toes. *Rudiger!* He was sitting in an armchair next to Daddy's Barcalounger, the two of them laughing at the TV, the sound blaring, Daddy slapping Rudiger on the arm and saying, "Good one," drinks in front of them on folding tray tables. She recognized the theme song to *The Rockford Files.*

Daddy looked up and said, "Katie!"

Rudiger stood up, smiling.

Styles darted toward her, whimpering with joy, his whole body wagging, and flopped onto his back. "Hello, little man." She knelt and started rubbing the dog's belly. She looked up. "Hi, Daddy. And Rudiger, look at you. My God, you're here."

He looks fantastic. Those brown eyes, tanned, trim, looking cool and relaxed in Levis and a polo shirt that showed off his biceps. He no longer shaved his head; his brown hair had grown in to a crew cut. *I don't care how much plastic surgery it took to make him look like this, the man is gorgeous.*

Daddy stood and Rudiger walked to her, leaned over and kissed her on the cheek.

"Katie, great to see you."

She couldn't respond. *What's he doing here?* She looked up at him.

When Styles had seen Rudiger approach, he'd jumped up and run across the room for a ball. Now he trotted to Rudiger, dropped it at his feet and crouched.

"Not now, buddy," Rudiger said. He turned back to Katie.

At that moment the elevator rumbled, its door opened and Flora stepped out holding a platter of food. "Oh, Ms. Katie, welcome home." She headed for the chairs in front of the TV. "Kale over creamy polenta with lardons and shitake, portobello and chanterelle mushrooms. Special order by Mr. Rudiger for Mr. Dolan." She placed the platter on one of the tray tables in front of the chairs. "I get your plates," she said and started back toward the elevator.

"Get an extra for Katie," Rudiger said.

Flora waved her arm, got back in the elevator and closed the door. It thundered to life.

Styles was still sitting in front of Rudiger, poised.

"Go see your mommy," Rudiger said. He didn't move. "Go see Mommy," he said again. The dog turned and walked back to Katie. He sat down next to her, still staring at the ball at Rudiger's feet.

I don't believe this.

Flora came back downstairs and served them their kale and polenta. Katie ate, stewing, Daddy asking her about her trip, Katie responding in monosyllables, Rudiger alternately eating and eyeing her.

Katie ate a quarter of her portion, said, "I need a shower," and went upstairs. When she got to her room she couldn't help noticing that Rudiger's bags were in the room next to hers. She felt a flash of anger. *The man's moved right in.*

After she'd showered and changed into pajamas she heard a soft knock on the door.

It was Rudiger.

"You might as well come in. Seems like you think you own the place anyhow."

Rudiger frowned. "What's that all about? Your dad is upset. He thinks there's something wrong."

She gritted her teeth. *Thinks?*

"There is," she said.

"What?" he said, looking clueless, no idea.

Katie said, "In the first place, you obviously talked my father into putting some ridiculous satellite dish on the roof that's big enough to communicate with Mars. And my dog—*my* dog—is ignoring me in favor of you."

"He likes me. I like him. We play ball a lot."

"And you and my father, you've turned him into a frat boy, the two of you sitting around yukking it up, drinking and laughing at dumb-assed *Rockford Files* like you're teenagers. It's a wonder you don't have beer cans sitting around you on the floor."

She paused a moment.

"You done?"

"And you swiped a piece of my living room furniture."

"I'll put it back. I just wanted to sit and watch TV with your dad."

"That's part of a matched Ralph Lauren set. Two chairs and a sofa. Saddle leather. Do you have any idea how expensive it was for me to have that stuff flown in from the U.S.?"

Rudiger just shook his head.

"And you've even co-opted Flora. You have her cooking these gourmet recipes for you."

"It's not that exotic. Kale over polenta with bacon and mushrooms. Your dad said the kale by itself was getting boring. I found something called a Kalendar online. Some guys in New Jersey made a calendar with kale recipes for every week of the year. I printed it out for Flora, had her spruce up the kale for him, because I gather you're big on him eating his organic vegetables."

"What the hell, Rudiger, you can't have been here for more than three days and you've taken over my house." She was aware she was starting to shout now.

"You need to calm down. Lower your voice."

"I don't need to do anything. This is my house. I can yell all I want."

Rudiger didn't respond, just shook his head again. That made her madder.

"You know what you are—"

He walked up to her, put his arms on her shoulders and said, "I thought you'd be happy to see me. I was looking forward to seeing you. I missed you, thought maybe you missed me, too."

"Don't touch me!" She stepped back from him.

"Why are you so pissed off? I've never seen you like this."

"You don't know me well enough to have ever seen me like this or any other way."

"I think I got to know you pretty well."

"In what, ten days?"

Rudiger paused. "Yeah." He stepped toward her again. She stepped back. She wanted to smack him, but she also wanted to kiss him.

He took another step toward her. She took another step back and her leg hit the bed and she fell backward onto it,

Rudiger kept coming forward, lay on top of her and pushed her shoulders back down as she tried to get up. He kissed her.

She hadn't forgotten. *Man, what a kisser.*

She kissed him back, put her arms around him. After a minute she rolled away from him and stood up.

She adjusted her pajamas, looked at him and smirked.

"That's more like the Katie Dolan I know," he said. "What was that all about, you going ballistic?"

She felt the blood rush to her face, embarrassed. "I don't know. Forget about it, will you?"

"Okay."

After a moment Katie said, "So what's up? What brings you to Cape Verde?"

"What do you think? I was looking for you."

"So you missed me?"

"I already told you that." Rudiger added, "And my $30 million."

I knew it. She glared at him. "So that's your game plan? Step one, get laid. Step two, poke her in the eye about the 30 million bucks."

"Your dad would be disappointed if he heard you talking like that."

"Don't use my father against me."

"When did you get to be so edgy? I thought a place like this mellowed somebody out."

"I'm not edgy. I'm just fine. I just don't like it when somebody gets in my face."

"How about you peel yourself off the ceiling and we talk."

Katie paused. He had a point. She was beginning to wonder herself why she'd gotten so excited. Did she feel guilty about the $30 million? Or was she just stunned by, maybe afraid of, the blast of emotion she'd felt when she'd walked in and seen Rudiger. It made her feel like she'd lost some control.

Katie said, "Okay, let's talk."

"Did you think I wouldn't notice when you sent me a DHL package that was $30 million light?"

"Of course not. But remember what you said to me in New York. If you had it to do all over again, you'd figure out a way to make it work on only $10 million."

Rudiger laughed. "I should've said $40 million."

"Serves you right."

"Okay, so kidding aside, can I please have it back?"

Katie felt like her stomach was falling. She didn't respond.

"Katie?"

Katie still didn't say anything.

"Katie, what's wrong? What did you do with it?"

"I invested it."

"Is that why you were in Geneva?"

"Yeah."

"Invested it in what?"

"In an LBO fund, yesterday morning."

Rudiger's face softened. "That's okay, just don't honor the commitment when they try to draw down the funds."

Oh boy. Katie just looked at him.

"Katie?"

"It's a little different than that. I funded the whole $30 million up front in exchange for a piece of the sponsor's action."

Rudiger shook his head. "Oh, jeez. Who are these guys?"

Katie felt boxed in, then cleared her throat and realized she needed to put the best spin on it she could. She put on her lawyer face, like when she worked for the Manhattan DA's Office and stepped in front of a jury. She started talking.

———

Katie slept in the next morning. When she got up she opened the sliding doors and walked out onto the second-floor balcony. She leaned on the railing, felt the breeze, smelled the salt air of the ocean, felt the warmth of the sun on her face. She looked down and immediately saw Daddy, Rudiger and Styles walking along the beach.

She took in a sharp breath, then tears flushed into her eyes. Daddy had never done that before, and it was like planning the D-day invasion to get him to take his daily walk up the road. And they weren't daily; he skipped them half the time. Obviously Rudiger was a good influence. That made her feel guiltier about last night; she'd been horrible to Rudiger, still couldn't figure out what made her fly off the handle like that.

Rudiger had the Chuckit! launcher with him and he was throwing the ball, Styles racing ahead to retrieve it and then trotting back. That made her smile.

She glanced down at the table on the deck and saw the Private Placement Memorandum sitting on it. Rudiger must have been reading. She felt a wrench of discomfort, figuring he'd be having another session with her after he finished it. Last night she'd seen his face fall after she'd told him she invested the full $30 million up front. When she gave him her best pitch to describe the Ducasses' firm, their previous four funds' results and how Fund V was structured, including the 5% kicker she'd gotten for investing up front, his face was completely expressionless, unreadable. It was like negotiating with the Russians.

She turned around and walked back inside to take a shower. About an hour later she heard Daddy, Rudiger and Styles come back inside the house. She was finishing breakfast in the kitchen and Styles ran up to greet her, ball in his mouth. "Hello, little man." She put her plate with the rest of her eggs on the floor for him, then walked downstairs. Daddy was in his Barcalounger, the TV off. His eyes were fluttering. She saw Rudiger reading at the table on the deck.

"Hi, sweetie," Daddy said.

She kissed him on the forehead. "Hi, Daddy. I saw you walking on the beach. You were gone a long time."

"I guess today we went a couple miles."

Katie could hardly believe it. "That's fantastic. Are you feeling stronger?"

Daddy smiled at her. "Not at the moment. I usually nap when we get back. But yes, overall it's really helping me. Rudiger is a clever guy. He keeps me going farther each day. He's a good talker, and he knows how to keep my mind off it when he senses I'm getting tuckered out."

Katie kissed him on the forehead again, started toward the doorway to talk to Rudiger, then thought better of it and stopped. *Let him finish. Then I'll hear it.*

Flora arrived around noon and made them all a lunch of local shellfish over a fresh salad. She brought Rudiger his plate out on the deck. By then he appeared to have finished the Private Placement Memorandum and was staring at his iPad. Maybe surfing the web, doing research.

After lunch Katie walked upstairs to unpack, then drove into Sal Rei to pick up a few toiletries. She browsed the open market but didn't buy anything. She had a cup of tea at an outdoor café, then drove home. When she pulled under the carport and walked inside, Rudiger was sitting at the table on the deck, still staring at his iPad. He must've heard her come in but didn't look up. Katie was beginning to get anxious, waiting, wondering what Rudiger could be doing all this time.

She went upstairs to change into her workout clothes, then got on her off-road bike and went for a ride on the trail in the dunes to the hotels about five miles up the beach. She worked the trails up there for half an hour, pushing herself hard. Then she rode home, sweaty and worn out, putting in a total of about 15 miles. Rudiger was still staring at his iPad on the deck, didn't look up when she walked inside the house. Daddy was napping in his Barcalounger with the TV on, the volume low. She walked past him and up into the kitchen.

Flora was there. "Oh, Ms. Katie, I finish. Laundry is all done, beds made. Mr. Dolan say he want steak, so I put three out. Mr. Rudiger know how to cook them good on the grill. Salad is made and in the fridge, organic Swiss chard wash and prep for cooking."

"Thanks, Flora. See you tomorrow."

After Flora left, Rudiger walked in, looking relaxed.

Katie tensed.

He smiled and said, "Hi."

"Hi," Katie said.

"Your dad just woke up. Flora told me she left some steaks out. I turned the grill on, so we can eat dinner in a half an hour or so. That okay?" He was acting like nothing happened.

"Sure. Let me know when you're about ten minutes away and I'll cook the Swiss chard. I'll set the table out on the deck."

Rudiger said, "You want me to fix you a drink? Your dad and I are having one."

"Sure. I'll be right out. I just need a quick shower."

"Dark rum and soda with lime, right?"

Katie nodded, wondering what he was thinking.

———

Rudiger watched Katie during dinner. What she'd said last night was partly true: he really had only known her for about ten days. But being with her felt like it did when you reconnected with a lifelong friend; even after years, you picked right up where you left off. Same Katie: same attitude, same lively eyes, same tight little body. After they cleared dinner Rudiger told Frank, "I'm gonna hang out here with Katie a little while. I'll join you shortly." Frank went inside and sat down in front of the TV.

Rudiger said to Katie, "How about I make us both another drink and we talk?"

Katie looked guarded but nodded. Rudiger went inside and came back with their drinks. He sat down next to her and looked out at the ocean.

Okay, it's time.

"Something's fishy," Rudiger said.

Katie just looked at him.

Rudiger said, "Five funds in ten years, each one bigger than the last, it's just not how these LBO guys operate."

Katie sighed, now looking impatient.

It started to piss him off. *Where's she get off acting like that?*

Rudiger went on. "And these rates of return, IRRs of 32%, 37%, 41% and 29% net to investors in each of their four funds." He looked Katie in the eye. "You know the old saying: 'If it seems too good to be true, it's too good to be true.'"

"Rudiger, but you've been on the lam now for over ten years. I hate to say it, but you're out of touch."

"I stay pretty current. I can't call all my old contacts on the Street anymore, but I read the *New York Times* and the *Wall Street Journal* pretty much every day, and my bankers in the Cayman Islands are plugged in. I stay current on the phone with them, and periodically Pierre, my lead banker, flies to Antigua and we talk over dinner. I'm down there to review my investments at least once a quarter, too. And besides, I did some research over the last 24 hours."

"So all day today when you were staring at your iPad you weren't just sulking?"

Now he felt a burst of anger. "Don't be a smart ass. Yeah, I was surfing the web. Banque d'affaires Ducasse has a really slick web-site that talks about five generations of discreet advisory services akin to the Rothschild family, Lazard Frères, blah, blah, blah. But nothing much about them shows up anywhere else, except that Philippe Ducasse's great-grandfather was in the commodities trading business back in the late 1800s and somewhere along the line either he or Philippe's grandfather created a piddling private advisory business."

"So they *are* an old-line Swiss financial advisory family."

"If you can call it that. Nothing shows up of any major note to even put them on the same page, let alone five pages behind the Rothschilds or guys like André Meyer, who made Lazard into a powerhouse. But an interesting nugget showed up about André Ducasse, Philippe's father. About 40 years ago he was involved in a scandal in New York City, where he opened a branch of the family business. Seems he was advising wives of some of his father's wealthy clients in the States on some of their personal investments. Wives of clients he seems to have been very close to, if you get my drift. Some of the money from the investments André was advising them on started disappearing. The U.S. Attorney's Office began getting complaints from the husbands that maybe André wasn't just dipping the wick in their investment accounts. When the Feds started asking questions, André fled back to Switzerland, and the Feds could never convince the Swiss to give him up for prosecution in the U.S."

Katie said, "Maybe they never had anything on him other than some jealous husbands."

"The Swiss are an insular bunch who protect their own."

"Where are you going with this?"

Rudiger just stared at her, his jaw set, until she finally averted her eyes, then said, "I'm saying maybe your new pal Philippe Ducasse is a chip off the old block. Only he's doing his father one better. Having outside bankers, your Mr. Bemelman at ASB being one, profile wealthy women who don't know squat about finance, then sending them to Ducasse to invest in his new LBO funds. Handpicked investors who are too dumb—"

Rudiger saw Katie wince as he said it, didn't care, kept going.

"—to know any better or might even be too embarrassed to tell their husbands about it if they lost the money."

Katie made eye contact again. "But Ducasse thinks I'm divorced."

"Even better. Target divorcées and widows. Nobody to sic the authorities on him like an avenging angel."

Katie had her arms folded across her chest, her lips taut. "I think you're just making a stink because you're pissed off about the $30 million."

"*Of course* I'm pissed off about the $30 million. But it's not just that. It's that this whole deal stinks. This will be their fifth fund in ten years. Nobody invests money that fast and gets those kinds of returns. Funds like this usually have a window of seven or eight years for them to invest the money, with the option to take a few more years to liquidate any remaining investments before the fund is dissolved. Lots of times they're fully invested after a few years, but it still takes longer than it has for these guys to have deals pay out."

Rudiger could see Katie shifting in her seat, looking uncomfortable with where he was going. *Good.*

Rudiger said, "And after reading their Private Placement Memorandum, a couple of other things jumped out at me."

Katie looked away again.

"Having the ability to automatically have distributions from an earlier fund invested into a subsequent fund is something I haven't heard of before—"

"Like I said, you're out of touch."

"—but the thing that really gets me, and I checked with Pierre in the Caymans about it, is this notion that if you commit to a certain amount of money and fund it up front you get a cut of the sponsor's return. Ducasse gets you to stretch to fund $30 million instead of just committing to the $15 or $20 million you intended, and they give you five percentage points of their 20%

carried interest." He leaned forward for emphasis. "Nobody does that. Nobody."

"So what are you saying?"

"That this whole thing smacks of a new variant on a Ponzi scheme. New investors putting money in that pays out the old investors, so the old investors think they're doing great, but the sponsors are skimming money off and living the good life."

"I know what a Ponzi scheme is, Rudiger. I've prosecuted a few, remember?" she said, her lips curled with anger.

He leaned in, his face close to hers. "Yeah, but this is a new wrinkle. In this case, for example, investors in Funds II and III are paying out Fund I, and III and IV are paying out Fund II, etcetera."

"But Ducasse told me a lot of the investors from the early funds have continued to commit money to the later funds."

Rudiger laughed. "Even worse. Those investors are putting their new money in to pay themselves out on their old money, thinking they're getting a great rate of return on the earlier fund. It's like biting yourself in the ass and not even knowing it."

Katie's eyes were wide now.

Rudiger said, "It all goes back to what I said about these rates of return. If it seems too good to be true, it's too good to be true."

Katie licked her lips, then took a sip of her drink, her hand shaking as she did so. "So should I ask for my money back?"

Rudiger laughed again. "You mean *my* money." He paused, then said, "You don't get it, do you? If these guys are doing what I think they're doing, there's no way they're gonna give the money back."

Katie winced again. "So now what? Should we blow the whistle on them, have them investigated?"

Rudiger shook his head. "In the first place we're dealing with the Swiss. I already told you, they protect each other. In the second place, we have nothing but suspicions and my speculation to go on. You'd need to send in a forensic accountant to figure out what's really happening, and good luck getting the Swiss authorities to do that. And even if we could convince them to do it, it would take a year to unravel everything. After that if there was any money left it would take even longer to get anything back. And then what? Five or ten cents on the dollar on the $30 million?" Rudiger shook his head again. He looked Katie in the eye. "You got conned."

Katie's face had lost its color, her eyes looking panicked. "What can we do?" she said, almost inaudibly.

"I was hoping you'd have some brilliant idea, because I can't think of anything."

Katie stared back into his eyes. She didn't respond.

"I think I'll go in and watch TV with your dad now." Rudiger picked up his drink and stood up. He took a step toward the house and stopped. "Actually there's one thing you can do, something that was on my mind when I decided to come here in the first place."

She turned and met his gaze.

"You can apologize."

Katie's lips parted as if she was going to say something, then she turned her head and looked out at the sea.

Just like I thought.

Rudiger walked away.

———

Katie felt like she couldn't breathe, and then when she did she started hyperventilating as the tears came. She closed her eyes and shook with sobs. She didn't know how long she sat there crying, but it was long enough for her to be totally drained of energy. And pride.

She let out a long sigh, wiped her face with her hands and stood up. She wanted to go inside and talk to Rudiger, but she was afraid it would upset Daddy to see her like this. Instead she walked around to the front of the house, climbed the steps and entered through the main door on the second floor. She showered, changed into pajamas and then stepped outside her door to see if Rudiger had come up to his room yet. His door was still open and she heard him and Daddy laughing at the TV downstairs. She pulled her door shut and waited to hear Rudiger come upstairs. She fell asleep listening for him.

The next morning she awakened early. She checked Rudiger's room. The door was open and he'd already left. Downstairs she found Daddy sleeping in his chair again. She turned off the TV and looked outside to see Rudiger sitting at the table on the deck, a cup of tea in front of him, his gaze focused on his iPad.

She walked out on the deck and stood next to him, butterflies in her stomach.

"Good morning," she said. "Have you had breakfast yet?"

Rudiger looked up and smiled. "No. You?"

Katie shook her head. "Would you like some?"

"Three eggs over easy would be great."

"Do you mind if I join you?"

"Of course not." He smiled again. "It's your house, remember?"

Katie brought their plates of eggs out on the deck ten minutes later. She sat down next to him and said, "You must know I'm sorry, don't you?"

"Is that my apology?"

Her throat started to burn and tears welled in her eyes. She took in a deep breath, let it out. She leaned toward him, looked into his eyes and placed her hand on his forearm. "I'm sorry. And not just for taking the money in the first place, but for screwing up and losing it."

"Thank you. It's okay."

She sat back while he started eating, said, "About nine months ago, after I finished the house and we moved in, I took stock of my situation. Living is cheaper here, and even with my $10 million cut I have more than I'll ever need, including taking care of Daddy with the best doctors."

Rudiger nodded without looking up from his eggs.

Katie was aware her pulse was elevated, felt her legs weak from nerves. "I was going to send you the $30 million in bearer bonds in another DHL envelope. I had all these clever ideas for a Post-it note stuck to it."

Rudiger now looked up at her.

"'Just kidding.' 'Oops. Forgot these.' My favorite was 'Holy cow! I just found these in the bottom of my suitcase.'"

Rudiger said, "I like 'Just kidding' the best."

Katie started to feel her throat burn again. *Why does he have to seem so reasonable about it?* She said, "It was one of those things you think of and then just never get around to doing. They just sat in my safe deposit box in the bank. I never cashed them in."

"Until just recently, you mean."

"Yes. For what it's worth, my idea was to invest the money and pay you back, and then split the profit with you."

"I still would have preferred you sending them back and saying, 'Just kidding.'"

She said, "Believe it or not, I actually thought scamming you at your own game was kind of funny."

"In a way, so did I, at least after you sent me the $10 million. For a while there I thought you'd stiffed me completely."

She said, "I don't need much to live on. But I'd like to make sure Daddy's last days are as pleasant as possible, and that I can give him the best care until . . ."

"I don't want any of your money, if that's where you're going with this. It's not about that."

Now she couldn't keep the tears from falling. She said, "Thank you, by the way, for being such a good friend to Daddy. And I'm so sorry about those ridiculous things I said the other night. You've been great to him. You've got him walking, laughing, and his energy and spirits have never been better since we've been here. I can tell he really likes you. So thank you."

Rudiger took his napkin and reached over to wipe away Katie's tears. "I really like him, too. And Styles. They almost make me feel like I'm part of a family."

Katie was looking at the ground, fighting tears again. "I can't help going back to it. I'm mortified that I got conned out of your money."

"You're a criminal prosecutor, not a corporate deals lawyer. An experienced corporate deals lawyer might have had it jump right out at her, too, like it did at me. But you were out of your element. And if it's any consolation, even some top-notch corporate lawyers I know have a part of their brains that's tone-deaf when it comes to numbers. Don't take it so hard."

Katie let out a long sigh. "At least that makes me feel a little better."

"Good," Rudiger said. "I feel better, too." He finished his eggs, then leaned back in his chair and said, "I was up early, thinking.

We need to figure out a way to get the money back from these guys."

"How the hell do we do that?"

"Beat them at their own game."

"How?"

"I haven't figured it out yet. I've got a couple of ideas. But our next step should be for me to meet these guys."

————

Rudiger watched as Katie's face went from a blank look of confusion to a smirk.

She said, "Let me guess, you want me to bring you to Ducasse as a friend who's interested in investing in Fund V, right?"

"Works for me."

Katie stood up from her chair.

Rudiger figured he'd better tell her. He said, "There's something you should know before you call him."

Katie sat back down.

"I found out through some of my sources in Antigua that Charlie Holden knows where you are, knows you own a big house, even knows you spend a lot of money on doctors for your dad."

Katie's face went slack, then hardened.

Rudiger said, "Did you use Angela's passport to fly over here?"

Katie nodded.

"I thought so. Holden must have guessed that because the only way you could've gotten into the safe deposit box in New York was as Angela. Then he probably did a computer search of the INS's records and found you flew here on a passport as Angela."

"But that means he must've even had somebody sniffing around here in Cape Verde to find out the rest."

"That would be my guess."

"Wow, I really screwed up that one, too."

"You won't be going anyplace ever again as Angela. And not anyplace anyhow for at least 3 to 5 days. In addition to finding a place on this island I can buy a suit, I'll need to get my documents guy to get you a new identity to travel with."

"Rudiger, there's something else."

"What's that?"

"I used Angela's passport for my trips to Geneva, too."

"Charlie must've been asleep at the switch, then, because if he'd had the INS watching, you'd have been picked up at the airport in Geneva. You dodged a bullet."

———

Ducasse sat in his office, realizing he was clutching the edge of his desk so tightly that his fingers were beginning to hurt. He could feel perspiration soaking his forehead.

He kept replaying the conversation he'd just had at a café around the corner with the man he'd been referred to. The man spoke with an American accent and called himself Strasser.

Immediately after Ducasse had sat down, Strasser told him, "The guy and the girl you wanted me to follow, they're very lovey-dovey."

"You're certain it was them?"

"Two nights in a row. Positive ID from the pictures you gave me. I got a good look at them under the cast-iron light above the doorway as they left your building. The guy is maybe in his late 20s, blond, trim and good-looking, well dressed. The girl's a knockout brunette with a slim body and nice shape beneath that expensive suit."

Knowing where this was going, and hearing the man's detailed descriptions, started to make him nauseous.

Strasser leaned forward, locked his dead eyes on him and said, "You realize I don't take on jobs like this just to perform surveillance, don't you?"

Ducasse wondered if Strasser expected a response.

When Ducasse remained silent, Strasser said, "The only reason I did this surveillance work is if it's a means to get to a job, a real job, for me at the end of it. A job in my real line of business. This will be easy and clean if you want me to do them. Tell me now or I'm out of here. Is that what you want?"

Ducasse couldn't bring himself to answer. He stalled. "How would you go about it?"

"They have dinner after they leave work. It's fully dark by the time they finish. They'll undoubtedly head back to his apartment again. Lots of dark alleys, narrow streets. I'll make it look like a robbery gone bad."

"Will you attract any attention?"

"You hired a professional. I use a silencer on my gun."

Ducasse had to clear his throat before saying, "Do it."

Strasser said, "Cash in an envelope with the concierge at my hotel again. Don't try to cross me up, because I know who you are."

Ducasse didn't know how long he'd sat, staring at the door to his office, when he was startled by a knock.

Father walked in. He closed the door, stopped and widened his eyes. "Is everything all right?"

"Yes, I was just thinking about something."

"You look like you're about to faint."

Ducasse forced himself to smile. "I'm quite all right, I assure you." He motioned to one of the chairs in front of his desk.

"I'll stand. I just stopped by to tell you that Mrs. Stoltz has definitively backed out."

"Yes, I've already heard."

Father stepped back, put his hand on the doorknob and smiled. "Ah, well, not the end of the world."

Ducasse just looked at him.

Father's smile faded. He took his hand off the doorknob and said, "Maybe I should sit down after all." He walked over and sat. "Suppose you tell me what's going on."

Ducasse leaned back in his chair and exhaled. "It's not as simple as that." He averted his eyes. "Remember the young man in accounting I told you had gotten close to Mrs. Stoltz's niece?"

Father said, "Look at me. What's going on?"

Ducasse cleared his throat, leaned forward and put his elbows on his desk. "Mrs. Stoltz called Wolfe in accounting to say she was declining to invest."

"She called our *controller* to decline?"

"Yes. And Wolfe told me her tone was strained, her voice shaking. After he got off the phone with her, he came directly to see me. He was perspiring, nervous as a hen."

"Get to the point," Father said.

"Wolfe says Stroheim, the young man in accounting close to the niece, has come to him repeatedly asking about some of the financial results on various deals in our funds. Wolfe thinks Stroheim has figured it out."

"My God," Father whispered. His words hung in the air for a few moments before he said, "And undoubtedly Stroheim told the niece, who told her aunt, and that's why she backed out and didn't have the nerve to call either of us to say so." He paused. "What are you going to do?"

Ducasse averted his eyes again.

Father said, "I said, what are you going to do?"

Ducasse made eye contact with him again. "I've just spoken with someone about it. He's going to check into it for us, see how far it's gone."

Father looked at him for a long moment before saying, "I hope this young man Stroheim has the good sense to keep his mouth shut in the future."

Ducasse felt pressure in his chest as he nodded in response.

———

Strasser was hiding in the shadows of the recessed entrance to a town house across the street when he saw the two kids step out of their office door at 4 Rue Beauregard. It was early evening, just dusk.

Working late again.

Strasser followed them up the narrow street to Rue Etienne-Dumont, where they turned left. After they made the turn they started holding hands, walking close, their bodies touching.

Young love.

They were oblivious to anything but themselves, so he picked up his pace and closed to within ten yards of them.

They continued down Rue Etienne-Dumont to Place du Bourg-de-Four and spoke to the maître d' at a restaurant on the square. Strasser stopped, pretending to check his cell phone, and saw them being seated at one of the tables outside on the sidewalk.

He found an outdoor table at a café across the square from which he could observe them, sat down and ordered a tea. After his tea arrived he glanced back at the table where the kids were looking at menus. He'd have time to order dinner himself before he got to work.

———

Two days later at 7:00 a.m. Ducasse sat in his office, feeling relieved, drinking a cup of excellent espresso from his favorite café on Place du Bourg-de-Four, taking in the calming effect of his possessions and mementos surrounding him. The office was quiet, none of the staff in yet. His door was open.

Father strode in, a newspaper in hand, his face grim. He closed the door and threw the paper on Ducasse's desk.

"Even if you haven't seen this I presume you know all about it."

Ducasse felt his blood rise but kept his demeanor calm. He glanced down at an article in the paper about the murder of two young Banque d'affaires Ducasse employees on the streets of Geneva. Ducasse said, "I've read it. An apparent robbery in which they resisted and were both shot dead."

Father slammed his hands onto Ducasse's desk and shouted, "My God, you said you were having someone check into the situation for us, not commit some atrocity!"

Ducasse sat back in his chair and regarded Father. He waited a moment before saying evenly, "What would you have had me do?"

"I thought you were going to pay them off."

Ducasse chuckled. "For how long? Forever? And what if they wouldn't have taken the money, then what?"

Father slumped into a chair. "You've crossed the line."

Ducasse leveled his eyes at him. "We've way too much at risk."

"This isn't how we operate."

"It is now. We raised the stakes years ago. You can't expect the benefits without some costs."

Father hung his head.

Ducasse said, "You'll get used to the idea, as did I." He stood and walked around his desk to stand over Father.

Father appeared dazed but stood and looked him in the eye. He turned, walked to the door, opened it and left without another word.

Ducasse's hands were shaking as he walked over to close the door. Father was right: he'd crossed the line, but there was no turning back now.

———

It took four days for Rudiger to get Katie's documents. They left for Geneva the next day. When they checked into the Hotel d'Angleterre, the receptionist said, "Ms. Elizabeth Davenport. Mr. James Scott Rockford, correct?"

They both nodded.

"Traveling on one reservation, two single adjacent rooms." Katie pondered that. Rudiger had booked the reservations, and she figured he didn't want to seem presumptuous by reserving a single room. But adjacent rooms showed he was at least thinking about her. She went to sleep remembering his kiss back at her house. She got her wake-up call at 6:30 a.m., alone in bed.

Katie was in the lobby at 7:30 a.m., ready for breakfast, when the elevator opened on a demigod in a midnight-blue chalk-striped suit inside it, a simple blue pin-dot tie against a white shirt, silver cufflinks glistening on French cuffs. She felt a tremble between her thighs. She'd never seen Rudiger in a suit before. *God, he's beautiful.*

He smiled at her as he stepped out of the elevator. She saw him look her up and down. He'd probably never seen her in a suit, either. This was one of her best, a Ralph Lauren Collection navy pinstripe. They walked into the restaurant. All throughout breakfast, she couldn't take her eyes off his hands. They were tanned, manly, perfect. Now she remembered how they felt on her body. She had trouble putting thoughts in a line until in the cab to Ducasse's offices he said, "We should assume when we get over there that they're videotaping everything, or at least recording it."

Katie nodded.

"So let's not say a thing or even indicate anything with our body language that's anything other than the way we're representing ourselves. Me, John Rudiger, a friend of yours interested in investing in Ducasse Fund V, and you, Angela Conklin, in character. Okay?"

"Got it," Katie said, feeling Rudiger's hip and thigh against hers in the back of the cab, wanting to rest her hand on his leg.

At Ducasse's office the receptionist showed them to a first-floor conference room. It smelled like fresh paint and new leather. Katie saw Rudiger walking around and eyeing the oil paintings of the Ducasse ancestors. At one point he stepped so close to one that she could swear he was sniffing the old man.

What's he doing?

The door opened and Philippe Ducasse entered, followed by two young associates carrying bound books and papers. Ducasse said to Rudiger, "My great-great-uncle Nathaniel. Painted in the 1700s. One of our oldest." He turned and walked to Katie and smiled, his business smile. "Angela, how nice to see you again." He kissed her on each cheek. Then he walked to Rudiger and extended his hand, Katie guessing that Rudiger was assessing the firmness of his handshake. "You must be Mr. Rudiger."

They sat, exchanged pleasantries, poured tea. After about five minutes Ducasse said, "Please forgive the smell of fresh paint. We recently renovated this conference room, and we're christening it today." He pushed a button under the conference room table that opened a panel displaying an LCD screen. He took Rudiger through the presentation that Katie had seen on her first visit.

Afterward he said to Rudiger, "Any questions?"

Rudiger said, "I already read Angela's copy of your Private Placement Memorandum, so I'm up to speed. I'd put in $10 million in a month or two, then another $30 to $50 million in 60 to 90 days when some of my other illiquid investments pay out. But the only way I'd do it is if you'd give me the same deal as Angela—a 5% cut of your 20% carried interest."

Ducasse arched his head back as if he was surprised by Rudiger's bluntness. He said, "I don't really see how I could do that. Our current investors in Fund V haven't been offered those terms for only a $10 million investment."

Rudiger said, "Hear me out. I know your other investors probably don't make proposals like this, but we Americans can be a little brash." He smiled. "But there's more to my pitch. I have a few deals that I'm really interested in myself that I might lose if I can't fund them today, and I don't have the cash on hand to do them myself. But if we invest together, you can fund the portion I can't. So here's the back end of my pitch. If I invest $10 million in a month or two and you give me Angela's terms, I'll give you an exclusive on any deal I see for the next 60 to 90 days, including the deals I'm currently working on. The first deal I'm thinking of is probably going to take $100 million of equity, backed by $900 million of debt, but it's a home run based on a deal I did in the States about five years ago. That deal's paid out with IRRs over 70%." Rudiger folded his hands on the table. *Those hands.* "Interested?"

Ducasse settled back in his chair. "Well, that was a tease. Care to give me a little more detail on this investment?"

Rudiger leaned forward like a sportscaster eager for a baseball star's interview. "Five years ago I invested in a propylene deal in Houston, Texas. It was on the site of a defunct ExxonMobil refinery. But the concrete pads were there, a lot of the building structures, gas, water and electrical lines, roads, pipelines, emissions permits, whatever. Long story short, to build out a full-fledged state-of-the-art propylene plant on that site cost 30% less than to do a greenfield plant on a de novo site. I funded most of the equity, assisted by a number of private equity funds. I've got another site where I could cookie-cutter the same deal, only over on this side of the Atlantic. The Houston plant took us three years to build out. With that experience behind us, we could do the new one I'm talking about in a year and a half, allow us to tie up the whole European, African and Middle Eastern markets for propylene. I've already bought the site, an old refinery, for only $2 million down and a note for the balance."

"Was this Houston deal the Milprow Straights propylene plant?"

Rudiger raised his eyebrows. "You're familiar with it?"

"Yes. I didn't know you were involved."

Rudiger didn't blink, immediately came back with, "I invested through a blind offshore partnership in the Caymans."

Ducasse said, "The returns were extraordinary."

"Yeah, it was a great deal, and this next one should be even better."

Katie watched as Rudiger took Ducasse through his own pitch, seeing the difference between a metrosexual dilettante droning on about a stodgy old firm and some private investment results, and a man who could use his wit, intellect, overall energy, and even his hands to make his investment idea really sing. *Amazing.*

In the end Ducasse agreed to consider Rudiger's pitch, saying he'd consult with his lawyers about the possibility of accommodating his request in light of his ability to deliver transactions to the new fund.

"Yeah, and there's just one more thing. I noticed in your documents that you pay a .5% origination fee to intermediaries who bring investors into Fund V, and to advisors who present deals that you invest in. I'd expect the same thing for Angela for any money I invest, and for me for any deals I present that you invest in."

Ducasse didn't respond at first, then nodded.

"Good," Rudiger said. "If you do the propylene deal I'd expect that .5% on the full $1 billion plant cost."

Ducasse didn't respond.

"Up front, at the time I invest," Rudiger said. "I'm sure you'll get your mind around it. You've got it baked into your documents, right?" He sat back in his chair, looked over at Katie, then back at Ducasse. "I consider this has been a very productive day." He pushed his chair back and stood up. "Angela? How about I take you to some of the places I know in Geneva, and then we have a quiet dinner?" Katie stood up, a little afraid of Ducasse's reaction, then smiled as she saw him stand and watch Rudiger stride to the door of the conference room. Rudiger turned back as if it was an afterthought and extended his hand to Ducasse. "A pleasure, Philippe. We'll be in town until tomorrow." He handed Ducasse a business card. "You can reach me on my cell. I have one other meeting with another investment group tomorrow, then tomorrow afternoon I fly to Paris, then London for three other meetings. I hope I hear your response, at least in concept, by the time I leave Geneva."

He turned to Katie. "Angela, shall we?"

Katie walked toward the door, turned as she passed Ducasse and said, "Thank you for your time, Philippe."

They left without looking back. In the hallway Katie said, "Did you intentionally dis him as you were leaving? You walked right past him, then only gave him a perfunctory handshake."

"Yeah. Why wouldn't I? The prissy little jerk's got $30 million of my money." A moment later he said, "I saw you looking at me like I was crazy when I was sniffing that painting. Great-great-uncle Nathaniel, painted in the 1700s, my ass. That was fresh oil paint, still gassing off. I could smell the linseed oil when I walked into the room. Bush league. Even a half-assed forger knows to add lead naphthalene to the paints to speed the drying."

Katie laughed.

Once they were inside a cab, Rudiger said, "Well, I think we dangled the bait as well as we could. Now let's see if he'll take it."

Katie grabbed one of his hands in both of hers, couldn't resist. "Oh, I think you did more than that, Rudiger. I think he bit hard and you set the hook. Turned the whole thing around on him."

Rudiger shrugged. "We'll see if he calls me back today or tomorrow morning."

"For somebody who said he only had a few ideas, seems like you thought through that deal you pitched to Ducasse pretty clearly."

"I had four days to do some more research, make some calls and check things out."

"What the hell is propylene, anyhow?"

"Plastic. They make everything from plastic garbage bags to car dashboards to carpets out of the stuff. It's a huge business.

Over $65 billion a year worldwide. Ducasse's Fund III documents showed a small investment in a similar plant in Algeria that never fully panned out. One of the few deals they acknowledged wasn't a home run. So I think I found an idea that will appeal to his ego. Everybody likes to look like a hero on a concept that once blackened his eye. And besides that, the best way to scam a greedy guy is to tickle his greed."

Katie sat back and smiled. "I can't wait to see how it unfolds. But now I'm looking forward to the sightseeing you promised, a quiet dinner and flying back home tomorrow to see Daddy and Styles."

"Yeah, with one stop first."

Katie sat up. "What?"

"The more I think about it, I'm convinced Ducasse is in with both feet. We're flying to Morocco tomorrow afternoon."

"What for?"

"You'll see."

CHAPTER 5

Holden was looking at the memo that Shepherds and Johnston had prepared for him on the latest developments in extradition laws and treaties, the two men seated in front of his desk in his New York office. He looked up and smiled. "Oh, it's Johnston. With a *T*. Why didn't you tell me?"

Johnston laughed.

"So you guys don't think a snatch-and-grab from Cape Verde works?"

"I don't think the attorney general will buy it," Shepherds said. "We've only used that approach for drug lords and terrorists. And not even for that lately. That was de rigueur during the Bush administration, renditions of terrorists to Guantánamo, or to black ops locations in countries where they didn't care what we did to make prisoners talk. But today?" He shook his head. "I don't think so."

Holden could see Johnston squirming in his seat. Holden looked at Shepherds and said, "What's the big deal? We aren't talking about bringing them to some black ops site, waterboarding them or hooking up car batteries to their gonads until they confess. We're talking about grabbing them and bringing them back to the States to stand trial."

Shepherds said, "And what if we went ahead without the AG's knowledge or approval, and somebody asks you if you knew anything about it, or even orchestrated it? If you admitted it you'd get fired. If you were put on the stand and lied, you could potentially get disbarred for it. Are Conklin and Katie worth risking that?"

Holden felt his reaction viscerally. "I've been after this SOB Conklin for over a decade. And there's not much I wouldn't do to bring in that little wise-ass, Katie. She swiped millions right out from under our noses, bullshitting me the entire time." He looked at Johnston. "You look like you have something to say."

Johnston said, "The term is *irregular rendition*. The laws are on the books, and they say that we can do a snatch-and-grab—an irregular rendition—"

Shepherds said, "You mean kidnapping—"

"—of wanted felons and prosecute them in the U.S., as long as it doesn't violate an extradition treaty we have with the country where we apprehend them."

Shepherds said, "Yes, but we don't have an extradition treaty with Cape Verde."

"That's the point," Johnston said.

Holden got it. "I love it. We snatch them from Cape Verde, where we're not violating any extradition treaty because we don't have one. So who cares how we got them here? Once they're here, they're here. Conklin and Katie, the two of them hung up on a meat hook. Beautiful."

Shepherds said, "I understand that. But any irregular renditions that have ever been done have been limited to risks to national security, like terrorists, or major risks to the public interest, like drug traffickers, or those who are suspected murderers. I'm telling you the AG won't let us do it. But even if he did, the snatch-and-grab would probably be ruled an illegal seizure and a judge would let them walk. And then we could never prosecute them again under double jeopardy."

Holden said, "Alright, so how about this? We knock them out and grab them in Cape Verde—"

"—knock them out?"

"—yeah, knock them out. Have a CIA team slip them a mickey, or whatever it is they do, and then drop them someplace, say the UK, where folks like the Brits will work with us. We call the Brits and tell them we have a lead that two felons are on the loose and we think we know where they are. Conklin and Katie wake up in a London train station with a hangover and the Brits arrest them, then extradite them the usual way. Does that work for you?" Holden looked directly at Shepherds. Shepherds didn't say anything for a moment, so Holden added, "And I know AG Martin better than you do. You might think this is stretching it, but I think I can get him to buy it."

Shepherds thought for a moment, then said, "Aside from the fact that it sounds like a cheesy spy movie, it leaves open the question of culpability. How did they get to the UK in the first place?"

Holden shrugged. "Culpable deniability. Damned if we know. We just got this anonymous tip they were there."

Johnston was smiling. Shepherds said, "Okay, but what about resources? You're talking about an expensive operation."

"Leave that to me. I'll talk to the AG. If he signs off on it he'll talk to the FBI or the federal marshals' office. They'll send five, six guys in there on a private jet or a Blackhawk and it's done. I'll handle it."

———

Rudiger and Katie landed in Oujda, Morocco, in the evening, so it wasn't until the next day they rented a Jeep. Rudiger made a stop at a bank he was directed to by his Cayman Islands bankers and then drove out into the desert. Monotonous miles of sand. Sand in their eyes, their mouths tasting of sand. As they drove, Rudiger wondered what was up with Katie. She seemed tentative, not quite herself. Maybe she was still mortified about getting conned out of the $30 million, but he thought something else was bothering her, too. He'd booked separate rooms again at the hotel in Oujda, not wanting to seem pushy, and intentionally hadn't made a move on her because he thought if it was going to happen, it would just happen.

About an hour into the drive she said, "Where are we going?"

"The northeastern corner of Morocco, right on the Algerian border."

She was quiet most of the rest of the drive, but as they drove over the hill and approached the site she leaned forward and stared.

"It's beautiful, isn't it?" Rudiger said.

Katie looked from the site to Rudiger, back to the site and back at Rudiger again, her mouth open. "You're kidding, right?"

Rudiger laughed. "No. Everything is here, just like I was telling Ducasse about that Houston plant. Look at the infrastructure." He looked out the windshield and pointed. "Foundations, roads, electrical lines, water, even a pipeline that comes in from the Algerian national oil company."

"You can't be serious."

"Of course I am. It's a defunct refinery that we're going to repurpose as a propylene plant."

"It's a rusting pile of garbage," Katie said. She pointed through the windshield. "Half of the equipment's lying on the ground, worthless. It looks like a meteor hit the place."

"The existing equipment doesn't matter. All that stuff gets torn down and the new equipment for the propylene plant gets put in."

"Are you actually talking about building the thing?"

Rudiger laughed. "Hell no. But we just have to make it look like we're going to."

Katie shook her head. "You're crazy, you know that? We'll never pull this off."

"Watch me. And where's that mischievous Katie Dolan I knew in New York a year or so ago, who had a blast putting on a wig and big-boob falsies to go into a JPMorgan Chase branch on Pine Street and lift $50 million in bearer bonds from a safe deposit box?"

Katie sat back and exhaled. "Okay, I'll play along for now. So who owns this thing?"

"The guy's name is Carter Bowles. He bought it about five years ago, what for I'm not sure, then he went bust and disappeared, I guess to hide from his creditors."

"So the plan is to buy it from him and use it for the deal with Ducasse?"

"No. The whole thing is a sham. We show the property to Ducasse, but that's as far as it goes. We get him to invest the money based on our plans to build a propylene plant on the site."

Katie shook her head. "This will never work. They'll have lawyers crawling all over the place. Title searches, due diligence on environmental issues, engineering studies, the works."

"We'll make them up."

"You can't make up things like a title to the property, for starters."

"That exists. It's someplace where they file those things, in Bowles' name."

"Yes, but we don't have Bowles."

"We get somebody to play him."

"There'll be engineering studies, architectural plans. Have you thought about that?"

"Sure. Why do you think I got to know so much about that Houston propylene deal? I found documents on it from when it went public, and everything's there. All their old engineering studies, architectural plans, everything."

"Yes, but that's for a deal in Houston."

"I'm having them knocked off. Some guy with a CAD/CAM program, or whatever they do this stuff with, is working on it right now. Did you ever hear of Fiverr?"

"Fiverr?"

"It's an online service in India. For five bucks you can get somebody to do just about anything—write your college paper, do market research, create advertising, anything. They'll also do more complicated projects for a negotiated fee. One of my sources in New York has worked for years with somebody over there through Fiverr who knows how to do this stuff. He contacted the guy for me and assured me he's fully vetted him. After I personally checked his references and saw some samples of his work, I pitched him to create the plans we'd need for this project. I sent the guy the link for the Houston deal, and he's working on it right now, knocking off the exact same plans, changing all the names, locations, whatever. He's smart, he'll know what to do. My source in New York has three other guys working on the Private Placement Memorandum, the business plan and the PowerPoint management presentation. I paid them two grand against a final price of ten grand. We'll have everything in a week, in plenty of time for edits."

"What about a law firm?"

"You're a lawyer. You can draft all the documents in your sleep, right?"

Katie turned and looked out the windshield again. "It's not that complicated. Letter of intent, a purchase agreement, a partnership agreement, financing documents." She turned back to Rudiger. "I can draft whatever we need. But there are things that have to exist that we can't make up. Building permits. Easements. Environmental permits. I could keep going all day."

"We'll get the locals to issue them."

"How?"

"You're forgetting about Antigua. I got pretty good at getting to the right officials, paying them off for whatever I needed. And Antigua's pretty squeaky clean. We're in Morocco, the corruption capital of the world. Remember that movie *Casablanca*? Claude Rains as Captain Renault witnesses Humphrey Bogart shooting the Nazi major dead and then says to one of his patrolmen, 'Round up the usual suspects.'"

"But you don't know anybody here."

"I found a guy who does. He specializes in smuggling untaxed cigarettes. European, Asian, American, any brand you want. He knows everybody in Morocco, has to be bribing half the government."

"How'd you find him?"

"You think I'm playing Angry Birds on my iPad all day? I found a record of his arrest by searching the Internet."

"Arrest?"

"What, are you losing your nerve? Yes, arrest. He got off, surprise, surprise. The article had his whole background. So I called him. He wasn't that hard to find."

"And he's agreed to help us?"

"He's on the way here now to meet us. I offered him a 10% cut. He'll make it work. He pays the bribes out of his cut. He tells me it won't cost more than $200,000. I'm going to advance it to him for his expenses when he gets here."

"How do you know he isn't just going to skip with your money?"

"That's a chance I'll take on the theory he stands to make $3 million or so for only a couple of weeks' work."

Katie thought for a moment. "Are you going to have him play our seller, this Carter Bowles?"

"No, the seller is an American."

Katie nodded, looking out the windshield again.

"I'm having your dad play him."

Katie snapped her head around to look at him. "Rudiger, you can't involve my father in something like this."

"Why not? He loves the idea."

"You *talked* to him about it?"

"Yeah, I called him this morning before breakfast. I told him Ducasse had conned his little girl out of 30 million bucks and we have a plan to get it back."

Katie's mouth opened.

"At first he was dumbfounded, said he didn't know you'd taken that kind of money out of our New York adventure—"

"I never told him."

"—and then he was mad as hell at Ducasse, said to count him in."

Katie said, "You're a piece of work, you know that?" She leaned over and kissed him, then pulled back. "You didn't tell Daddy I took the $30 million from you, did you?"

"You think I'd rat on you to your father?"

She kissed him again. Rudiger put his arms around her and pulled that tight little body against his. It was happening, right here in the front seat of a Jeep in Morocco.

Then it wasn't.

Rudiger heard the sound of an approaching car, then saw a Range Rover pull up, trailing dust. The Rover stopped and the driver got out. "That must be our guy, Mec. I can't imagine who else would be out here in the middle of nowhere."

Katie slid across to her seat and climbed out the passenger-side door just as Rudiger stepped out. A man who looked like a light-skinned Arab, close-trimmed beard, strode around from behind the Range Rover. He flashed a toothy smile. "You must be Mr. John Rudiger." Katie walked around the front of the Jeep.

"And you must be Ms. Katie." They all shook hands. Mec said, "I am Elijah Jelloun. But everybody call me Mec." He turned to look at the site. "Man, you got big nerve trying to sell somebody this place. Almost as much as me." He laughed and showed that toothy smile again.

Rudiger said, "Leave that part to me."

"Okay. You do your part, I do mine."

Rudiger said, "Katie is a lawyer. She can help you figure out all the permits we'll need and the people you need to get to."

Mec pulled a paper from his pocket and handed it to Katie. He said, "My list of permits we need. From my people in the government departments. I don't think they missed nothin'. The more permits, the more they get paid." Katie put the paper in her pocket.

Mec said, "When do we start?"

Rudiger said, "Probably next week, maybe the week after. We need to have some documents prepared, put in place some theatrics to make a good show. We'll need two full days undisturbed on-site once we start. You have that covered?"

"I got it. No police, no military. Nobody bother us." Mec squinted at Rudiger. "What you mean theatrics?"

"We're gonna put on a little play. Make it look good for our mark, so he has no choice but to believe it's all real."

He saw Katie shaking her head.

"I have a friend in Hollywood who produces films. I spoke to him last night, then this morning again. He found me a friend in France who produces films for StudioCanal. His friend's gonna pull together a crew for us, nothing too elaborate. Thirty or forty actors to play bankers, lawyers, a half dozen of them each, because they travel in packs. A CEO and CFO of our new company, a couple of engineers, construction foremen, you get the picture."

Mec was looking at Rudiger with wonderment in his eyes. "What can I be?" he said.

"Mec, you're Mec, our local guy who handles everything."

"I could play a banker, or a lawyer. You should see me in a suit."

"You have any uniforms, like for security guards or police?"

"Anything you want."

"How about this: head of global security for John Rudiger Enterprises, Inc., on-site to keep order and make sure the workers don't slack off?"

"You kiddin? I'm on that like flyshit. With a uniform with epaulets."

"Right, and do you have any other guys who can be your lieutenants, with uniforms?"

"Done and done."

Rudiger said, "We could use some extras, too."

"Extras?"

"Yeah, you know, the groups of people who mill around in the background in a film, crowd scenes, things like that. We'll need about 50 construction workers. It would be great if they spoke French, because we'll have French actors playing the foremen telling them what to do. I can't imagine that will be too expensive, will it?"

"Leave it to me," Mec said.

"Here's for your expenses," Rudiger said, opened the door of the Jeep and reached into the side pocket for an envelope. He walked over and handed it to Mec. "As we agreed."

Mec nodded.

Rudiger said, "Alright, I'll be in touch. You know where to reach me if something comes up."

They all shook hands and Mec climbed into his Range Rover and drove off.

Katie said, "You're going all out. How much is all this going to cost?"

"Maybe a million. You have to spend money to make money, and we're talking about making $30 million, net of Mec's cut."

"I hope your French producer hired a good director, somebody who can orchestrate this whole thing."

Rudiger said, "The producer's got a screenwriter drafting a script right now. He tells me it'll be just like shooting a scene from a movie. One day of dress rehearsal, the next day live. These guys are pros."

Katie sighed. "Yeah, but what about my father?"

"Are you kidding me? He's watching *The Rockford Files* right now, boning up on his moves." Rudiger pulled out his iPhone and looked at it. "I haven't heard from Ducasse since we left Geneva."

"You worried?"

"A little. I expected him to jump all over the idea. We just have to operate under the assumption he's going forward."

———

Rudiger and Katie flew back to Cape Verde that afternoon and spent the next three days preparing. He received emails from his contractors in India with attachments of the Private Placement Memorandum, the PowerPoint presentation, business plan and the engineering plans and blueprints. Katie worked on the legal documents: a purchase agreement, partnership agreement and various financing documents, all modeled on the publicly disclosed documents from the Houston deal.

It was the best she'd felt in a long time. She was happy to be working on something, but more than that, she was content. Each morning she sat at her desk facing the ocean, typing on her laptop computer to create the legal documents, a photo of Mom and Daddy on the desk next to her. From there she watched Rudiger return to the house from his morning run along the beach. After he showered she'd make breakfast for all of them and they'd sit and laugh about the deal around the table on the deck. She hadn't seen Daddy so animated since before Mom died. It was as if some benevolent spell had been cast on the household.

After breakfast she'd go back upstairs to work at her desk. From there she'd watch Daddy and Rudiger take their walk on the beach, Rudiger throwing the ball and Styles chasing it. In the evenings they had cocktails together, then dinner. Katie remembered what Rudiger had said about Daddy and Styles almost making him feel he was part of a family. She felt that way about Rudiger now. She'd watch Daddy and him talking together about TV shows, movies or just horsing around, like a couple of old college buddies reminiscing.

At dinner the first night they were talking about the deal and Daddy said to Rudiger, "Mec, that's a funny nickname."

"It means 'dude' in French."

Daddy raised his eyebrows. "Dude. Jeff Bridges in *The Big Lebowski.*"

Rudiger said, "I think the Dude's *still* looking for that rug of his."

They both laughed.

Katie felt warm in her chest. *My frat boys.*

That night she went upstairs before Rudiger and Daddy finished watching TV. She showered and went to bed, remembering Rudiger's kiss in the Jeep earlier that day, the firmness of his hands on her as he pulled her body against his. She left her bedroom door partway open, watching and listening for him, ready to go to him. She fell asleep before he came upstairs, and she was awakened to Rudiger whispering her name, standing next to her bed. She held up the sheet and he slipped into bed beside her. She felt the magic of his hands on her body.

Every night after that she waited to hear him come up. When he got out of the shower, she'd tiptoe from her bedroom to his.

She didn't want it to end.

One morning later in the week she came downstairs to show Rudiger revised drafts of the documents. He was working on his iPad at the table on the deck. He looked up and smiled. "Hey, good-looking."

She sat down next to him and kissed him. He tasted like Earl Grey tea.

Rudiger said, "Ducasse just called."

Katie felt a flutter of excitement.

"He wants to move forward. I told him we had two other interested parties and that we'd proceed on the same track with everyone, first come, first served, because we only want one partner. I told him I'd get back to him with a date in a week to ten days for a presentation and site visit."

"That's great. Although we'll have to hustle to get ready by then."

"I don't know. You look like you're almost finished with all the legal documents. I spoke to the guys in France earlier. The script is finished and the cast has done three or four read-throughs together already. They start rehearsals tomorrow."

"Aren't you even going to look at the script?"

"I don't need to. I sent them the Houston deal Private Placement Memorandum, PowerPoint and business plan. I made up my own Q-and-A for them and I'm working on the CEO and CFO bios right now."

"There are a lot of moving parts here. Not much time. I wish I was as confident as you are."

"I wouldn't say I'm confident. I just feel it in my bones that we're going to pull this off."

Katie laughed. "I think that would be the definition of confident."

———

The next morning Katie got up with Rudiger for a run on the beach.

"I thought you did off-road biking to stay in shape," Rudiger said.

"I mix it up."

They were about a half mile into it when Rudiger said, "Your dad told me you were a great runner in high school."

"Yes, I had a fabulous trainer, Mr. Cain. He took me from having some raw talent to a whole different level. Training with fartleks."

"What?"

"It's a Swedish term for combining high-intensity interval training with continuous training. Sprints for 50 to 100 yards, then gliding, then another 50 to 100 yards, and so on like that for two or three miles at a time. Then jogging a quarter mile around the track, then another two to three miles of fartleks, repeat until you throw up."

"Sounds like fun."

"Tears at your lungs. Hurts like crazy, but it conditions you for the race."

"Your dad said you always ran from the front. This coach taught you that?"

"No, I got that from the neighborhood, Cobble Hill in Brooklyn. When big brother Mike wasn't around, I had to fend for myself. Outrunning the Johnson brothers, or Dennis Clark and Mike Slee from over on 8th Street. But Coach Cain taught me how to *stay* in front against great runners. The fartleks conditioned me to give a runner who was challenging me a 20- or 30-yard sprint, beat him back. Sometimes it took three or four sprints to break them, but I almost always did. There was a guy named Dick Stowe on my team who never gave up. I'd have to give him six or seven intervals during a race to finally beat him. One time in my junior year I was coming out of the final turn and he kicked past me on the straightaway into the finish, but after that I made sure he never stayed close enough to do that again."

"Remind me never to challenge you to a race."

———

Eight days later Rudiger rented them a private jet and he, she, Daddy—with his iGo—and Styles flew to Oujda, Morocco. Flora and her husband, Carlos, would house sit. Katie watched Daddy laughing and motioning with his hands over dinner at the Royal Hotel, clearly excited about playing his upcoming role, even though it wasn't a big one. The next morning they rented a mini-van with a pneumatic lift on the back that held an ATV for Daddy to drive around in the desert sand instead of using his wheelchair. They hired three bellmen at the hotel to go upstairs and play with Styles at the end of each of their shifts, and to feed and walk him.

Katie could see the tops of the defunct refinery equipment appearing over the crest of the last hill as they drove to the site. She hoped to find it transformed, but felt a sag of disappointment in her chest as they approached. Two large tents had been erected in front of the site, and about a dozen people in suits milled around the entrance. She saw Mec standing erect, in a uniform, with epaulets no less, and ten other men in similar uniforms standing in a line for about 100 yards in front of the chain-link fence with their arms folded in front of them. But that was it.

"Not bad for starters," Rudiger said.

He looked over at Katie, then stopped smiling. Her disappointment must've shown on her face.

He said, "Relax. This is just the core team. Tomorrow you'll see the whole show."

They stopped and got out, then got Daddy settled into his ATV. Mec walked over first.

"How you like my security ensemble?"

"Clothes make the man," Rudiger said, "and you're the man."

Rudiger headed toward the larger of the two tents with most of the people inside it. Katie started to follow him when Mec said, "Ms. Katie. I get everything on my list plus those you added. All the permits, even a clean title search. The whole kitchen sink."

Katie laughed and thanked him, then followed Rudiger into the tent. Two men, presumably those playing the CEO and CFO, were giving a presentation at a podium in the front of the tent, a PowerPoint projected on a screen behind them. About 20 other people were seated in rows of chairs, listening. One of the men in front was going on about the propane-to-propylene price spread. A man in the audience raised his hand and asked a question, and the other man giving the presentation fired back a response, then another question from a woman seated in the rows of chairs, and so on. Katie wasn't wowed, but she had to admit it looked authentic.

After a few minutes a man walked over to Rudiger. "John?"

Rudiger said, "Yes. Michel?"

"Yes." They shook hands. Rudiger turned to Katie. "Michel Baptiste, this is Katie Dolan. Katie, Michel is our executive producer from StudioCanal, the man making it all happen."

Katie smiled.

Rudiger said, "How do you think it's going?"

Michel said, "Fine, just fine. Dorian and Christophe are doing some ad-libbing with their answers, but this is good because it means they are comfortable with their lines, as well as the materials that you sent. I expect no issues unless there are questions not addressed by the materials."

Katie got some comfort from that.

Michel said, "I told Mec I would feel more comfortable if our men playing the foremen of the work crews in the yard would have an opportunity to do at least one dry run with the extras. Mec has arranged that for tomorrow morning."

They stayed for two hours, seeing three full runs of the presentation and question-and-answer sessions.

When they got back to the hotel, Rudiger waited until he and Katie returned to their room before saying, "You're like a dark cloud. If you don't snap out of it, you're gonna bring about whatever it is you're afraid of."

Katie felt her anger begin to stir. "I'm concerned, that's all."

"More like worried."

"Well, somebody has to focus on the nuts and bolts, make sure we think of everything, because you only seem to be seeing the big picture."

"Do you call setting this whole thing up, pulling all the documents down off the web, arranging everything with the contractors in India to knock off most of the documents and all the engineering studies, finding and cutting a deal with Mec, even drafting the CEO and CFO biographies, only the big picture?"

Katie sat down on the bed and sighed. "You're right, but there are a thousand more details to get right, and if we screw just the wrong one up . . ."

Rudiger sat down on the bed next to her.

Katie said, "What if Ducasse isn't as stupid as you think he is? What if he has really sharp lawyers—hell, just mediocre lawyers— and they do their own due diligence on our CEO and CFO and find out their bios are fabrications? Or they call the Paris office of the law firm we're supposed to be using and on whose letterhead we've drafted phony legal opinions, and find out the partners our actors are portraying don't exist? We're busted."

Rudiger put his arm around her, kissed her and said, "I think we should just chalk this up to stage fright for your upcoming performance as Angela Conklin."

His kiss didn't calm her.

He said, "That's a role you've performed beautifully. Just focus on that and let everybody else focus on their roles, and we'll be fine."

Katie looked him in the eye, felt a twist of annoyance and said, "You're taking this the wrong way. You think I'm crumbling with nerves. The more I think about that little eel Ducasse and his pompous old father, the madder I get and the more I want to do more than get the money back. I want to bring them down."

"So do I. It was my $30 million. Plus, I just found out I need it more than ever."

"Why?"

"I was down to my last $4 million before I left Antigua."

"What? How?"

"Tech stocks. Up 50% six months after you sent me the $10 million, then recently Apple took a dive, and my bet on the new BlackBerry Z10 smartphone fizzled. And today I just learned that my insurance company put a hold on paying the $12.3 million for my house burning down."

"Your house burned down?"

"Yeah. I didn't really have a choice. I put a dead backup battery on my alarm system before I left the house, so when the power went off the alarm wouldn't work. The insurance company found out the alarm company's software detected the battery switch ten hours before the fire. Now the Antiguan police are reopening their investigation because they suspect I may have conspired with the guy they nailed for torching my house. The insurance company won't pay until it's resolved."

Katie shook her head. "So you conspired with the guy?"

"No. I did it myself."

Katie felt a wave of unease. "All the more reason we need to look sharp here. And I think you underestimate Ducasse. I don't. We need to act as if we're dealing with people who are as smart as us on the other side."

"That's the way I've approached this whole thing."

Katie said, "Well, if I were Ducasse, I wouldn't buy what I saw today. And we go live tomorrow, our only shot at this."

————

Ducasse and his entourage arrived late that night, so Rudiger, Katie and Daddy didn't meet them until they all had breakfast the next morning. The staff at the Royal Hotel pushed together a group of tables for ten in the main dining room. Ducasse introduced his team: two associates from his firm, a partner and two associates from his Swiss law firm and a propylene industry consultant. Katie noticed that Rudiger didn't flinch when the industry consultant was introduced to him, but she felt a stab of anxiety.

The man better be an idiot.

Ducasse and his people in two Range Rovers followed Rudiger, Katie and Daddy in their minivan out of town into the desert. As they approached the site, Katie could hear the sounds of heavy equipment from a quarter mile away. When they got closer she heard saws, grinders and hammers as well.

They started up the final hill and Rudiger picked up his iPhone to make a call. "Okay, Mec, now," he said.

A few moments later a huge dump truck roared toward them, passed and headed off into the desert in the opposite direction. Katie looked over and saw Rudiger grinning.

As they rode over the crest of the final hill, she could hardly believe what she saw. A phalanx of 20 to 30 Range Rovers and Jeeps were parked in a semicircle off to one side of the two tents. About 30 people in suits were milling in and out of the main tent, and men in work uniforms and hard hats walked in and out of the smaller tent.

Three large caterpillars on tracks moved around inside the site, pulling over pieces of the rusting equipment. Foremen in hard hats directed teams of laborers who were using acetylene torches, saws, grinders and sledgehammers to cut up the debris. Other foremen directed teams that lugged the broken pieces into piles that two front loaders were lifting into dump trucks. Five more dump trucks were lined up behind them, waiting.

Mec stood outside the main tent wearing his uniform and observed as Rudiger and the other vehicles approached. He held up his hand to stop them, no-nonsense authority in his eyes, then waved to the left for them to park. His men were again lined up in a row for about 100 yards of the chain-link fence in front of the site. Another dump truck full of debris rumbled through the open gates and passed them as they parked the minivan.

"That's a helluva show," Katie said.

"Worth every penny."

They all piled out of their vehicles and Rudiger handled the introductions, then herded everyone toward the main tent. Katie couldn't help but smile. Not only was the demolition site abuzz, so was the main tent. At least 30 suits were in the tent, all actors hired and rehearsed by Michel Baptiste—some playing the role of company management, some their lawyers, some their bankers, some their bankers' lawyers and some the project engineers. Most were seated in rows of chairs waiting for the presentation, many milling around, drinking tea or coffee and talking. An 8' x 10' artist's rendering of the completed propylene plant stood on an easel in the front of the room off to one side. The catering table on the right was lined with breakfast snacks—fruit, croissants, bagels and accompaniments, Danish—coffee, tea and other beverages. The table on the left had piles of bound copies of the PowerPoint presentation, the Private Placement Memorandum, the business plan and draft copies of a purchase agreement, financing documents and the other legal documents. Two-inch-thick copies of engineering plans with a stack of folded copies of blueprints sat next to them.

Katie felt a swell of energy as Rudiger, looking resplendent in a navy suit, strode to the front of the room, stepped to the podium and said into the microphone, "Good morning, everyone. I'm John Rudiger of John Rudiger Enterprises, Inc., the equity sponsor of this project. Welcome today to all of you from Banque d'affaires Ducasse and advisors as potential participants in this transaction. With us today from our management team are Dorian Marchand, who'll serve as CEO of the company, and Christophe Renaud, who'll be CFO. We have representatives of the newly established Moroccan office of our law firm, Barnard, Montigny and Pineau, based in Paris, with offices in London and Milan." About six people stood up and turned around, nodded.

Rudiger continued with the introductions of Tepper & Wilbanks, their engineering firm, six bankers from BNP Paribas in Paris who were proposing to do the construction financing, three bankers from Bank of America Merrill Lynch in London, who were contemplating providing the secured project financing once the facility was in place. Both banks had a group of lawyers. After he finished he invited Ducasse to introduce his team. Ducasse stepped to the podium and had each individual introduce him- or herself by name and state their position with their firm. After that, Rudiger stepped back up and introduced the CEO and CFO, who started their 35-slide PowerPoint presentation. Questions and answers at the end were lively. There were moments when Katie thought she was watching a movie, including jokes followed by strategic bursts of laughter that were baked into the script, and a few spontaneous ones she didn't recognize from the prior day. Katie tensed as Ducasse's industry expert, a German named Schoenfeld, stood up and asked a few tough questions that Marchand handled. Then Schoenfeld said, "Allow me to give a summary of my understanding of your profit thesis. Number one, propylene production from heavy feed crackers is uneconomic today."

Marchand nodded his agreement.

"Number two, low natural gas prices provide downward pressure on propane prices as a feedstock."

Marchand nodded again.

"Number three, higher oil prices are driving a higher propane-to-propylene spread, which in turn will maintain a high EBITDA margin for years."

Marchand stepped to the microphone and said, "Exactly. Add to that the facts that conventional propylene production capacity has recently been significantly reduced and that propylene demand is in brisk recovery. It all spells a recipe for record high propylene prices and a record high propane-to-propylene spread."

Schoenfeld continued to stand. He said, "Yes, but what about the fact that JP Propylene has recently finished plans for a 1.8 billion pounds per year propylene plant, 50% larger than what you propose, located on the northern coast of Algeria? It would have strategic access to Algerian natural gas and propane supply pipelines and Mediterranean port access to the same customers you propose in Europe, Africa and the Middle East."

Marchand looked down at the podium as if studying his notes for a while. When he looked back up, Katie saw his eyes looked glassy. He cleared his throat.

At that moment Rudiger stood up on the aisle and said, "Perhaps I should answer that, since that's been a factor in my firm's decision to go forward with this project." He walked to the front, said to Marchand, "Thanks, Dorian," and stepped in front of the microphone. "There are two major reasons we don't think that's a concern. First, JP Propylene is relying on some of the same potential investors that we are, and we have the advantage of first mover status in locking down investment capital to preempt JP Propylene. Second, we're well out in front of them. We can get up and running about two years before they can. JP Propylene proposes a greenfield plant on a de novo site. As you know, we're retrofitting a former refinery site, which gives us a host of advantages: existing infrastructure such as roads, electric, water, pipelines, etcetera, to jump-start the project and make it about 30% cheaper than a greenfield plant. As you may have noticed behind me"—and Rudiger turned his head as if to look at the site through the back of the tent, at which point a loud crash from the demolition resounded—"and may have heard"—and a rumble of laughter went through the room—"my firm elected not to wait for all the capital to be in place to commence demolition so we could move the project along. We've funded the initial efforts entirely ourselves, and we believe that could give us as much as an additional six months of lead time over JP Propylene.

"In addition, with our first mover status, we'll have already locked in strategic customer relationships. As such, we believe that

JP Propylene will determine that there will be reduced demand for their product. Their math won't work for their required return on investment and their Algerian plant will never be built.

"I should add that I'm aware, confidentially, that JP Propylene is considering another plant on the Saudi peninsula in a joint venture with Saudi Aramco that would service the Middle East and Far East. And yet they only have management resources and funds available to build either the Algerian or the Saudi plant. So we're convinced we'll be the determining factor in assuring that their plant will get built in Saudi Arabia instead of Algeria."

Schoenfeld hesitated for a moment, then nodded and sat back down.

After the presentation Rudiger found Katie, Schoenfeld and Ducasse standing together and talking.

Schoenfeld said to Rudiger, "Interesting insight into the JP Propylene situation. I was completely unaware of the proposed Saudi plant."

Rudiger said, "Please don't tell anyone where you heard it, since my source would be very embarrassed if it got out."

Ducasse said, "Angela was just telling me that she's considering an investment directly in the project."

Rudiger smiled. "Yes, but she's been very coy about how much."

Katie smirked at him.

Ducasse said, "And I *was* surprised to see the activity on the site when we arrived. I had no idea you were commencing operations."

"Like I said up there just now, I intend to strike while the iron is hot."

Katie saw Daddy wave them over to where he was sitting near the back of the tent. Rudiger said to Ducasse, "Philippe, I introduced you to Carter Bowles, the man who sold us the property, at breakfast, but from where you were seated you didn't have much opportunity to speak with him. He's over there." Katie and Rudiger walked Ducasse over to Daddy.

Daddy, looking dignified in a suit with a string cowboy tie, said to Rudiger, "You know, John, I hadn't seen all this material before. This old cowboy is having second thoughts about selling." Katie felt a jolt of alarm. She darted a look at Rudiger, whose face was expressionless.

Daddy said, "This project is much more attractive than I had realized. Would you consider not paying off the note 100% and letting me roll some of the principal into the new project?"

Rudiger said, "That's an interesting idea, Carter, but I'm not sure there will be room in the deal." He looked at Ducasse.

Ducasse said, "Yes, I believe the deal will be fully subscribed, and you've already sold the property, have you not, Mr. Bowles?"

Daddy pursed his lips and shrugged. Katie had to stifle a grin.

On the way back to the city an hour later, Katie turned to see Daddy snoozing in the back of the minivan. She said to Rudiger, "Was that little ditty with my father something the two of you scripted at the last minute? It gave me a scare."

"No, that was pure ad-lib by your dad. I think he's been watching too many old episodes of *Dallas*." Rudiger laughed.

"And what about your response to Schoenfeld's question on JP Propylene?"

"That was a Hail Mary, pure fiction. But it looks like it worked."

They were in Daddy's room fixing drinks at five o'clock when Rudiger's phone rang. He answered it, listened for a moment, then smiled and said, "That's great news, Philippe, I'll be happy to have you on board. Let's sit down together and work it out tomorrow." He hung up. "That was Ducasse. He's in. He wants to fund the full $100 million of equity for the project."

Katie kissed him, then Daddy. She said, "Champagne!"

Daddy said, "The hell with champagne, let's get a bottle of Jameson's."

CHAPTER 6

That night Rudiger awakened to a sound he couldn't identify. He sat up in bed, alarmed, looked to see Katie wasn't in the bed, then heard her voice. "Breathe!" she said, "Breathe!" He felt a bolt of panic, jumped up and ran into the living room. He saw Katie standing over Frank through the doorway adjoining their rooms. Frank sat in his wheelchair, gasping for air, his eyes showing terror.

"What's wrong?" Rudiger said.

"An attack," Katie said, her voice urgent. "A bronchospasm, but he's coming around."

Katie held a rescue inhaler in Frank's mouth, gave him another spray. "It's okay, Daddy. It's passing."

Frank's breathing slowed, his eyes closed and he nodded to her. Katie waved Rudiger off, and he went back to bed. A half hour later Katie came to bed.

"He's sleeping, breathing normally," she said.

"Has that happened before?"

"A few times in the last year. Dr. Dewanji says it comes on after a very stressful day or if he gets overly excited. Today may have been too much for him."

"What was that inhaler?"

"A bronchodilator. Relaxes and opens the airways."

"Maybe you should show me where you keep it, just in case he has another attack and you aren't around."

Katie nodded. Rudiger could see she was still rattled. He put his arm around her and pulled her to him. She rested her head on his chest. She said, "It's times like this I have to force myself to face the reality that he won't be here forever." A few moments later he felt her tears on his chest.

———

The team of six arrived shortly after dawn at Rabil Airport on a G650. Their man met them on the tarmac with two SUVs. Stevens, the team leader, waved his men into the SUVs and crackled them all on the radio.

"We're five minutes away," Stevens said. "I don't see any reason to wait. The target site is isolated, no resistance or weapons expected, low probability of observers. We go in now. Jenkins is watch from the shore side, Golub from the beach. The rest of us go in and surround the house. Weapons live. Stone, Harris and Kaminsky, you are with me, shooters with your dart guns. The four of us go in, snatch-and-grab our two targets, then we're out. Subdue any witnesses, but no terminations."

Stevens waved Jenkins to start driving. He headed out on the main highway and within minutes found the turnoff for the long driveway into the target property. Hardscrabble volcanic rock and low-lying shrubs, reminding him of the plains in Afghanistan.

Stevens felt for the dart gun in the holster on his hip, fingered the M1A he held.

With any luck, they'd be in and out of here within half an hour, then drop their targets at the airport in Lisbon. From there the targets would be sent off to wherever. Stevens didn't know and didn't care. All that mattered was that this looked to be an easy job for once, then some R & R.

They bounced up the rocky road slowly enough to avoid raising too much sand and dust. As they approached the target location, he saw a huge satellite dish on the roof of the house. He motioned for Jenkins to stop, and the other SUV fell in behind. They all got out and moved forward, crouching over their M1As. When they got to the crest of the hill, Stevens waved them all onto the ground and said into his radio, "Golub and Jenkins, use your binoculars. Golub, go around the house and report from the beach. Jenkins, get as close as you can from this side and tell us what you see." Stevens noted that two SUVs were parked under the carport. He pulled his copy of the photos of the two targets from his pocket, a man and a woman.

Five minutes later Jenkins crackled the radio. "A woman moving around inside the kitchen. Can't see her face but slight build, maybe 5'3" to 5'5". Looks like target one."

A few minutes later Golub was on. "A man on the deck outside. Tall, maybe 6'2", dark hair. He just walked back inside."

That was good enough for Stevens. He looked down at his other men lined on the hill, then waved "Go," with two fingers. The other three of his men ran down and surrounded the house. Stevens trotted down the grade after them. When he reached the deck of the house facing the ocean, he saw the sliding doors on the ground floor were open. He clicked on the radio and said, "Okay, Stone, Harris and Kaminsky, with me now, we're going in." The men fell in behind him and the four of them entered the ground floor, weapons pointed. Just as they entered, a woman carrying a laundry basket reached the bottom of the stairs and started across the room. She saw them and dropped the basket, her eyes like saucers.

"Down, down, don't move," Stevens said. The woman fell to the floor facedown, her arms and legs outstretched. He didn't need to look at the photo again to tell she wasn't target one. Stevens ran to kneel next to her, motioned to his men, who entered the other rooms on the first floor.

"Where are they?" Stevens said.

"No home," the woman said.

Stevens waited until his men came out of the rooms, shaking their heads, then immediately ordered them upstairs. He heard them walking around, checking rooms. His radio crackled. "Got the man, bringing him down."

They pushed the man down onto the floor next to the woman.

Damn. He wasn't target two. Stevens pulled the woman up to face him.

"Where are they?" he said.

"They fly out two days ago."

"Where?"

She shook her head. "Don't know." Her eyes showed enough fear that he figured she wasn't lying.

"Who?"

"Ms. Katie, Mr. Dolan and Mr. Rudiger. And . . ."

"And who?"

"Styles."

"Who?"

"Pitbull. I wish he remain here. Then you no be so rude."

Stevens glared into her eyes. "Don't call anyone."

The woman didn't respond.

"I said don't call anyone, you hear? You do, we'll come back for you."

The woman still didn't respond.

"Tell me you understand."

The woman moved her head up and down.

———

Katie and Rudiger rode the elevator down to the second floor of the Royal Hotel. He had arranged for the meeting with Ducasse in a conference room he'd booked in the business center. They were dressed down from the day before, Rudiger in jeans with a sports jacket over an open-necked shirt, Katie wearing pants and a blazer over a shirt with an Hermès scarf tied around her neck.

Rudiger said to Katie, "You still seem concerned."

"No more than usual. I'm convinced the only way to hold this together is to fast-track it. Otherwise there's too much room for slipups." The elevator door opened and Katie walked out first. She said, "Remember our agreement. I'm the bad guy, you're the good guy." They started down the hall toward the conference room.

Rudiger said, "Okay, Counselor."

Katie smirked and stopped to let Rudiger enter first.

Here we go, Rudiger thought. He pushed the conference room door open and walked in. Ducasse and his senior lawyer, Rupert Stillman, stood up, both smiling. Ducasse's clothing was his usual over-the-top, a hammer-and-nails suit with peaked lapels, purple shirt and lavender tie with a lavender pocket square. Stillman wore lawyer's gray, a muted tie.

Ducasse's brow rose with surprise when he saw Katie walk in. He recovered and smiled.

Rudiger and Katie walked to the end of the conference table where the two men stood. Katie didn't offer her cheek to Ducasse, but instead extended her hand and shook his.

Ducasse said to Rudiger, "I thought we'd agreed it was to be business principals and one senior legal advisor only."

Rudiger said, "Yes. You didn't know? Angela is my lead lawyer."

Ducasse said, "I had no idea."

Katie said, "My private practice is limited to my long-standing relationships, and John is my most important client."

They all sat.

Rudiger said, "As I said on the phone, Philippe, I'm really pleased you've elected to step up. We only want one equity partner, so this fits the bill."

Rudiger could see Ducasse's gaze moving from him to Katie, a look of disbelief when he took her in. He was obviously mystified that she wasn't just some wealthy divorcée without a clue. Rudiger had to keep himself from grinning.

Ducasse looked back to Rudiger and said, "We're pleased as well." He turned to his lawyer. "Rupert?"

Stillman said, "We picked up your draft documents yesterday, and much appreciated the completeness of the package and the obvious care that was put into them." He inclined his head at Katie. "The financing documents are in good order as well."

Katie said, "We've been negotiating them for a few weeks and they're almost done. A $900 million construction loan with $900 million of takeout debt and a $200 million revolver once the construction is complete."

"There was one minor omission," Stillman said, and he picked up two copies from a stack of documents piled in front of him and handed one each to Rudiger and Katie, "a letter of intent to memorialize our understanding that you'll shut down all other discussions and negotiate with us exclusively until we sign the final contractual agreements."

Katie took Rudiger's copy and placed it on top of hers in front of her, pushed them back toward Stillman. "No, that wasn't an omission," she said, then to Ducasse, "As John told you, we've been dealing with a number of potential equity participants on a first-come-first-served basis."

Ducasse furrowed his brow and said to Rudiger, "I don't understand. Yesterday you said we had a deal."

"We do," Rudiger said. "A handshake. We're prepared to go full out with you to get this signed up and closed as soon as possible."

Ducasse said, looking back and forth from Rudiger to Katie, "But this is very unusual. We reached an agreement, so there should be no hesitation about memorializing the agreement in a letter of intent. It will establish our exclusivity and give us an adequate window of time to sign the final contracts and close the transaction."

"We aren't prepared to do that," Katie said. "If we sign such a letter of intent with you, we'll have to shut down discussions with any other potential equity participants. Anyone waiting in the wings will go away. If for some reason we can't come to terms with you, then we're left high and dry."

Ducasse sat back in his chair as if he needed a moment to think. He looked at Stillman, then back at Rudiger. "We've never done a transaction this way before."

Katie said, "I'm aware you'd much prefer to lock us up with a letter of intent, then take your time and do it the old-school way. But this is standard procedure in the modern world, and John won't do it any other way."

Stillman said, "And what is your proposed timetable?"

"I don't see any reason why we couldn't have all the agreements fully negotiated, sign them and close in a week to ten days."

Ducasse's eyes widened.

"You said yourself, Rupert, that the package of documents is complete. We have all of our due diligence disclosures prepared, even filed for all the necessary approvals and permits, as evidenced by the fact that we've commenced demolition."

Stillman didn't respond. Ducasse looked at him as if for an answer.

Katie said to Rudiger, "Why don't we give Philippe and Rupert a few minutes to think it over privately." She stood up.

Rudiger followed her lead. He said to Ducasse, "We'll go get a cup of tea."

Ducasse smiled and stood, his composure returned. "Thank you. Please give us ten minutes or so, and then we can talk things through."

Katie and Rudiger left. He grinned at her as they walked down the hall.

"What?" she said.

"I have this image of you in your blue bathing suit the day we met in Antigua, and I keep forgetting you were an Assistant DA in Manhattan, then a prosecutor with the U.S. Attorney's Office. I've never seen you in action."

"I don't mind saying I was one of the best young prosecutors in our office. You should have seen me in front of a jury, cross-examining a hostile witness."

"I prefer the image of you in the blue bathing suit."

They had a cup of tea in the downstairs lobby.

Katie said, "I'd love to hear what's going on up there."

"I'll bet Ducasse still hasn't recovered. Did you see his face when he saw you walk in? And then when I told him you're my lead lawyer?" He laughed.

"I have to admit I enjoyed pushing him around a little."

"You really spun him. Angela Conklin, former $30 million patsy, now in-your-face lawyer."

Ten minutes later Rudiger checked his watch and said, "Okay, showtime again." When they walked back into the conference room, Ducasse and Stillman were still seated at the far end of the table. They both stood again, Ducasse with his genteel smile. When Katie and Rudiger sat back down, Ducasse said, "Thank you for the time. We talked it over, and we think we have a way to proceed that should make both parties comfortable." He turned to Stillman.

Stillman said, "We propose a simple letter agreement in which we confirm our willingness to proceed together on an exclusive basis, but which won't preclude you from maintaining contact with other parties. In the event we two can't come to terms, and you fund the transaction with another party within 30 days, you agree to reimburse our expenses."

Ducasse added, "We'll be spending a great deal of money in legal and other professional fees."

Rudiger said, "We already have, and we'll be spending just as much, maybe more than you going forward."

Katie said, "And there's no way to police the letter agreement you propose. If we can't come to terms with you, it could be because you dig in your heels and are unreasonable about certain conditions."

They paused.

Ducasse looked at Stillman for a long moment, then at Rudiger. "Very well," he said. "We'll do it your way. But only with a timetable that assures us that we have your full attention. We'll go back to Geneva, fully digest and mark up all the documents, and expect to be back on-site here at your local law firm's offices in three days. Then we'll negotiate nonstop until we either have a deal or not. Agreed?"

Rudiger's mind whirled. *Our local law firm's offices?* That's one he hadn't planned on, figured the negotiations would be conducted with long-distance conference calls. He said, "Our law firm just set up their new local office and they're living out of boxes. I suggest we work here. We can book a couple of conference rooms at the hotel for the duration."

They shook hands on it and Ducasse and Stillman left.

After they closed the door Rudiger took Katie in his arms and kissed her.

———

When they got back to their room after leaving Ducasse and Stillman, Rudiger saw Katie plunge her hand into her bag and pull out her cell phone. She put it to her ear, checking her voicemail. She started pacing and her face darkened.

Rudiger felt a flash of alarm.

Katie dialed a number and he heard her say into the phone, "Flora, it's Katie." A long pause. "Flora, slow down." Another pause, this one much longer. Katie told her, "Don't worry about the house, just lock it up and leave. Right now. Go to the hotel and call me if anything else happens. I'll talk to you later." She hung up and turned to Rudiger, her face drained of color.

"What's wrong?" Rudiger said.

"I had my phone turned off during the meeting. I got a voicemail from Flora, called her back. She's frantic, said four men stormed the house with guns, put Flora and her husband on the floor, searched the house. When the men figured out no one else was home, they demanded to know where we went. She told them we flew out two days ago, she didn't know where."

Rudiger's spine went stiff. He started trying to figure it out. Maybe a case of mistaken identity? *But they stormed the house with guns.*

"It doesn't make sense," Rudiger said.

"Flora said there were at least four inside the house, and she thinks she saw another one or two outside. It was a trained team from the sound of it, maybe some kind of black ops." Katie was looking off at the wall, thinking.

Rudiger said, "After us?"

"I can't think of any other explanation. This could be something I've heard of but never seen done before. It's called a snatch and grab."

"A what?"

"I forget the legal term for it—oh yes, 'irregular rendition'—where we go into another country, grab a fugitive and bring him back home for prosecution."

"Is that legal?"

Katie said, "I've only heard of it for terrorists. People we would make disappear to Guantánamo. But I thought we'd stopped all that. And I've never in my entire time working for Holden ever heard of him considering something like this."

"I thought if they didn't have an extradition treaty with the U.S., that something like this was illegal."

She looked Rudiger in the eye. "Legal isn't the primary consideration in our case. They grab us, ship us back to the U.S., and we have to fight our way out of it on the grounds we were illegally extradited. Otherwise we stand trial. They throw us in jail while we wait to see who wins that argument."

"Not one I want to fight out if I can avoid it."

"Me neither." Katie shook her head. "That was a real screw up, my using that fake Angela Conklin passport to go to Cape Verde in the first place. That let Holden track me there."

"It was a nice place while it lasted. But I can't see going back there now," Rudiger said. "But there is one good thing about this."

"Which is?"

"They don't know where we are now."

Katie nodded.

Rudiger said, "Still, maybe we should change hotels. And register using different names and passports than we did here."

—

They were seated in Holden's office in front of his desk, Shepherds and the new guy, Johnston.

"So what went wrong?" Holden said.

"They weren't there, that's all," Shepherds said.

"I know that, but did we figure out where they are?"

Johnston said, "Nothing on the commercial airlines, so we checked the charters."

Shepherds said, "The day before our team went into Dolan's house, a chartered Gulfstream flew into Oujda, Morocco, with three passengers, four if you count the dog."

Johnston said, "The manifest said the passengers were James Scott Rockford, Elizabeth Davenport and Fred Beamer. And a dog named Styles."

Shepherds laughed.

Holden said, "What's funny?"

Johnston said, "Rockford, Davenport and Beamer."

Shepherds laughed again.

Holden felt a ripple of annoyance. "I said, what's funny?" He stared directly into Shepherds' eyes, then Johnston's.

Shepherds said, "They're all characters on *The Rockford Files*, the old TV show."

"Jim Rockford, the star of the show, and Beth Davenport, his lawyer and sometime girlfriend."

Shepherds said, "And Fred Beamer, an auto mechanic and wannabe private eye, who always got Rockford into all kinds of trouble."

Johnston said, "Played by James Whitmore—"

"Alright, knock it off," Holden said. "So what does that mean?"

"I think, sir," Johnston said, "that means they're all traveling under a group identity, obviously fictitious, and that they've got a sense of humor about it."

"So it sounds like it's them," Holden said.

"It has to be," Shepherds said.

Holden thought for a moment, then said, "Alright, so find them, wherever they are in this Oujda, Morocco. Under those names, or as John Rudiger and Katie Dolan, or Walter and Angela Conklin, whoever."

Shepherds said, "It won't be easy. There must be 30 or 40 hotels in that city, and we don't have any jurisdiction to allow us access to hotel records. We'll have to phone the hotels and ask to speak to one of them by name to know if they're registered there."

"What, you can't make 30 or 40 phone calls?"

Johnston said, "They're traveling with a dog. We'll just Google hotels that are dog friendly. There can't be that many in a primarily Muslim country."

"There you go," Holden said. "So find them, and fast, because before long whoever was at Dolan's house will tip them off we're looking for them, if they haven't already, and who knows where they'll bury themselves next."

———

Ducasse and Father were having lunch in the private dining room of their offices in Geneva. The waiter had just finished clearing the plates for their *céleri rémoulade* appetizer and they were waiting for their entrées. Father reached to the center of the table and picked up the decanter of red burgundy. He raised his eyebrows at Ducasse, who nodded, and Father poured him a glass, then one for himself.

Father said, "So what's your conclusion about this LHIW Propylene deal?"

"I'm going to do it."

"How much?"

"It's all or nothing. The whole thing."

"That's $100 million."

"It's only 5% of our new fund. Within the limits we've disclosed to our investors."

Father said, "Still, we've never committed that much to any one deal."

"You're forgetting I know the business from the Tetra Propylene venture from Fund III, which failed—"

"Yes, failed."

"—but which allowed me to understand the Houston deal that Rudiger was the primary investor in, and gave me the insight that his LHIW Propylene deal in Morocco is really a cookie-cutter of that deal."

Father said, "It damages us too much if it fails."

Ducasse was beginning to get impatient. All Father thought about was how much money he could pull out and when. Ducasse said, "This man Rudiger is a sophisticated financial player."

Father paused. "Maybe. But if the deal falls flat it will impact us severely. We have to strike a delicate balance here."

Ducasse laughed. "Don't worry, Father, we'll both still be able to take out however much we want. Remember, this is a $2 billion fund we're raising. Plenty of room to support our lifestyle. And if the LHIW Propylene deal doesn't work, we'll simply fabricate a few more successful deals." Ducasse sat back in his chair and sipped his glass of burgundy. He said, "But that's not the delicate balance I'm concerned about."

Father said, "What is?"

"Keeping Angela Conklin from getting suspicious."

"Why? You said yourself she fit the profile perfectly: divorced, wealthy, financially unsophisticated and relying on someone like Bemelman to help her make decisions. Even Bemelman thought she was an easy mark."

Ducasse waved his hand. "Bemelman is an idiot. This Rudiger is a real financial man, and I've just seen how our demure Mrs. Conklin operates as a sharp-witted attorney, a side to her I never knew about."

Father laughed. "She can't be that sharp-witted. She's in for $30 million, funded up front."

Ducasse felt a tremor of annoyance. *He's not getting it.* "Put Mrs. Conklin together with Rudiger and it's a dangerous combination. Rudiger is way too financially savvy to fit our profile. If he looks closely at our numbers, we may have a problem. And as I said, Mrs. Conklin is no shrinking violet. You should've seen her negotiating with us in Morocco. I swear it's a different person than the one I've known here in Geneva."

Father said, "So retreat."

"I can't. As you said yourself, she's in for $30 million and the two of them are very close."

"Retreat and declare victory. Figure out a reason and give her back her money. Be done with them both."

What? Give it back? "You must be joking. That's the last thing I'm going to do. No, I think the solution is to fund Rudiger's project, keep his mind on that and off of us."

"Buy him off?"

"So to speak."

Father said, "I'm glad it's not our money you're throwing around."

"Me, too. But I'm not thinking about that. I'm thinking about how much we could stand to make in this deal if it works as planned."

Father reached for his wineglass, took his time picking it up and sipping it. He said, "People in our position can't afford to get too greedy. Taking a moderate amount from time to time is tried and true. Taking too much, reaching for the stars, will get us caught. Remember that."

———

Later that afternoon Katie smiled as she watched Daddy walking on the crowded streets of Oujda, gesturing and laughing with Rudiger. Rudiger had Daddy's iGo in a backpack, Katie walking Styles on a leash. Katie looked around. Oujda was a continual surprise, a mix of 12th- and 13th-century Arab buildings of sandstone, with their curves and domes, and modern steel-and-glass skyscrapers. Seeing Daddy enjoying being out among the people on the street made her wonder if it might be a suitable home now that staying in Cape Verde no longer seemed safe.

"Styles! Stop pulling," she said.

"He's not used to being on leash," Rudiger said. "You want me to take him?"

Katie shook her head, kept walking.

Most of the passersby on the street either gave Styles a wide berth, or approached to pet him as if they'd never seen a dog in the city streets before. "He's friendly," Katie would assure them, and then Styles would sit, his tail wagging, mouth open and tongue hanging out with his pitbull smile, loving the attention.

When they got back to the hotel after their walk, Daddy sat down in a chair and fell asleep almost immediately. Styles curled up at his feet. Rudiger and Katie went next door and closed the door that connected their adjacent rooms.

"Hi," Rudiger said and kissed her.

"Hi," she said and eased him backward onto the bed, sat him down and then climbed on top of him, started taking off her shirt, then her bra. She lay down on top of him and kissed him again, more urgently.

They made love.

Afterward, Katie pushed her hair out of her face, said to him, "You think we have a chance?"

"A chance at what? You still concerned about our deal?"

Katie stroked his chest. "No. I mean us."

Rudiger turned to look her in the eye. "We seem to be doing fine."

"That's not an answer."

"Can you be more specific?"

"A chance for us to be together, for something more than a week or two of . . ."

Rudiger smiled. "I'm here, aren't I? Cape Verde is a long way from Antigua."

"Yes, but are you here for your $30 million or for me?"

"Both. And for an apology. But I already got that. Put it this way, I wouldn't be here if it wasn't for you."

His words warmed her, then she thought for a moment. She was still uncertain. She said, "Are you sure?"

Rudiger rolled onto his back and looked at the ceiling. He said, "I have this perspective that people don't always know entirely what they're doing, at least on the surface. You sent me the $10 million in bearer bonds without concealing the return address in Cape Verde. Whether you knew it or not, I think you wanted me to know where you were." He turned to look at her.

Katie felt her face burn, a wave of anticipation course down her body.

Rudiger said, "And as for me, why would I come here if I wasn't looking for you, even if I told myself it was only about the money?" He paused. "But I never told myself that." He leaned over and kissed her. "So if you're asking me if we have a chance, I don't know. But I know what I'm doing here, and I'm pretty sure you want me to be here."

Katie stroked his cheek, then pulled his face to hers and kissed him.

"Yes, I want you to be here, and I don't want you to leave," she whispered.

———

Stone had been sitting in the lobby of the Hotel Babel Nador for four hours. He was ready to switch off with Kaminsky for the next surveillance shift. The team was rotating through five hotels each day, 12 to cover in all from the list Stevens had gotten from HQ. Stevens plus five teammates at five hotels each day, with one floater playing leapfrog as relief so there were no coverage gaps.

This was the second day with no activity. Stone sat up as he saw a trim, strawberry-blonde-haired woman, maybe 5'4", walk into the lobby with a brindle pitbull on a leash. He pulled the photograph out of his pocket, checked it and felt a blast of adrenaline.

Gotcha.

He punched his cell phone for Stevens.

"Yeah?" Stevens said.

"Got her. Lobby of the Hotel Babel Nador with the dog. Positive ID from the photograph."

"Okay. We're all on the way."

Stone adjusted his earpiece so he was certain he could hear Stevens on the line.

The radio crackled. Stevens came on. "Positive ID on target number one. Hotel Babel Nador, Stone on-site. Rendezvous ASAP in the lobby."

Stone waited. Twenty minutes later the full team of six had arrived. Stevens walked into the men's room. Each of them followed at one- or two-minute intervals. Once inside, Stevens hung around until the last guest left, then locked his heel against the door to hold it shut.

Stone leaned against one of the sinks as Stevens addressed the team. "Okay, listen up. We hang out here at the hotel, mill around, eat dinner, drink coffee, do whatever. We wait until target number two, the man, is identified, and when he enters, Stone, you ride the elevator up with him to his floor, identify the room, then come back downstairs. Then we regroup and plan our acquisition."

Stevens paused, looked at them, each one in turn, and each nodded to Stevens.

Jenkins said, "I already notified our pilot and our drivers. Two units are parked outside. There's a service entrance in the back where we can take our targets out into the alley, should be no problems. Then to the airport and the G650."

Stevens said, "Okay, we wait for target two."

Stone was in the lobby when target two entered, again a positive ID from the photograph, grainy as it was. Stone stood up and followed the target into the elevator. The target pushed the button for the 10th floor. Stone stepped forward and hit the 10th-floor button again. "I always do that," he said and shrugged. The target smiled.

When the door opened on 10, the target hesitated for so long that Stone felt he had to walk out first. He headed down the hall, hearing the target's footsteps behind him, Stone waiting.

Damn. He could see the exit to the stairwell at the end of the hall, but that was a last resort. If the target didn't stop at his room by then, Stone would have to go through the ruse of patting his pockets, pretending to look for his key to let the target pass.

Lame.

But halfway down the hall he heard the target stop, slide his card key in the lock and open the door.

Stone counted, *One Mississippi, two Mississippi,* after he heard the door open, then turned back to see the door swing closed. Stone was back in the elevator in a moment and clicked the radio, said, "Room 1012." When the elevator doors opened, he walked through the lobby to the revolving doors, crossed the street into a tea salon. He sat down and waited. Stevens was the first to arrive, said, "Good work. Now we go live."

———

Upstairs, Kaminsky was positioned in front of the targets' door, wearing the outfit of one of the service staff, God knows where he got it. Stone would make sure he gave Kaminsky megatons of crap about how cute he looked in it. Kaminsky held a bottle of champagne in an ice bucket and two glasses in his hand.

Stone, Harris and Jenkins converged and pressed their backs against the wall near Kaminsky. Golub and Stevens came out of the door to the stairwell at the end of the hall, approached with their hands in the pockets of their jackets, live weapons in them.

Kaminsky knocked on the door. After a moment it opened a crack, the chain on it. Kaminsky said, "Champagne."

The woman's voice said, "I didn't order champagne."

"Compliments of the management."

Kaminsky drove his shoulder into the door, snapped the chain and pushed inside, dropping the champagne and glasses, pulling his dart gun out.

Stone was the first in behind Kaminsky, his dart gun drawn. He saw the dog, a pitbull, leap for Kaminsky's arm as he grabbed the woman and she yelled, "Hey!" The dog gripped Kaminsky on the wrist above the hand he held his dart gun in. The dog spun his head back and forth, snarling, all four feet off the ground. Kaminsky howled in pain and went down. Stone heard the snap of Kaminsky's wrist breaking as the dog brought him to the floor.

Stone aimed his dart gun and fired, hit the dog square in the side and it went limp in an instant. The woman stood looking at his gun with her mouth open. She inhaled and Stone knew she was going to scream, so he raised his gun and shot her in the chest. She went down like a sack of potatoes.

Harris and Jenkins by then had run to his right, grabbed the man, target number two, already unconscious with a dart sticking in his chest, and held him up. They dragged the man out. Stevens and Golub carried the woman out, each one supporting her under an armpit as if she were too drunk to walk.

Stone turned as an older man in a wheelchair with oxygen tubes in his nose rolled himself through the doorway from an adjoining room. He was shouting, Stone couldn't tell what; it was unintelligible. Stone aimed his dart gun at the man and shot him in the chest. His head slumped to the side.

Stone headed out of the room, his heart pounding.

CHAPTER 7

Holden was just finishing up a meeting in one of the conference rooms, discussing the final draft of a complaint on an insider trading case he'd been working on for 18 months. The attorney general was on the speakerphone from DC. The room was full of about a dozen of Holden's staff members and smelled like burnt coffee. Five minutes ago when he saw the meeting winding down, Holden had turned around, called Stephanie on his cell phone and asked her to have Johnston and Shepherds join him in the conference room when this broke up.

"Alright, guys, great job," Attorney General Martin said.

Holden said, "Thanks, Dan." He heard the AG click off the line. "Okay, guys, that's a wrap. We're on our way. We break this one on Monday."

Holden's junior attorneys stood up, headed through the door. Holden saw Johnston and Shepherds standing outside. He stood up, gave them a big smile. "My men of the hour. Snatch-and-grab Johnston and irregular rendition Shepherds. Come on in, guys."

They sat down across the conference table from Holden, Johnston eyeing him.

"What's wrong, Johnston?" Holden said.

Shepherds laughed. "I don't think he's ever seen you smile like this before."

Holden smiled more broadly. "Get used to it, Johnston, you're one of my stars now."

"Yes, sir," Johnston said.

"And quit calling me sir."

Johnston squirmed in his seat, like it was impossible for him to do it.

Holden shook his head, saw Shepherds laughing again. Holden said, "Okay, so are the Brits playing ball with you guys? If not, I can call Commissioner McPherson again."

"Everything's going as we'd orchestrated it," Shepherds said. "The Brits have released to the press that two U.S. fugitive felons have been positively ID'd in the UK and are believed to be attempting to leave the country. Conklin's and Dolan's photos have already been submitted to the press, soon to be on TV screens throughout the country, hopefully before the arrest."

Shepherds looked over at Johnston.

Johnston said, "We're monitoring them where we dropped them. The plan is to wait for them to wake up, and then apprehend them with a combined team from Scotland Yard and the London police. They tell us it should be a photogenic moment."

"I love it," Holden said. "They gonna get this on TV, too?"

Johnston nodded. "That's the plan. The Brits will leak the impending bust to the press, and there'll be TV crews on the scene."

Holden said, "The whole British Empire coming down on them—the Ruler of the Queen's Navy, Her Majesty's Secret Service, Scotland Yard and all that, splashed across all the networks and CNN. That's even better than dragging them out of their apartments in handcuffs at 6:00 a.m. in front of the cameras, then having them do a perp walk into the courthouse for their arraignment. Great work, guys. So now we wait, right?"

Shepherds said, "It shouldn't be long."

"Then we push through the extradition papers," Holden said, "fly them home and roast them over an open fire."

———

Rudiger heard a voice echoing in his head, like it was coming from inside a tunnel. He tried to open his eyes but couldn't.

Take it slow.

He remembered the sensation, from when he was in college and drank tequila. His mind worked but his body didn't. Brain telling muscles to walk, muscles and bones like rubber.

He waited, breathing. He smelled peanuts. His mouth tasted like garlic and metal.

Now he heard people talking, British accents.

He was able to open his eyes. He was in some kind of lounge, people milling around, nice cushioned chairs, classy. *What the hell?*

He could move his head now. He inhaled and exhaled. That helped. He looked around. It was an airline lounge. He looked down, saw he was sitting in a wheelchair. Now he remembered. Morocco. *Who were those guys?*

Where's Katie? He looked to his right, then left, saw her sleeping with her head slumped to the side in another wheelchair. He sighed, relieved.

He tried to lean forward to stand up, couldn't do it. He glanced to his right, saw a copy of an *American Way* magazine, picked it up and squinted at the sticker on the bottom.

American Airlines Admirals Club Lounge, Heathrow Airport.

He sat back and breathed, trying to will his body to work. After a minute he was able to push himself to a standing position.

The woman across from him in a cushioned chair said, "Are you alright?"

"Never felt better," Rudiger said. At least his brain said it, but he wasn't sure what came out of his mouth.

The woman looked at him with her lips parted, her brow furrowed. He sat back down. He reached over and shook Katie's shoulder. She didn't respond. He waited another moment, then pushed himself to a standing position again. This time he was able to walk to the chair next to the woman who'd spoken to him. He sat down with a grunt, looked over at her and smiled.

He said, "A red-eye, that's all," sure the words came out intelligibly.

The woman smiled back. "Ambien," she said. "It gets me through every time."

Rudiger looked over and saw Katie opening her eyes. He waited until they stopped looking glassy, then walked over to stand in front of her.

"You okay?" he said.

She didn't respond, just looked around, running her tongue over her lips. "Thirsty," she said.

Rudiger turned and walked over to the food counter, carried back two bottles of water. He opened one and lifted it to Katie's lips. Only about half of it went into her mouth, the rest down her chin, but she responded with a smile. He opened the other one and drank it in a few glugs. Katie was blinking her eyes now, looking around, much more alert.

Rudiger sat down in the wheelchair next to her. She looked over at him and whispered, "I remember now. Where are we?"

Rudiger whispered back, "London Heathrow Airport, American Airlines Admirals Club."

"Where's Daddy? And Styles? They shot Styles! I saw it!"

"It was a dart, same as the ones they shot us with."

"He's so small, it could kill him." Her brow wrinkled with anguish.

"He weighs about 80% of what you do, and he's tough. He'll be fine."

"Oh my God, what about Daddy? He's so sick. If they shot him with one, it could kill him." Now she looked panicked. "Where are they?"

Rudiger shook his head. "I assume still back there." He rested his hand on Katie's arm. "I really think they're both okay."

Katie nodded but didn't look convinced.

Rudiger's mind was waking up. He felt in his pockets. His wallet and passport were gone, but his iPhone was still there. He looked over and saw Katie's handbag hooked over the arm of her wheelchair.

What the—?

He said, "All my ID, money and credit cards are gone, but I still have my phone. Check in your bag, see if you still have yours."

She reached in, came back up with her phone in her hand. "No money or ID, but the phone's still here."

Rudiger said, "What's up with that?"

Katie's eyes were focused now, looking at the phone. She turned to Rudiger and motioned with her finger for him to come over. He leaned his head toward her and she whispered in his ear, "They can track us through our phones' GPS, and I'm sure they've set them up to listen in to what we're saying. If that's the case, they know we're awake now, so we need to react."

Rudiger tried to digest it, leaned back in his chair. It didn't make sense. He said, "You think you can stand up?"

Katie tried. She sat back down, hard. She took a few breaths and then tried again, balanced herself.

"Let's walk over to get some coffee or something," Rudiger said in a normal voice. He left his phone on the wheelchair, then hooked his arm through hers and they walked.

Over at the coffee station, Rudiger said to Katie, "Any idea what's going on? No question that was a snatch-and-grab, like you'd described. But what are we doing here? I'd have thought we'd wake up on a plane back to the States, in handcuffs."

"The only thing I can figure is that Holden's worried about the irregular rendition not holding up in front of a judge. So they dump us here in the UK, the Brits arrest us and then we get extradited the normal way. They know we're awake now, so we need to get out of here before the police come for us."

Rudiger shook his head. It still didn't make sense. "Why haven't they pounced on us already?"

"Maybe they don't want it to look like an obvious setup. If a U.S. judge sees we were dropped here only to be served up to the Brit police, he might throw out the extradition."

"Are you okay to run?"

Katie said, "Give me a minute."

Rudiger knelt and pulled off one of his shoes. He reached in, peeled up the leather on the bottom and removed something, handed it to her. "It's three $100 bills in a tiny plastic bag. I started keeping them in each shoe when I went on the run 11 years ago."

Katie said, "Remind me never to underestimate you. So what's the plan?"

"Like you said, first, get the hell out of here."

Katie said, "We need to slip our phones into somebody else's bags or purses, throw Holden off."

Rudiger said, "I'm thinking of pulling the fire alarm and running, disappearing into the crowd in the confusion. You able to run now?"

Katie reached in the refrigerator, pulled out a bottle of water, opened it and drank most of it. "No choice. I'll have to do the best I can."

Rudiger checked each direction. Nobody seemed to be watching them. He said, "You know Fortnum and Mason in London?"

"On Piccadilly."

"Right. If we get separated, I'll meet you in the 1707 Wine Bar."

Katie said, "I'll find it. And it's better if we do separate. They'll be looking for us together. Okay, let's do it." They walked back to their wheelchairs, picked up their phones and Katie dropped them into other passengers' handbags. Then they walked to the reception area of the Admirals Club.

Rudiger grinned at the lady with the nice smile behind the nameplate that said VERONICA COOPER-MULLEN. When she looked away he pulled the fire alarm. He held on to Katie's arm until at least a dozen other people ran out the front door, then let go. After she reached the terminal, he yelled, "Bomb!" He waited another few moments until he heard people repeating the word in the terminal, then ran out the door.

———

Katie ran through the door of the Admirals Club into the terminal, shielded by a group of four or five others. She felt a jolt at the sight of 15 or 20 policemen rushing toward the sound of the alarm in the club. She and Rudiger may have just barely escaped; that team must have been coming for them. She forced herself not to look back to see if Rudiger was okay, did her best to put one foot in front of the other as fast as she could, still wobbly from the drug.

A crowd of panicked travelers stampeded onto escalators to the lower floor. The sign said TO BAGGAGE CLAIM AND GROUND TRANSIT.

Katie ran toward it, her heart pounding and her head throbbing, the drug still affecting her.

By the time she neared it a crowd of hundreds of travelers had jammed the top of the escalators to the point where no one was moving. Katie ran to the windows and looked down to see the roadway to orient herself, turned right and ran toward the opposite end of the terminal. She knew American Airlines was Terminal 3. Terminal 1 was about a half mile away. She figured all the shuttle buses would either be clogged with people or not running because of the alarm. She'd find a way downstairs and run to Terminal 1. When she got to the end of the terminal, she found a stairwell, ran down into the baggage claim area, then outside. Once outside, she started running on the roadway toward Terminal 1. The air was cool and it stung her lungs, but it felt great because it was clearing her mind, helping her body respond.

Now she was running smoothly, feeling natural in her Nikes, her stride steady, her heart pumping like it did in the first lap of a half-mile race when she was in high school.

Just then Katie could swear she heard footsteps behind her. She figured it was someone else running from the chaos at Terminal 3. She glanced back, felt a stab of shock. An English cop in stride with her, even catching up. She turned around and picked up her pace.

Oh, man, I don't believe this.

"Caitlin Dolan," the cop said, sounding like he wasn't even breathing hard. "I am placing you under arrest."

You've gotta catch me first. In the neighborhood she would've yelled it back over her shoulder.

Give him 20.

Katie sprinted for about 20 yards, remembering her training under Coach Cain. Now she didn't dare turn around to look because she knew she was in a race. She was just barely into the run, maybe four tenths of a mile to go to Terminal 1. She glided, listening behind her.

Still there. The man had guts, and he wasn't some 40ish doughnut-eating New York cop. She wasn't in top shape herself, but she was still in kick-ass condition for somebody her age, and he was keeping up.

Break him.

She gave him another 20, then extended it to 30 yards, then glided again.

She listened behind her. The cop had caught up, maybe ten feet behind her. Her lungs were on fire already, and still at least a quarter of a mile to go. But her legs were holding up. Thank God for those off-road bike rides she did out in the rocky hills of Cape Verde, and for her runs on the beach.

She gave him another 20, then glided again, recovering.

Thirty seconds later he caught back up, maybe 15 feet behind her.

She started to feel desperate, like maybe she didn't have it in her anymore. She hadn't gotten a good look at him; maybe he was some young buck in his 20s who could still run forever.

Get it out of your head. You're a Dolan.

She straightened up her form, got her arms moving in a line, gave him another 20. Again he was there behind her. She listened for his breathing, his stride. Smooth, no strain in his breath. She judged he had a lot left.

She could see the terminal in front of her now, up close. Maybe only a 220 away, an eighth of a mile, half of the last lap, coming down the straightaway heading into the final turn. She tasted sweat in her mouth, heard her breathing labored in her ears. She couldn't let him catch her with his kick at the finish. She had to break him now.

Now, Katie, she said to herself. She waited. *Now.* Still she waited. *Now!* she screamed to herself. She sharpened her form again, took off, gave it everything she had, knowing she'd finish with almost nothing.

After a hundred yards she could feel the burn in her legs, afraid she would cramp up, so she eased off, listening behind her.

Oh my God, he's still there. The man must be a machine.

She was coming up on the terminal now, only 100 yards away, her legs stiffening, her pace slowing and he was behind her 20 feet, maybe closer. Her brain flashed with panic.

She decided.

She stopped, turned around and saw the look of surprise on his face as he pulled up, trying to stop, and Katie slammed her hands into his shoulders as she kneed him square in the balls. He collapsed without even a groan. He lay curled up in a fetal position with both hands between his legs. She waited to hear him inhale and then gasp. "Sorry," she said and then ran for the terminal.

She entered the first door she encountered, stood looking behind her, doubled over, panting, sweating. The cop was still down, not moving. She forced herself erect and walked down the aisle along the baggage claim conveyors, looking for a currency exchange. She saw one, decided to pass it and look for another farther down the terminal. She found one and stepped to the window, pulled the three $100 bills from her pocket, unfolded them from the plastic and stuck them into the cup under the glass. She affected a French accent and said, "English pounds, please." She was holding on to the counter, aware she was soaked with perspiration, afraid she might collapse.

The woman behind the glass looked at her, then at the bills for a moment as if she didn't know what to do.

"It's U.S. currency."

"I'm aware of that," the woman said. She picked them up, placed them on the counter beside her and pulled a marker from a drawer in front of her. She swiped the marker across the bills, waited a moment for the ink to dry and then examined them. She pursed her lips.

Come on.

The woman picked up the phone and made a call. Katie looked around behind her. No sign of the cop from the roadway, or any other police, not even any commotion and seemingly no awareness of the alarm in Terminal 3. She turned back around. The woman was now hunched over, speaking into the phone, Katie unable to hear what she was saying. Now she was looking at the bills, and Katie could see her reading the serial numbers off to someone. Katie started gritting her teeth, her muscles tensing.

Come on, come on.

Katie felt her legs cramping. She wanted to sit down, take the weight off her legs, but she held herself up by the counter.

After maybe a minute the woman finally hung up the phone, looked at Katie, flicked the microphone back on and said, "Sorry about that. Just a precaution with bills this old. After commission that will be 173 pounds, 90 pence. How would you like your currency?"

"One hundred in 20-pound notes, the rest broken into 10-pound notes, please."

The woman counted out her currency, slid it into the cup under the glass, stuck the receipt with it and smiled.

Katie picked up the money, shoved it in her back pocket and headed to the door for taxis and got on line. It took her five minutes, every so often glancing back behind her, before she reached a cab. "Fortnum and Mason, on Piccadilly," she said into the driver's window, then slumped into the backseat.

It wasn't until they were on Piccadilly, the cab bogged down in traffic, that Katie saw an electronics store.

"I'll get out here," she said, paid the driver and hurried inside. She bought three prepaid cell phones and a half dozen time cards. After she paid she asked the cashier, "Any chance I can log on a computer to activate these?"

The salesgirl directed her to a display of computers and said, "They're all on our wireless network, please help yourself."

Katie sat down and logged into the site for TracFone. She activated all three phones and put 180 minutes on each. On the remaining cards she had a total of 540 more minutes.

Her hands were trembling as she dialed Daddy's cell phone. It rang ten times, her nerves twisting. It went to voicemail.

"Daddy, it's me. I'm okay, Rudiger's okay. I'm so worried about you. And Styles. When you get this please call me back on this number as soon as you can. I love you. I hope you're safe." She hung up and clenched her jaw, tried not to cry, but she couldn't stop the tears.

It took her a few minutes to collect herself, and then she got up and left the store and hailed another cab. The cab had just dropped her outside Fortnum & Mason when the cell phone rang. She felt a blast of adrenaline.

"Daddy?"

"Katie. You're okay?"

"Yes, yes. And you?"

"A worse hangover than I've ever had from Jameson's, but I'm fine. Styles is okay, too. It was him that woke me up, tugging on my shirtsleeve. I don't know whether he knew it or not, but the battery on my iGo had run out—I didn't have it plugged in—and if he hadn't woken me up when he did, I might not have gotten up at all. Where are you?"

"In London. Rudiger and I woke up at Heathrow. I'm going to meet him now. We split up to get away. We're both fine."

"Who the hell were those guys?"

"Some team Charlie Holden sicced on us. Trying to bring us back to the U.S. to prosecute us. I'll explain it all later. You and Styles get out of there, but don't go back to the house. Call me on this number and let me know where you are. I love you."

"Love you, too, Katie."

She hung up and walked into Fortnum & Mason.

———

Ducasse sat in the comfort of his office, his enclave. Being surrounded by the enveloping closeness of his books, mementos, photographs, paintings of family patriarchs and the cushioned leather chairs had a calming effect on him. Right now he needed it. He sat back in his chair, his elbows on the arms, his hands steepled in front of his mouth, listening to Stillman, his lawyer.

Stillman, always a level head, but never reacting with the degree of urgency or passion that Ducasse did. Too careful, too methodical. Ducasse was growing impatient, but he let Stillman finish before saying, "So, Rupert, what do you think we should do?"

Stillman said, "Give them another day. Don't act irrationally. These things happen in deals."

Ducasse leaned forward, propped his elbows on the desk, said, "It's completely mystifying to me that Rudiger hasn't been in touch. We were to have started negotiating the final documents to the deal this afternoon, and no word on scheduling—"

"Yes, but Philippe, as I said—"

"—all this despite my leaving multiple voicemails for Rudiger, Angela and their Moroccan lawyers. Still nothing after 24 hours."

Stillman opened his mouth as if to speak, but Ducasse raised his palm to stop him.

Ducasse continued. "I'm extremely suspicious, even smelling something foul." He now leaned back in his chair and regarded the ceiling molding. "What has Rudiger been saying from the outset, and what did Angela reinforce in our recent meeting with them in Morocco?"

Stillman didn't respond, either assuming the question was rhetorical or that Ducasse would answer himself.

"That he was visiting with multiple parties to find an investor, and then subsequently, that they were negotiating with multiple parties on a first-come-first-served basis." Ducasse lowered his gaze to look Stillman in the eye. "So what does this delay sound like to you?"

"It could be anything, and I understand that it could be—"

"Well, it sounds to me like he's negotiating the deal with another investor as we speak, and he's squeezing us out. I'm not going to stand for it. I'm going to say in my next voicemail to Rudiger that if I don't hear back from him within hours, that we're going to walk from the deal ourselves."

"Philippe, you said yourself this is a very attractive transaction, modeled on one with heroic rates of return. I implore you not to do anything rash."

"I don't enjoy being taken for granted, manipulated or trifled with."

Stillman extended both arms and motioned with his palms toward the floor, as if to tell him to calm down. Stillman said, "Here's my suggestion. Send one of your young associates back to Morocco to visit their lawyers' offices to find out what's going on firsthand. If he leaves now, he can be there this evening, and on-site at their lawyers' offices first thing in the morning."

Ducasse regarded the ceiling again, letting it sink in. Stillman did have a point. He wouldn't want to do anything to jeopardize his participation in the deal. And having clear knowledge of where he stood first thing in the morning would probably suffice. Still, he almost choked on the words as he said, "Thank you, Rupert. Wise counsel."

———

Rudiger was halfway through an order of Scottish salmon with toast, accompanied by capers, chopped onion and a touch of Dijon mustard, complemented by a glass of white burgundy, when he felt a hand on his back.

He turned to see Katie, looking drawn, her face damp with perspiration. She managed to smile and sat down next to him at the wine bar.

"What'd you do, run all the way here?"

"I'll tell you about it later." She leaned over and whispered, "We're scrambling for our lives and you're drinking wine?"

"That's why they call it a wine bar."

Rudiger kissed her, then turned and motioned with his head to the bartender. "This is Horatio. What would you like?"

"First, a glass of water. Then some food." Horatio pushed a menu in front of her and turned to get her a glass of water.

Katie whispered, "Can we talk here?"

"Wait." Horatio placed Katie's water in front of her, then walked down to the other end of the bar. Rudiger said, "I've been thinking about it. We'll need money and documents to get out of the UK. It'll take a few days to arrange new passports through my documents guy in New York. I can get money wired by the end of the day through my bankers in the Cayman Islands. We'll need phones, too."

Katie pulled one of the prepaid cell phones out of her pocket, placed it on the bar.

"I've got three of them, all activated."

Rudiger said, "Great work. It's a start. You call your dad?"

"He's okay. Turns out they *did* dart him. Styles woke up first, then woke up Daddy. I told him to get out of the hotel, go someplace safe but not back to the house."

Rudiger thought for a moment, watched Horatio come back and take Katie's order for a salad Niçoise, then move to the register. He said, "I was supposed to call Ducasse last night to confirm our negotiations in Morocco for this afternoon."

"He'll survive," Katie said.

"I don't know. He's an antsy little flake." He looked up at the clock over the bar. "It's about 11:15 a.m. on the Continent right now. I'll wait until about 12:30 Geneva time to call him. Try his office line and figure I won't get him because he'll be at lunch. Leave a voicemail, think of something to stall for time. We can reengage with him once we regroup and figure things out."

"We need to get the hell out of here."

"That's what I said earlier."

"I got chased by a cop back in the airport, who knew me by name, said I was under arrest."

Rudiger glanced over at her, said, "You were right about Holden, then. What did you do?"

"I turned around and kneed him in the balls."

Rudiger grimaced. "Where'd you learn that trick?"

"I grew up in Brooklyn, remember?"

"I'll bet that made you a popular girl." Rudiger thought a moment. "It's not gonna make you popular with the Brit police. We should change our appearance, maybe dye our hair, wear glasses. My documents guy in New York has our photographs. I can ask him to change our hair color for the new passports."

Katie said, "We'll also need to find a place to stay. We can't check into a hotel without a passport or some ID. Maybe find a newspaper, rent a room in someone's house on a day-to-day or week-to-week basis."

Just then Rudiger looked up at the television at the far end of the bar. A newscaster was talking into the camera. A grainy photograph of Rudiger and a recent one of Katie were on the screen beside him. He felt a rumble of dread.

"Oh, man."

Katie snapped her head around to look at him. "What?"

"Don't look. Our pictures are on the TV screen. Just walk away. I'll meet you out front."

————

When Ducasse returned from lunch, he checked his voicemail and found one from Rudiger.

Rudiger said, "I'm terribly sorry, Philippe, but Angela and I, believe it or not, were mugged in Oujda. Our cell phones, IDs, money and credit cards were stolen. If you've been calling our cell phones, that's why you've been unable to get through. We were both roughed up and spent the night in the hospital for observation. We were just released. We'll be up to speed again in a day or so, and I'll be in touch about the timetable to resume negotiations on our deal. I hope you'll understand."

Ducasse sat back and said, "Oh my." He listened to the next voicemail, surprisingly also from Rudiger, who said, "Philippe, it isn't lost on me that with all our discussions of other parties we'd been soliciting for this deal, and our insistence upon having the flexibility to maintain contact with them throughout our negotiations with you, that you may be suspicious that we're doing the deal away from you with someone else. Please understand that neither Angela nor I are in the habit of getting mugged, or spending time in the hospital. It's not something we would make up. So please put your mind at ease. We have a handshake on a deal with you and we're committed to moving forward. I hope to speak with you in the next day or two."

Ducasse reached forward and pushed the button on his intercom to his assistant.

"Yes?"

"Frederick, I need you to contact Stefan Blastin for me. He should be on the way to the airport by now."

"Right away, Philippe. I'll reach him on his cell."

"Thank you. Put him through when you get him."

No sense in sending the young man to Morocco, at least for now. Blastin had protested that it was his wife's birthday, after all. *Plus, this way I'll save us the airfare* and *look like the benevolent boss.*

"The words 'ham-handed' come to mind," Attorney General Martin said. "They ran right past 15 or 20 cops? How did the Brits let that happen?"

Holden said, "I wouldn't say it was just them."

"What do you mean?"

"I worked out the plan in advance with them." Holden shifted in his seat, looked across his desk at Johnston, then Shepherds seated in front of his desk. He was glad he hadn't put the AG on speakerphone.

"Plan?" Martin said, sounding annoyed.

"Instead of just bringing them home, we decided to drop them off at Heathrow, out cold in wheelchairs, wait for them to wake up and arrest them in public."

"Why the hell'd you do that?" Now sounding angry.

"First, because we were concerned that we might not get the snatch-and-grab past a judge back here in the States. So we wanted the Brits to arrest them and extradite them the usual way. Second, the Brits leaked the whole thing to the press and they had camera crews on-site to film it, give us a splashy bust on the news."

"Charlie, we've known each other, what, 20 years? This is the biggest boneheaded move I've ever seen you pull."

"I take full responsibility for it," Holden said.

"*You're* taking full responsibility?" Martin said, outraged. "It doesn't matter. *I'm* the one who looks like an idiot down here in Washington. I had to move mountains to get resources for that kind of an operation, and now I have to go back and explain that one of my most experienced guys screwed it up."

Holden closed his eyes and hung his head.

Martin said, "That was an amateur screw up, trying to stage your bust for the cameras. It's like doing a touchdown dance before you get to the end zone, then having the other team strip the ball from you and recover the fumble—"

"Yeah, got it."

"—and then having to watch the replay on the big screen in the stadium ten times."

"I'm sorry, Dan."

"Nobody cares if you're sorry!" Martin yelled. "Do you have any idea where they are?"

"No. But we lifted all their IDs, credit cards, cash and passports, so they're running around with only the shirts on their backs. We assume they're still someplace in the UK."

"Well, *that* really narrows it down. And based on history, this guy Conklin figured out how to deal with that a long time ago. You've been trying to nail him for, what, 11 years?"

Holden didn't need to be reminded.

Martin left a long pause before saying, "You damn well better find them, or I'm not going to be able to give you air cover on this one, Charlie." He hung up.

CHAPTER 8

Rudiger put a rush on their passports, so his documents man in New York only took two days to express them to the flat they'd rented from a university professor on sabbatical. By then they had new credit cards and cash. They'd changed their appearance as well. Katie had cut her hair short and dyed it dark brown. Rudiger had dyed his hair and the beard he'd begun to grow blond. They'd bought nonprescription cosmetic contact lenses, Katie's colored brown and Rudiger's blue.

Katie called Daddy their second night in London to tell him they would leave the next day. They left the flat the next morning, had a car service drive them to the Folkestone Terminal in Cheriton to take the Eurostar train through the Eurotunnel to Paris.

"Our train leaves in about 20 minutes," Katie said to Daddy over the phone.

"In that case I'll see you in about three hours."

"What?"

"Yeah, I booked a Gulfstream G650 through the charter company we used to go to Morocco. Styles and I landed in Le Bourget Airport in Paris about an hour ago."

"Daddy, that's crazy," she said, even though she was thrilled.

"No it isn't. How else would you get home?"

She laughed. "We'd fly commercial."

"I wouldn't hear of it."

"Daddy, what's gotten into you?"

"Whattaya mean? A business mogul who just sold his defunct refinery site for millions can't fly to Paris to pick up his daughter and her boyfriend?"

"You're too much."

"Call me when you get to Paris. I'll be waiting at the Le Bourget Airport." He hung up.

She laughed and turned to Rudiger. "Daddy's still in character as Carter Bowles. He chartered a private jet and flew up with Styles to pick us up in Paris. This whole propylene deal has been really good for him."

Rudiger smiled. "It's probably easier to get through passport control and out of France that way than it is flying commercial," he said, his smile fading. "But the passport control here in Cheriton is the one I'm concerned about."

Katie said, "I hear passport control at the Cheriton terminal is more relaxed than at the airports."

Rudiger shrugged. "I don't know. But if they're gonna get us, this is where it'll happen."

When they got out of the car they split up. Katie could see Rudiger about ten people in front of her in the line for passport control. She felt a rush of energy as she saw him sail through. When it was her turn, the agent looked at her as if studying her face for too long, gave her a flutter of apprehension, then stamped her passport, handed it back and waved her through. Rudiger was nowhere in sight on the platform. They'd agreed to sit in the third car, but not together. She entered the car, walked up the aisle until she saw Rudiger, passed him and sat down about ten rows in front of him.

She let out a sigh. *Okay so far.*

The trip was uneventful. When they arrived in Paris they took a taxi to Le Bourget Airport. Katie's eyes teared up and her throat went lumpy when she walked into the terminal and saw Daddy and Styles sitting side by side. She waved. Daddy showed no recognition, but Styles started prancing in place, whimpering and wagging his tail. "Daddy!" she called out. He did a double take and then his face lit up. He let go of Styles' leash, and Styles ran to her, the entire rear half of his body wagging. He greeted her, then Rudiger. They walked to Daddy.

"I didn't recognize you," he said.

She hugged him. "Thank God you're safe,"

She turned to Rudiger, beaming, and said, "We made it."

"Yeah, looks like it. And tomorrow, we'll get our deal with Ducasse back on track as well," Rudiger said. He kissed her.

Katie reminded Rudiger that Charlie Holden had no jurisdiction in Cape Verde, no way to get local police to watch for them at the house, and after they'd escaped in the UK it was unlikely Holden could mount a similar snatch-and-grab. Nonetheless, when they arrived they went directly to the ClubHotel Riu Karamboa, where Frank had booked them adjoining rooms. Frank said, "I brought your luggage back from the hotel in Morocco."

"Wow, that's a relief," Rudiger said.

Katie looked at him. "Rescued from 20 years in prison and you're concerned about some clothes and luggage?"

"My Rudiger passport, other IDs and credit cards, along with a couple of other identities are in the false bottom of my bag." He shrugged. "I guess I'm a little sentimental about Rudiger."

"Whatever," Katie said and walked to the minibar. "Anyone else joining me for a drink?"

Frank said, "I've got a bottle of Jameson's in my room." He rolled himself through the doorway adjoining their rooms and came back with a bottle. Rudiger walked over and helped Katie fix drinks, then they all sat down around the table on the balcony. The air was warm and dry, the smell of barbecue cooking and the sounds of people getting lively in the bar adjacent to the pool downstairs.

"It's a hell of a lot better than being in that clammy air of the UK," Rudiger said.

Katie said, "It's just good to be back home—well, sort of home. And knowing that we're all safe." She turned to Frank, put her hand on his forearm. "I was so worried about you when I woke up in Heathrow, Daddy." She looked down at Styles, who was curled up on the floor between them. "You, too, little man." She looked back up at Frank. "My heart just about exploded when I saw them shoot him. I didn't realize it was a dart."

Frank said, "It's all over now. And I think when the soreness in my chest from that dart wears off I'll be able to laugh about the whole thing. Even now, I have to admit I haven't had this much excitement in as long as I can remember." He laughed. "Well, I guess I can laugh about it already." Rudiger smiled. Katie laughed. "And look, I got a souvenir from the escapade." He reached beside him in the wheelchair and came up with a gun in his hand. "One of their dart guns, with a full magazine of sedative darts."

Rudiger saw Katie's mouth drop open. "How'd you get that?" she said.

"It was laying on the floor when I woke up."

Rudiger said, "It must've been from the guy that Styles took down and snapped his wrist. Fell out of his hand and slid away and nobody noticed in the confusion."

Frank handed Rudiger the gun.

"It's light," Rudiger said, hefting it.

"All plastic, even the CO2 cartridge is plastic. It doesn't register in metal detectors or on X-rays. I know because I had it in my luggage when I flew back here from Morocco."

Rudiger handed it back.

Katie looked over at Rudiger and said, "So tomorrow it's back to business."

Rudiger said, "Yeah. I'll call Michel, our movie producer, first thing in the morning, see if I can line up his actors who played our lawyers for the day after tomorrow, then I'll call Ducasse and set it up at one of the hotels in Oujda."

After their second round of drinks, Rudiger walked into the living room and returned with a glass ashtray. He said to Katie, "We'll need to show some bruises from our mugging. Give me a shot in the forehead with this so I can walk into the negotiations with an egg and bruise on my head."

"I'm not going to hit you in the head with that."

"Come on, it won't hurt that much."

"Would you hit me with that if I asked you to?"

"Of course not." They all laughed.

Later, Rudiger noticed that Katie didn't even cast a disapproving eye at Frank when he suggested a third round.

Rudiger kept watching Katie as she alternately watched her father and smiled back at him as they talked. It dawned on him that during the whole episode in the UK he hadn't really worried about her. He guessed it was because he knew she could take care of herself. But now he felt a rush of emotion, relief that she was safe.

———

The next morning Rudiger called Michel, arranged for the actors who played the lawyers on their last trip to Morocco. The actor playing one of the junior lawyers was busy filming a movie, but the rest were available. He tentatively planned for them to fly in the next afternoon, with negotiations to start the following morning. He called the Atlas Orient hotel, made reservations and lined up two conference rooms.

Then he took a deep breath and called Ducasse.

"Philippe, it's John Rudiger." Listening for Ducasse's tone, trying to take his temperature.

"John, I received your voicemails. Are you and Angela alright?" Concern in his voice.

Rudiger chuckled. "Yeah. We had a bit of a scare. Jumped by four guys when we were walking someplace at night we never should've been. If you don't know a city very well, you can get yourself in trouble."

"It's shocking. Were you severely injured?"

"Some bruises and scrapes, but we're fine. So, on to our deal. I apologize again for the delay, but we're ready to proceed as you originally suggested: we work pretty much nonstop until we're finished. Can you and your team make it into Oujda tomorrow evening and be ready to start first thing in the morning the following day?"

"Absolutely. We've reviewed all the documents, compiled our comments and we're ready to go whenever you are. I'll call my attorneys and make the arrangements." Rudiger could hear the enthusiasm in his voice.

"Great. It's the Atlas Orient hotel. I took the liberty of reserving a block of rooms for you and your team. They're under my name. I've reserved two conference rooms for two weeks. Safe travels."

He hung up.

Rudiger sat back and smiled.

Katie, sitting adjacent to him on the sofa, said, "I only heard your side of it, but it sounded like everything is all set."

Rudiger nodded. "We managed to hold it together after all."

"Let's fly in early enough tomorrow so I can have multiple copies of all the documents produced and I can rehearse with the actors playing the other lawyers."

Rudiger said, "Good idea. And Michel's having a makeup guy flown down to touch us up with some bruises and bandages."

"Maybe I should've just brained you with that ashtray after all," Katie said.

They both laughed.

That afternoon they changed back into themselves: Katie bought a strawberry-blonde wig that matched her own hair color and Rudiger dyed his hair back to his natural color. They saved their colored contact lenses for later, and Rudiger bought a blond wig, just in case.

————

They left Frank and Styles at the hotel and flew into Oujda the next morning, again on a chartered jet. Rudiger had seen how disappointed Frank was not to be part of the show, so he promised they'd call frequently to update him on how it was going.

Katie put everything in place in the conference rooms herself. When the actors arrived she handed each of them some lines she'd scripted out for them.

"François, you're our environmental expert."

The man nodded, reading.

Katie said, "You don't have to hit the lines exactly, just pick up enough of the buzzwords to make yourself sound credible."

She turned to one of the others. "Alain, you're our permits and approvals man."

The man nodded.

And so on, six of them in all. Rudiger watched them go through two rounds of rehearsals, Katie playing the parts of herself and Stillman, and then motioning to each of the actors in turn for them to discuss their areas of specialty as lawyers. There was one point where David overacted and botched up some of the legal terms. Katie talked right over him, getting it right, and Rudiger felt like she would've even pulled it off in the meetings.

The next morning, after the makeup man visited their room, Katie assembled the entire team in the lobby coffee shop for last-minute questions. Katie then walked them all upstairs and stopped in front of the conference room door to let Rudiger open it and go inside first. He took a deep breath, smiled at Katie and said, "Break a leg."

She smirked at him. "What a ham. Let's get on with it."

Rudiger opened the door and was surprised to see only Ducasse and Stillman sitting at the far end of the conference table. *What the—?*

He smiled and pretended he didn't sense anything wrong. "Philippe, Rupert, great to see you," he said and strode into the room. Both of their faces were like stone. Rudiger reached the end of the table and extended his hand. Neither man stood up or reacted in any way.

Katie said, "Where's the rest of your team?"

Ducasse said, "Sent home yesterday evening." He said to Rudiger, "The only reason Rupert and I didn't leave with them is that I wanted to say to your face that you're a liar and a fraud. In fact, I'm now actually beginning to wonder who you are, if John Rudiger is a fiction perhaps as big as the scam you seem to have gone to such great lengths to perpetrate upon us."

Rudiger felt like his stomach was falling down to his feet, but he forced himself not to show any reaction. *Don't say anything. Just listen.*

Ducasse continued. "Shortly after we arrived in Morocco, one of our junior attorneys, Stein, called your local law firm with a question about BNP Paribas' financing commitment. No answer, voicemail and no reply. So he called the number on the BNP Paribas banker's business card. Same result. So then he called the Paris office of BNP Paribas and asked to speak directly to the banker, Levasser. When Stein reminded Levasser they'd met a week earlier on the LHIW Propylene deal in Morocco, and that he had a question on BNP Paribas' financing commitment for the deal, there was stunned silence on the other end of the line. Levasser told Stein he'd never been to Morocco, never heard of LHIW Propylene and there was no financing commitment. So we took it upon ourselves to go visit your local law firm's offices here in Oujda. The business cards your lawyers handed us"—and Ducasse now looked at the actors lined up behind Katie—"listed Suite 2720 in an office tower in downtown Oujda, a building which, it turns out, only has 17 floors."

Rudiger knew they were cooked, didn't need to hear any more, but Ducasse continued.

"Even though I knew what the answer would be, I nonetheless sent one of my young associates in an SUV into the desert to view the construction site. Nothing was happening." Now Ducasse stood up. "Quite an elaborate con. You must think I'm an idiot. I discussed the matter with Rupert, who assures me we would have a valid course of legal action against you for our expenses, but that the cost of pursuing the suit would likely make it inadvisable to file one. I'm unsure whether or not I agree; I'll wait until I return to Geneva to decide." He pushed his chair back. Stillman stood. "But I can assure you, if you ever show yourself in Geneva again, I'll have you arrested."

Ducasse and Stillman walked out of the conference room.

Rudiger turned and looked at Katie, his mouth dry, his legs feeling like he was standing in quicksand.

"Now what?" she said.

"I can't think of much of anything else to do except go home and lick our wounds."

———

On the plane flight back to Cape Verde, Katie reached across the aisle and took Rudiger's hand. She felt like she might cry.

"I'm sorry," she said.

"For what?"

"For everything."

"Everything? This wasn't your fault. We had some bad luck. If it wasn't for Charlie Holden's detour into the UK, I think we would have pulled this off."

"If I hadn't swiped your $30 million in the first place, if I hadn't let myself get duped by Ducasse, and if I hadn't used that phony Angela Conklin passport to fly to Cape Verde, none of this would've happened."

Rudiger softened his features. Katie's eyes were swimming; she knew she was now on the verge of tears. Rudiger said, "Why do women always look backward?" He paused, squeezed her hand. "We are where we are. Let's just deal with it."

That made it worse. He was like he was back in Cape Verde when he first learned about the $30 million. So reasonable, so even. "Why don't you just tell me I'm an idiot?"

He stood up, stepped over to her and kissed her, a long, tender one. He pulled back and said, "Because you aren't." He sat back down.

Katie waited a moment, then said, "So what do we do now?"

"Normally I'd say we regroup, then figure out what comes next. But in this case, I don't see any way forward with Ducasse."

"So it's kiss the $30 million good-bye?"

Rudiger smiled. "Well, unless he's gonna single you out to screw you out of the fund's returns he gives everybody else, bogus or not, you're gonna do quite well."

Katie bucked up, even smiled. "So that means in three or four years I should have your money back."

"And then some," Rudiger said, "if he raises a Fund VI."

He said nothing more, but Katie didn't believe he didn't see any way forward, certain that he was still turning it over in his mind, looking for an angle. She felt better after that, not giving up herself, either.

When they got back to the hotel at Cape Verde, Daddy was full of questions. Katie waved Rudiger off and took Daddy into the living room of his suite. She talked to him for at least half an hour, Katie explaining to Daddy and Daddy reacting, sometimes looking like he couldn't believe it, sometimes nodding. Afterward, Katie came back in and said to Rudiger, "He's upset. He feels like maybe he could've helped if we'd brought him along."

Rudiger shrugged. "I hope you told him that wouldn't have made any difference."

They had a quiet dinner that evening, barbecued spareribs ordered in from the restaurant downstairs next to the pool, because Daddy had been seduced over the past few days by the aroma.

"I'm sorry, guys, but I'm disappointed," Daddy said, putting down a few bones from his rack onto his plate.

"Really?" Rudiger said. "I think it's good stuff."

"Yes, Daddy, great stuff," Katie said, certain Rudiger had said it to humor Daddy, not too impressed herself but willing to say anything to make sure Daddy was having a good time.

"No," Daddy said. "Not the ribs. I'm talking about Ducasse. I can't believe you two are ready to give up on getting the money back."

Katie looked at Rudiger, who smiled back at her. Did he have an idea? She said, "We haven't given up." She set her jaw, straightened her spine, feeling like she was the Brooklyn girl with her attitude back. "We just need to figure out a way to still nail the little creep."

"That's my Katie," Daddy said.

———

The next morning Rudiger got up shortly after dawn, his usual time, and got dressed for a run on the beach. Katie stirred. "You coming?" he said. She climbed out of bed, Rudiger admiring her body.

"Quit leering."

"I'm admiring. You're beautiful."

She mouthed, "Thank you," cocked her head and put her hands on her hips, gave him a long look, then walked to the bureau.

Rudiger heard Styles whimpering in Frank's adjoining room, figured he needed to go out. He opened the door and walked inside, saw Styles sitting next to Frank's wheelchair and looking up at him, Frank asleep in front of the TV again.

Rudiger walked in, heard the oxygen concentrator running, the air hissing in the tubes as he approached Frank. He shut off the TV, then placed his hand on Frank's shoulder. Styles whimpered again. Rudiger got a flash of alarm.

"Oh no."

Frank's shoulder was rigid. Rudiger felt his neck. It was like cold marble, and he knew even before he didn't find a pulse that Frank was gone. Tears welled in his eyes. "Oh no, no, no." Styles whimpered again and lay down. "I know, buddy, I know," Rudiger said to him. He closed his eyes and felt a sag in his chest, his legs go weak.

He turned at a sound and saw Katie in the doorway, her mouth open, her eyes showing disbelief.

Rudiger said, "Katie, I'm sorry. So, so sorry," his voice hoarse with emotion.

Katie collapsed to her knees and put her hands to her face. "No!" she said. "No!" She fell to the floor and started sobbing.

Rudiger crossed the floor to her and knelt in front of her. He lifted her and took her in his arms. "I'm sorry," he said again, feeling like he'd been stabbed in the heart.

———

Katie was sitting on the sofa in her and Rudiger's room, Daddy not visible through the adjoining doorway, but she could still see Styles lying on the floor in front of his wheelchair. Styles wouldn't move, even when Rudiger put his leash on him to try and take him out for a walk. Ultimately, Rudiger unhooked the leash and left him alone.

Rudiger was now sitting next to her on the sofa, his arm around her, doing his best to console her, but there was nothing he or anyone could do to stop the tears that came in waves, then turned into sobs.

They waited. It had been an hour since Rudiger called the front desk to ask them to inform the coroner, then called Dr. Dewanji, Daddy's main doctor. He was the first to arrive. Rudiger showed him in. Dr. Dewanji was a wiry Indian man with sympathetic eyes and a soft voice. He walked to Katie and clasped both of her hands in his.

"I'm so sorry, Ms. Katie."

Katie could barely lift her head to look up at him.

"Your father was a true gentleman. I was proud to have been able to treat him." He glanced at Rudiger, who sat back down and put his arm around Katie again. Then Dr. Dewanji walked into Daddy's room. He stayed there for a few minutes, then returned and sat in the chair adjacent to Katie.

Dr. Dewanji said in his lilting tones, "I believe I can tell you some things that may be of comfort to you, if you are able to listen."

Katie raised her head to look at him.

He said, "I remember telling you when you first arrived that your father's condition had multiple complications, including his lungs, heart, liver and kidneys. That everything was failing. That you did the right thing by bringing him to this climate and giving him the peace of mind to know he was well cared for. The combination of physical care and mental and emotional serenity you provided him allowed him to flourish beyond what I would have ever expected of a man in the advanced stages of his disease. Rest assured he did not pass in a violent manner. I recall telling you this end for him was possible, and vastly preferable to the lingering dissipation normally associated with his primary condition, emphysema."

Katie tried to smile at the kindness in Dr. Dewanji's voice, but could only manage a nod of her head.

"I believe he simply went to sleep. No pain. And now he is with your other loved ones."

Katie's tears flowed freely again, but there was a sweetness in it, that she could believe Daddy was with Mom and Mike now. She looked up at Dr. Dewanji.

He reached out and squeezed her hand.

There was another knock at the door. Dr. Dewanji looked at Rudiger, then stood up. "I'll take care of this," he said, walked to the door and opened it. It appeared to be the coroner. Behind the man in the doorway, Katie saw two other men in the hallway with a gurney. Dr. Dewanji spoke in low tones to the first man for a moment, then closed the door and walked into Daddy's room. He snapped his fingers at Styles, who got up and trotted out. Dr. Dewanji shut the adjoining door behind him. Styles climbed up on the sofa next to Katie and lay down with his head on her lap with a grunt, then a long exhale. After about 15 minutes Dr. Dewanji came back into their room and sat down in the chair adjacent to Katie again. He said in his soft voice, "They're prepared to take your father away now. Would you like to spend a few minutes alone with him before they do?"

Katie nodded, slid out from underneath Styles and started to get up, then slumped back into the sofa. Rudiger helped her up and walked her toward Daddy's room. He left her at the doorway and she walked in herself, stood next to Daddy and looked down into his face for a long time. Finally she said, "I love you, Daddy." She leaned over and kissed his forehead. "Good-bye."

On the third day after Frank died, Rudiger, Katie and Styles sat in the backseat of Xavier's Range Rover, driving over Katie's long driveway from the highway to her house. She had a cardboard box on her lap with Frank's ashes in it.

Rudiger glanced over at her, wondering if she was really okay. *Give her some space.*

The previous day Katie had been a rock through the simple service at the funeral parlor. Flora and her husband, Carlos, and another half dozen employees of the hotel attended, people who'd gotten to know Frank during their yearlong stay there prior to moving into the house. Katie had insisted on a priest to say prayers, and Flora had arranged for the priest of her church to come in. Afterward, Rudiger, Katie and Styles rode with Frank's casket to the crematorium.

Now, when Xavier pulled his Range Rover under the carport, Katie walked onto the deck, put the box with Frank's ashes down in the center of the table. Styles ran in circles, wagging his tail, Rudiger unsure if he was looking for a ball or for Frank. Katie walked to the sliding doors, unlocked them and went inside. Rudiger just stood there, looking at the sea, listening, smelling the air, remembering Frank.

A few minutes later Katie walked back out with a tray of drinks. She put them down in front of three of the chairs, her rum and soda with lime, Rudiger's gin and tonic, and a Jameson on the rocks for Frank. Rudiger extended his hand, she took it and he pulled her to him, hugged her. He said, "One last drink. That's appropriate." They sat down, Styles lying down on the deck between them, his head resting on his front paws, ears pinned back.

Katie looked down at him and said, "It's as if he knows to be respectful."

"I think he does."

Katie picked up her drink and raised it. Rudiger picked up his, waiting.

Katie said, "A toast to Frank Dolan. A simple man, a loving father . . ."

"A good friend," Rudiger said. He clinked his glass against Katie's, then Frank's. Katie reached over and touched her glass to Frank's as well.

They both sipped, Rudiger watching Katie. She was holding up, done crying.

They drank in silence for about 15 minutes, Rudiger giving Katie as much time as she needed.

Then she turned to him and said, "You ready?"

"It's not up to me. Are you ready?"

Katie nodded.

"Are you sure you want to do it here?"

She smiled at him. "He was happy here. There wasn't much left for him back in Cobble Hill before we left. Yes, he still had friends in the fire department, but as time went on, fewer and fewer of them dropped by to see him. Mostly, he stayed in the house and watched TV."

Rudiger stayed silent, observing her.

"But here, well, mostly he watched TV," she said, smiled, then reached out and took his hand. "But after you arrived, he was a different person. He hadn't had a good friend, somebody he could talk to, laugh with and be himself with, for five or ten years, I don't even know how long. You gave him a life again." She squeezed Rudiger's hand and he saw tears welling in her eyes. "And the whole LHIW Propylene deal? He was like a different person. He was a simple man. For him to have taken it upon himself to charter a jet to get back to Cape Verde from Morocco is remarkable." She laughed, tears flowing down her cheeks. "But to have chartered a jet and flown to Paris to pick us up? That's not something I could ever have imagined him doing. You brought that out of him, Rudiger." She stood up and kissed him. He felt her tears dripping onto his face. She leaned back, looked him in the eye and said, "He loved you."

Rudiger felt his throat thicken. "Yeah," he tried to say, but it came out as a whisper. He cleared his throat, said, "I think he did."

Katie smiled. "I know he did."

She stood back up, took the box in her hands and opened it. There was a seal with a number on it wrapped around the plastic bag inside. Katie pulled it off and looked at it as if it were a sacred relic, then put it in her pocket. She picked up the box, held it against her breast and reached for Rudiger's hand. They stepped off the deck onto the sand, Styles following them.

Katie said, "The wind is blowing back toward the house from the ocean. We'll scatter him from the shore."

CHAPTER 9

Rudiger decided not to push Katie on the subject of Ducasse until she was ready. A week after Frank passed away, they were walking back to the hotel after a run on the beach when Katie turned to him and said, "I'd feel like we'd be letting Daddy down if we didn't figure out a way to go after Ducasse."

That's the Katie Dolan I know.

After a shower and as they started breakfast at the table on the balcony, Rudiger said to her, "We should brainstorm about how to get to Ducasse. I think we can forget about the LHIW Propylene deal, but—"

"What does LHIW stand for, anyhow?"

Rudiger said, "Let's Hope It Works."

Katie laughed.

"It was your father's idea. He said not to tell you what it meant, just wait until you asked, that you'd get a kick out of it."

Katie laughed again. "That's my daddy."

Rudiger said, "So maybe a way to start this off is to look at how we each would approach this in our former lives. How'd you go after Ducasse if you were still with the U.S. Attorney's Office?"

"First, I'd draft a complaint that would peel the varnish off the wainscoting in his office."

"What would you allege in the complaint?"

"That he defrauded at least three U.S. investors—my man at ASB in Geneva introduced me to them when I was considering investing in Ducasse Fund V—in a Ponzi scheme that bilked them out of their money to pay off previous fund investors, and fabricated rates of return to solicit and defraud new investors like me."

Rudiger said, "I did most of the research, but I could go back and do it in detail to give you the guts for that complaint, citing each of the deals from their first four funds that were bogus. Companies that I never heard of and found no evidence of, I'm sure never existed. And then those companies being bought out by other companies that also never existed. All to fabricate phony investment profits."

Katie said, "How would you go after Ducasse if you were in your former life?"

"Do the same research I already did, then find his weakest link."

"Weakest link?"

"Yeah, his accountant, his CFO, a junior associate, then show them the data and bluff them into confessing by saying they'd get immunity. Then use that confession against Ducasse."

Katie thought for a moment. "How about this? I put all that in the detailed complaint as if I'm still Katie Dolan working undercover for the U.S. Attorney's Office in a sting operation. We show it to Ducasse and say if he pays me, Katie Dolan, the $30 million that I invested under the alias of Angela Conklin on behalf of the U.S. government, I'll disappear with the money and bury the complaint so the U.S. Attorney's Office will never be able to file it to bring him down."

Rudiger shook his head. "All he needs to do is Google the U.S. Attorney's Office and find out you're no longer with them."

"I'm undercover. And so are you, Walter Conklin. We busted you, and you're cooperating as part of a task force to bring in white collar crooks."

Rudiger said, "I'm not sure it's enough, you and three other investors acting as witnesses." He thought for a moment, then said, "We need someone on the inside who really knows Ducasse's operation to give us his testimony, make Ducasse sweat. Didn't you say it was your banker at ASB who introduced you to him?"

"Bemelman."

"And the three other U.S. investors were also introduced to Ducasse by this Bemelman?"

Katie said, "Yes."

"Ducasse's fund documents say he pays origination fees of .5% for bringing in new investor money. So Bemelman is getting paid, and he's Ducasse's shill. We talked about this before we went to Geneva: Bemelman has a profile. Middle-aged, wealthy divorcées or widows, clueless about finance. He scans his clients for women meeting the profile, then feeds the easy marks to Ducasse."

Katie said, "I met three of them. That's exactly right."

Rudiger said, "Lonely women looking for a man, bowled over by Ducasse's impressive town house, vintage cars, exotic tastes, and susceptible to his advances."

"I'm sure one of them slept with him, because every time she mentioned Ducasse her face lit up. She was like the pimply faced high school girl who was finally getting laid."

Rudiger said, "So we go after Ducasse via Bemelman. We fly to Geneva and sweat him. We tell Bemelman I'm working undercover with you at the U.S. Attorney's Office. We say we've figured out the scam, show him our draft complaint and get Bemelman to flip on Ducasse, spill everything he knows in exchange for immunity from prosecution."

Katie was nodding. She said, "Then we add Bemelman's testimony to the complaint, and then—"

"Show it to Ducasse and put the wood to him," Rudiger said. "Okay. Let's see if we can make it work. You start drafting your complaint. I'll pull together my research on Ducasse's scam for you to use in it."

Katie looked skyward and said, "We're on it, Daddy."

———

Rudiger and Katie worked together on opposite sides of the table out on the balcony. Katie drafted a complaint against Banque d'affaires Ducasse, and Ducasse and his father individually, as if she were still with the U.S. Attorney's Office. Rudiger refined his research into Ducasse's phony deals.

It was like when the two of them had done their separate parts back at her house in pulling together the LHIW Propylene charade. But now it was bittersweet because Daddy wasn't there.

Early on, Rudiger said to Katie, "You don't need notes or source documents?"

"Only the stuff you'll be feeding me, but the complaint itself? I could do this in my sleep."

At the end of the first day, Katie handed Rudiger a 45-page shell of her complaint, listing 11 counts—securities fraud, investment advisor fraud, mail fraud, wire fraud, money laundering, providing materially false and misleading information, and so on. Under the first count, a heading in the middle of the page read: "The Ponzi Scheme to Defraud." It summarized Ducasse's entire modus operandi. A series of captions with half-page blank spaces beneath them read: Specification One, Specification Two and so on.

"The blanks below the specifications are where we'll drop in your information about specific fraudulent deals," Katie said.

After he finished reading the document, Rudiger said, "Why aren't you naming the women witnesses you call Sources X, Y and Z?"

"For now, we don't want Ducasse to know who they are and come after them."

"But you use Bemelman's name in here."

"That's under the assumption we can get him to flip, and—"

"Yeah, I get it. Trust me, we work him hard enough, Bemelman will flip. Then Ducasse will see that and know he's cooked."

Rudiger started feeding Katie the bogus deals and she dropped them into the complaint, fleshing it out.

They had a regular routine. Up shortly after dawn, a run on the beach, shower and breakfast, take Styles out for a walk and ball throwing with the Chuckit! launcher, then back to the hotel by 10:00 a.m. and work through until early afternoon, lunch, more work, then cocktails at 5:00 p.m. In the evenings they'd take walks with Styles, watch TV together, Styles curled up with them on the sofa. Once Styles was tired enough to want to go to sleep, they'd retire to the bedroom and make love. Katie hoped it could always be like this.

By the end of the third day she was satisfied with the draft of the complaint.

"We're in good shape. Once we talk to the three American investors and Bemelman, we'll have some changes to the document before we can use it. But for now, we're there."

"I'll book a flight and hotel in Geneva."

"I'll line up the three ladies."

Rudiger sat back in his chair. "We may have to hold off for a day or so. I called my documents guy in New York yesterday and have him working on something for us."

"Why can't we use the documents we left the UK with?"

"We can. This is different. He has all kinds of sources, hacks into various computer systems, has databases the cops, the FBI and Interpol use. I asked him to find out as much as he can about Bemelman. I also hired a Geneva PI firm to do some research as well. If we can dig up some dirt on him, great. But at least to know where he lives, whether he's married, has kids, whatever, will help us out."

Katie smiled. She was glad Rudiger and she were on the same side.

————

Two days later they left Styles with Flora at the hotel and flew a chartered jet direct to Geneva. They checked into the Hotel d'Angleterre and went downstairs to the lobby, where they would meet the first of the three "American Ladies," as Katie had come to call them. They sat in the lobby until an elegant woman with flowing brown hair, beautifully made up and wearing a stylish wrap dress, entered. Katie stood up and smiled.

"Stephanie," Katie said, "so glad you could come."

"My pleasure, Angela."

Katie introduced the woman as Stephanie Silverman and Rudiger as John Rudiger, a friend of hers. They sat down. Katie started off in a lowered voice. "Stephanie, some of what I have to say may surprise you, even shock you, so I didn't want to let on over the phone."

The woman's brow wrinkled.

"I asked you here to talk about the Ducasse funds."

"Is something wrong?"

"We think so."

Rudiger leaned forward and said, "We're more certain than that. I'm in the investments business myself, and I do a great deal of private consulting work, including with the U.S. Attorney's Office in New York. That's the assignment I'm currently working on."

Stephanie's eyes widened.

Katie said, "And that's my role here, too. My real name is Katie Dolan, and I'm a lawyer with the U.S. Attorney's Office in New York, working undercover." She pulled out her old ID from the U.S. Attorney's Office and showed it to Stephanie. "To get it all out on the table, we believe that Banque d'affaires Ducasse has conducted an elaborate Ponzi scheme with their various investment funds over at least the last ten years."

Stephanie's lips parted and her eyes looked glassy. "Is my money safe?"

"We don't know the extent of the situation yet," Rudiger said, "but we're certain as an investor in Funds III and IV that you've started to receive payouts."

"Yes, in fact I've gotten half of my money back already."

Katie said, "That's because we believe—"

"We're *certain*," Rudiger interjected.

"—that Ducasse's modus operandi is to take money from investors in subsequent funds, manufacture artificial returns to the investors in the earlier funds, and then skim as much as he wants out of the combined pot."

"It keeps working as long as he keeps adding new funds of bigger and bigger size," Rudiger said. "So your money is giving investors in Funds I and II very nice returns. And you'll do very well if Ducasse can raise Fund V. But someday when the music stops, everything will come crashing down with a thud."

"The rationale for the U.S. Attorney's Office getting involved," Katie said, "is based on the fact that U.S. citizens, such as yourself, have been defrauded in this Ponzi scheme, a violation of fraud provisions of the U.S. securities laws. In addition he's violated U.S. mail fraud, wire fraud, and money laundering laws."

Stephanie leaned back in her chair and rubbed her forehead, as if trying to digest all the information Katie had just dumped on her. After a moment she said, "So how does this involve me, aside from the fact that I may have been one of Ducasse's patsies?"

"What we're asking is for you to give us the details of your investment—amount, timing, when you received money back from those funds—for us to use in supporting the charges against him." Katie met her gaze, saw resignation, then sadness in her eyes.

"I feel so stupid. If Stanley were still here on this earth, he'd skin me alive." Stephanie looked away. When she turned back her eyes were moist.

In that moment Katie felt connected to her, got a terrible sense of loneliness. She felt her hatred of Ducasse flare.

Stephanie said, "Okay. I'll do whatever you ask."

Two hours later, the meeting with Valerie Seymour went about the same. After Valerie left, Katie said to Rudiger, "I think I'm going to cancel the next meeting with Melinda Chase."

"Why?"

"She's the one who I think might be sleeping with Ducasse."

"You afraid she might tip him off?"

Katie nodded. "I don't think so if she knew the truth, but it's a risk not worth taking. We'll get enough from Stephanie and

Valerie to give Ducasse a statistical sample of his widow investors' righteous fury that should scare him to death."

Rudiger said, "Okay, tomorrow we do Bemelman. If that goes as planned, we'll really scare the hell out of Ducasse."

———

The next morning over breakfast, Katie said, "Did your documents man or that private investigator ever turn anything up on Bemelman?"

Rudiger realized he'd forgotten to tell her. "Most of what I got was from the PI, Krause. Bemelman lives a pretty ordered life. He has breakfast every day at a café around the corner from his house, where he reads the newspaper. Then he goes to the office. He eats lunch at one of three places near his office every day, unless he's entertaining for business. After work he generally goes straight home. Except on Friday nights." He paused. "Then he goes to the Pâquis District to the apartment of his mistress, Gabriele Stoltzberg. Sometimes he stops and buys groceries first."

"What's the Pâquis District?"

"It's Geneva's red-light district, where prostitution is legal. Gabriele Stoltzberg is a registered sex worker, with a long record of drug arrests."

"Not the kind of thing that a buttoned-up Swiss banker wants getting around. That should help get him to cooperate."

After breakfast Katie called Bemelman. "Mr. Bemelman, it's Angela Conklin." Pause. "Yes, I happen to be in town and I was wondering if I could come to your office to introduce a friend as a potential client. He needs a local banker." Pause. "My pleasure. We'll see you at 11:00 a.m."

At 11:00 a.m. Katie and Rudiger went to his office and were escorted into a conference room. Bemelman came in smiling: a short, slim man in rimless glasses wearing a dark-gray suit with all three buttons buttoned, a white shirt and muted tie. His hair was combed straight back.

Katie made the introductions and they sat.

Rudiger's heart rate shot up; he got right to it, saying, "My name is John Rudiger and I'm an investment manager who also does consulting work, in this case for the U.S. Attorney's Office in New York. We are on the verge of filing a complaint and a formal extradition request to the Swiss government for Philippe Ducasse and his father, André, for 11 counts of violations of the U.S. securities laws, including securities fraud, money laundering, wire fraud, mail fraud and improper disclosure. Ducasse PE Funds I through IV, and its proposed Fund V, are part of an elaborate Ponzi scheme to defraud investors that's been continuing for ten years."

Rudiger watched as Bemelman's face lost any expression, began to look like a death mask.

Rudiger continued. "We have obtained the cooperation of two U.S. investors in Ducasse funds, and in addition, the woman you've known for the past year as Angela Conklin is really Caitlin Dolan, a lawyer at the U.S. Attorney's Office in New York working undercover."

Katie pulled out her old ID and showed it to Bemelman.

"The $30 million she invested in Ducasse Fund V, at your introduction, was the U.S. government's money, invested as part of this sting operation."

Bemelman took a breath and opened his mouth to speak but Rudiger raised his hand for him to stop, talked over him.

"At least two other investors and Ms. Dolan were introduced to the Ducasse funds by you as part of a profiling operation to obtain unsophisticated investors—widows or divorcées with substantial resources and little knowledge of finance—as part of the Ducasses' Ponzi scheme."

Rudiger nodded to Katie, who said, "If you agree to cooperate with us and provide details of the Ducasses' operation, I am authorized to offer you immunity from any prosecution in the United States and Switzerland."

Bemelman stood up and said, "I'm going to speak to my lawyer."

Rudiger said, "That's certainly your right, but we should tell you that this is an offer we'll only make you once."

Katie said, "We have other individuals with whom we'll be having this conversation. Insiders with knowledge of the Ducasses' operation. Whoever agrees to work with us first will be provided immunity. The others would be prosecuted along with the Ducasses."

Rudiger said, "In plain English, if you don't hit the bid, you're toast."

Bemelman said, "Kindly show yourselves out," then turned and left the room.

Rudiger felt like he'd been sucker punched. He slumped in his chair, turned to Katie. "I didn't expect that."

"Neither did I. I thought he'd roll right over."

They left the building and hailed a cab. Rudiger gave the driver an address.

"Where are we going?" Katie asked.

"To Bemelman's mistress' apartment." They drove into the Pâquis District, a seedy neighborhood of sex shops, bars and clubs. They stopped in front of a restaurant and got out. They walked to a door next to the restaurant that had buzzers for four apartments. Rudiger pushed one. A woman's voice came on the intercom.

Rudiger said, "Gabriele Stoltzberg, it's the police. I need to speak to you."

"What about?"

"About Hans Bemelman."

A buzzer signaled them to enter.

Rudiger and Katie walked up the stairs to the second floor. When they got to the landing, the door was ajar, the chain still on. A pretty woman in her 30s peeked out.

"Is he alright?" she said.

Rudiger handed her his card. "Please have him call me as soon as possible. It's important."

Rudiger and Katie left. They were sitting in their hotel room when Rudiger's cell phone rang.

"Alright, you have my attention. I am prepared to meet," Bemelman said.

Rudiger got a blast of energy. *Yes.*

He gave Bemelman their hotel room number. Twenty minutes later Bemelman knocked on the door. Rudiger showed him to a chair across from the coffee table and sofa where Katie and he sat down. Bemelman sat erect in the chair and said in a stern voice, "I am unaccustomed to treatment like this. I am a respected banker in the city and have been so for 25 years. I have been a faithful husband and devoted father for even longer."

Rudiger said, "The fact that you're keeping house with a prostitute and drug addict doesn't exactly square with that, does it?"

Bemelman said, "Gabriele Stoltzberg is my stepdaughter, not my mistress."

Whoa. Didn't see that one coming.

Bemelman said, "I insist you not involve Gabby in any of this, and I consider your visit with her today to be a breach of any professional protocol, not to mention common decency."

Katie said, "Mr. Bemelman, we didn't know. We're working on an investigation and are not attempting to harm anyone who is close to you."

Rudiger said, "Yes, this is about Ducasse, not your personal life."

Bemelman sat back in the chair and let out a long sigh. He hung his head for a moment, looked up into Rudiger's eyes, then Katie's. It was as if he was pleading. He said, "I have had this hanging over me for eight years, this sordid Ducasse mess that I allowed myself to become entangled in. Gabby had gone seriously astray, gotten involved with drugs, then prostitution in order to pay for drugs. My wife threw her out of the house and has had nothing to do with her ever since. It was after Gabby's third or fourth arrest, I don't remember, that Philippe Ducasse took notice of it in the newspaper and approached me. At that time he was raising their second fund. He was bold about it, made no pretense to conceal the fact he was aware of Gabby's arrests, and that a simple banker such as myself could use extra money to pay for legal fees. He offered me .5% of client funds I brought him, with additional monthly cash payments that would be undisclosed. I told Ducasse I thought it was unethical and declined."

Bemelman let out another long sigh. "Ducasse approached me again. He said he would only accept investors who fit a certain profile." He looked up at Katie. "A profile with which I understand you are familiar. I agreed to read the fund documents. After I did so I was suspicious about the extraordinary performance of Ducasse's first fund. I suspected what was going on. I declined again. He approached me yet again and offered me a $5,000 per month surreptitious cash payment in addition to the fees of .5%, with a $50,000 bonus paid up front. At that time Gabby showed receptiveness to entering a rehab facility. It cost $60,000. I returned to Ducasse and accepted his proposal, believing that it would be a short-term arrangement until Gabby was on her feet. I was wrong."

Bemelman paused again and sighed. The air seemed to be coming out of him. Katie stood up and walked to the minibar, returned with a bottle of water. She gave it to Bemelman.

He smiled for the first time, opened it and drank. "Thank you." He looked at Katie and said, "I must seem a rather pathetic man to you. But you have to understand, I raised Gabby from a child as if she was my own. She was just three years old when I married Hilda."

Rudiger was afraid to glance over at Katie, for fear she might be tearing up. Bemelman was starting to get to him, too. He felt sorry for the poor schmuck.

Bemelman continued. "Gabby went through rehab but relapsed almost immediately. I was able to afford counseling for her, and reluctantly got her a license as a sex worker so the prostitution arrests would stop. Her life since then has been a succession of rehabs, counseling and relapses." He looked at Katie again, then averted his eyes. "Her mother to this day believes I attend a regular card game on Friday nights."

He took another sip of water and paused for a long time. Then he took a deep breath and seemed to find a new reserve of strength. He said, "In a way your appearance today was a blessing. It helps me to find an escape from this corrupt scheme I've become an integral part of. And it does so in a manner that assures a measure of justice will be served and stops Philippe Ducasse from continuing his sordid games with people's lives. I'll do anything you ask, as long as you leave Gabby out of it completely and as long as we are able to destroy Ducasse."

Katie leaned forward and said, "Can you provide us with a list of your clients who invested in Ducasse funds?"

"Names, amounts and dates of investment," Bemelman said. "I have detailed records."

"About how many investors and how much money?" Katie said.

"Approximately 100, who have accounted for about 60% of funds raised by Ducasse PE Funds I through IV, or about $1.1 billion."

Katie paused a beat, Rudiger detecting she was as surprised as he was. Then Katie said, "How many investors do you estimate were U.S. citizens?"

"About a third of them."

Katie said, "Can you email that list later today?"

"When I return to my office."

Rudiger said, "Has Ducasse ever disclosed to you the true nature of his Ponzi scheme?"

"As I said earlier, I suspected from the moment I read his first fund memorandum. But he has never confirmed it to me, and I have never asked him. I have accepted his money, complicit with my silence." He hung his head a moment, then looked up again. "How do we proceed from here?"

Katie said, "I suggest I draft a sworn affidavit laying out the facts of our discussion today, incorporating the information from the list you will send me. I'll send my draft to you for your review and ultimate signature. Please add any additional facts that you believe will be helpful. All of that will be incorporated into our complaint to be used against the Ducasses. Once we have our documents in final form, we can make our move. Agreed?"

Bemelman nodded.

Rudiger showed Bemelman to the door.

Before Bemelman stepped out, he turned and said, "There is one other thing you should be aware of."

Rudiger and Katie both waited.

"A young man and woman who worked for the Ducasses were killed in an attempted robbery earlier this year. The young woman's aunt was a client of mine who fit the Ducasses' profile that I referred to them as a prospective investor. The young man worked in the Ducasses' accounting department, and after he began a relationship with the niece, the aunt backed out of the deal. I have always believed the young man uncovered the Ponzi scheme and advised the young woman to warn off her aunt. I have also always considered those murders suspicious, although the police never uncovered any connection to the Ducasses."

Bemelman opened the door and left, leaving Rudiger and Katie staring at each other in silence. Finally, Rudiger said, "I think I'll keep that PI, Krause, I hired to research Bemelman on retainer to watch our backs, just in case."

Later, Katie said, "Bemelman's as much a victim of Ducasse as he is his shill. In strict legal terms, I guess the worst thing he's done is take money under the table. If he was to tell the Swiss police everything he knows, he might get immunity."

"Maybe that's why he's kept such detailed records." Rudiger had a sour taste in his mouth. He thought a moment, then said, "I'm not sure how this ends, but it would be nice if we could avoid wrecking Bemelman."

———

That night after they made love, Rudiger turned to Katie in bed and said, "When I first went to your house and got to know your father, we were walking on the beach the last afternoon before you returned. He told me that after he died he hoped you could figure out a way to go back home to the States." He paused, then said, "I wouldn't mind being legitimate again, either. A second chance." He looked into her eyes in the faint light. He felt a swell in his chest, his emotions rising. "You and me going home to New York, playing house together. Seeing if we could make it work. I could go for that."

Katie kissed him. "Me, too." She stroked his hair. "It's a nice dream, but I don't see how I could make that happen. Unless I had something major to deal to Holden, he's got me and I can't go home."

"Your father said you were a crackerjack lawyer, and now that I've seen you in action, I agree. What does Charlie Holden really have on you?"

"I thought about that a week or so ago. I remember your story about that investor of yours, Myron, the bread-bag-closure mogul, who gave you the $50 million in bearer bonds that were never part of your hedge fund. So I guess technically Holden couldn't prove one way or the other that we took them, since nobody but you and Myron knew they existed. I could make the case that all I did was up and leave the U.S. one day with Daddy for Cape Verde without telling anybody."

Rudiger said, "That's encouraging."

"And then I remembered that I used Angela's phony passport to leave the country and go to Cape Verde. That's passport fraud, a felony."

She pulled herself close against Rudiger's body, rested her head on his chest. He closed his eyes and felt the calmness of being with her, focused on them together as if they were one. She said, "I thought about what Holden's got on you, too. You told Daddy you took $40 million of Myron's money, but the other $400 million or so that disappeared from your hedge fund was pure market losses, right?"

"Yeah, most of it after I left town when the Feds froze my fund's assets in losing positions and the markets continued to melt down."

Katie lifted her head and looked Rudiger in the eye. She said, "No harm, no foul on your part."

"But remember my CFO falsified our results, and I told him to keep cooking the books until I could manage my way out of it, and ultimately couldn't."

"Well that's securities fraud, a felony, and a big one. I recall Holden also had counts against you of obstruction of justice and flight from prosecution, also felonies. But for you, too, Holden wouldn't know about the $50 million in bearer bonds. Then there's the $40 million of Myron's money you took from your hedge fund."

"Actually, I had investment discretion for him, and he was dead by then, so I had his estate redeem the money from my hedge fund first before I swiped it, so technically I didn't steal it from the fund but from the estate's bank account after the redemption. And like I told your father, the guy had no will, no heirs, and I haven't the faintest idea what happens in that case. But I don't know how anybody would figure out what happened to the $40 million, certainly not Holden. I wired it to a bunch of different accounts in the Netherlands Antilles, Brazil, all over the place and finally to an account in the Cayman Islands."

Katie said, "Still, Holden's got you on a big securities fraud and some other felonies."

Rudiger said, "So we're both cooked."

"Yes. It was nice of Daddy to think of going back home to the States," Katie said. She eased herself up and kissed him again. "But it isn't going to happen, for either of us."

———

The next morning Katie was finished with the affidavit of Bemelman's statement, having received his detailed list of investors, amounts and dates of investment the previous afternoon. She spent another hour incorporating that information into the complaint, then emailed the draft affidavit and complaint to Bemelman. When she finished she stood up and walked into the bedroom, where Rudiger was sitting at the desk working on his iPad.

"I'm done."

Rudiger turned and smiled at her. "We're ready?"

"Once Bemelman sends his comments on his affidavit, we should be good to go."

"Now we show it and the complaint to Ducasse and sweat him."

Katie felt a surge of excitement, said, "What about this instead? Go to Holden with an airtight case. Barter the bust on Ducasse for letting us walk."

"Walk?"

"Yeah," Katie said, her scalp tingling. "What we talked about last night. Going home. Only now we have something to deal to Holden: bringing in Ducasse in exchange for dropping all charges against us. Or maybe we get a slap on the wrist, plea-bargain for some minor offenses and do community service for a few years. Holden gets a big, splashy international bust; U.S. investors defrauded, justice served. Holden files with the Swiss to extradite Ducasse to prosecute him."

Rudiger said, "It'll never happen."

Katie leaned forward, insistent, said, "Holden has to look like a complete moron for letting us get away."

"It was the Brits that let us get away."

"I know Holden better than you do. And I've also never seen an operation like they used to bring us to the UK. That's not within the U.S. Attorney's Office's or the Justice Department's mandate. It was some kind of black ops, Special Forces or the CIA. Holden had to go to the top to get that authorized."

Rudiger said, "How high?"

"At least the attorney general, and who knows where the AG had to go to get it approved and funded. It shows how hard Holden was willing to push to bring us in. Trust me, if we offer ourselves up as part of a package, Holden will deal. He looks like a fool now, and he wants us badly. That's a good combination for us."

Rudiger grinned. "Bringing down Ducasse and getting Holden off our backs forever. That's a deal I'd love to do. How do we make it work?"

"We brainstorm it out, I finish my complaint, email it to Holden and then call him to cut a deal. Then Holden calls the Swiss and they bring in Ducasse. Maybe we even fly home on the same plane they use to extradite Ducasse."

Katie couldn't stop beaming. *Maybe going home.*

———

Holden had just walked out of his office, heading to the conference room for a meeting with his staff on an insider trading case, when he heard his phone ring. Stephanie picked up, listened and said, "One moment, please."

Holden looked at her.

"Katie Dolan on the line for you."

Holden felt surprise wash over him, then a rise of excitement. "Who?"

"Caitlin Dolan, an attorney who formerly worked in this office for—"

"I know who the hell she is," Holden said, turning around and heading back into his office. *Everybody's a wise-ass.*

Holden picked up and said, "Well, well, well, if it isn't our own Katie Dolan. Is this a social call or can I do something for you?"

"Hello, Charlie, Mr. United States Attorney for the Southern District of New York. Congrats on finally getting promoted to the top job out there."

"Like I said, can I do something for you?"

Katie said, "Don't bother trying to trace this phone, it's a pre-paid cell and I'm throwing it away after I hang up. I called to offer you a deal."

You're offering me? "Yeah? What's that?"

"A ten-year $2 billion Ponzi scheme bust, tied up in a nice neat bow with Walter Conklin and me cooperating and providing testimony in exchange for immunity."

Holden laughed. "I must say, little lady, you never lacked for balls."

"Come on, Charlie, cut the bravado. I know you're interested."

Holden paused. It couldn't hurt to hear more. "Okay, shoot."

"The scheme is run by a private family-owned Swiss financial advisory firm. Starting ten years ago they raised four private equity funds, a total of $1.85 billion, and are currently raising a new $2 billion fund. It's a Ponzi scheme. Investors from the early funds are getting paid out from money investors put into the later funds."

"Swiss? What's our legal nexus? Who's been damaged in the U.S.?"

"Thirty-five investors in the funds are from the U.S. We've got testimony from two of them. We've also got the sworn affidavit of a Swiss banker at ASB who's been profiling and funneling easy marks to the fund sponsor, intentionally finding unsophisticated investors who won't suspect the scam."

"Could be intriguing, but you can't be serious about full immunity for Conklin and you."

"I am. I emailed you the draft complaint and our witnesses' affidavits ten minutes ago. I used code names for the target suspects and witnesses. Read them and I'll call you back tomorrow at the same time." The line clicked off.

Holden got up and walked out of his office. As he passed Stephanie's desk he said, "There's an email in there someplace from Katie Dolan with attachments. Print them out and have three copies ready for me when I get back."

––––

The next day at noon, Holden sat in the chair behind his desk, his computer screen pulled directly in front of him, waiting for a Skype call. Katie had called back that morning and Holden had agreed to the Skype call. Shepherds, Johnston, a computer tech and one of their goon squad guys who did enforcement work sat in chairs encircling his desk. The goon was recording the call.

At exactly noon, the screen flashed to Katie Dolan's face.

"Good afternoon," Holden said. He smiled, showing he was cooperating, receptive.

"Hi, Charlie," Katie said. "Who else is there?"

"A couple of my guys listening in. They read your stuff last night, too. Shepherds and a new guy, Johnston."

Holden moved closer to the screen. "You're looking tanned and relaxed, Katie. Being on the lam agrees with you."

"Let's cut to it, Charlie. I'm sure you're busy. I know I am."

Holden felt a flare of anger, reined himself in. He said, "How about you tell us what you want before we tell you what we think of what you've got?"

"I told you yesterday. Full immunity in exchange for our cooperation and testimony in a prepackaged Ponzi scheme bust."

"You're too smart, too experienced to believe that full immunity will ever happen."

Katie said, "I'm not sure we have much more to discuss then."

Holden knew she was bluffing, that she'd accept lesser charges, some fines and probably even some jail time for Conklin. He said, "Alright, but before we cut this off as going no place, let me tell you what we think of what you've got. We agree with your analysis that 35 U.S. investors gives us plenty of grounds for indictments based on U.S. securities violations, and based on the amount of capital invested, plenty of juice for getting the Swiss to cooperate for extradition. But two investors' testimony isn't going to cut it—"

"Come on, Charlie, you know as well as I that we can get more, maybe even a couple dozen."

Holden continued. "And your star witness, Mr. B, has some great stuff. But even he admits he's not on the inside, and that Suspect D never confessed to him it's a Ponzi scheme, just gave him profiles to bring helpless lambs to the slaughter. Incriminating, but not enough to convict."

"What about all the analysis of bogus deals? Twenty-one of 43 deals they did in the first four funds were companies they acquired that we can't find any records showing they ever existed. Same with the companies that bought them out to produce those home-run profits. And half the real deals were duds, modest returns at best."

Holden said, "But that's not proof, and you know it. The way to get proof is to go in there with investigators and forensic accountants to root it out. But is what you've got enough to get the Swiss to send in a team? I don't think so. We need more."

Holden watched Katie's face, her eyes. Not a flinch. *She's good.*

After a moment she said, "I worked with you long enough to know where this is going."

"You got it," Holden said. "We need to send you in there wearing a wire so we can get Suspect D on tape. He doesn't have to spill the beans completely—"

"He'll never do that," Katie said.

"—but enough to incriminate himself, so when we package it with what we already know we can convince him he's really fried. Then we get him to plea-bargain, or if necessary we go the full nine yards, extradite him and prosecute him."

He watched Katie again. She took a moment to think, then she said, "We're back to where we started. Full immunity, including from the IRS, so that any money we bring back into the U.S. has a free pass from any questions about where it came from."

Holden said, "Maybe you should let me run this up the flag-pole, see what I can actually deliver and then you and me talk again, Katie."

Katie's features hardened and she leaned in closer to the screen. She said, "You want to do a deal or not, Charlie? Don't give me a bunch of crap about having to go back up the flagpole. How far up the flagpole did you have to go to get that black ops team to do a snatch-and-grab of us from Morocco? It had to be at least to the AG, and he had to go higher because the Justice Department doesn't have those kinds of resources in-house. And I know for a bust this large you can get the AG to give us an immunity letter, including from the IRS."

"You're stretching it."

"Maybe it is a stretch," Katie said. "But I'm betting that you'll stretch it as far as you can with the kind of pressure you must be under after letting us slip through your fingers in the UK."

Holden decided to take it down a peg. He smiled into the screen. "Katie, let's just examine this practically for a moment. Look at Conklin's case. We're talking about a half-billion-dollar meltdown, embezzlement and then flight from U.S. justice. It's still a case the press refers to when we have a major insider trading, embezzlement or Ponzi scheme investigation. It's been on the top ten list for over ten years. Do you really think I can get Conklin full immunity after that?"

Katie said, "The trading records all still exist. If you haven't done the forensic work by now, you can, and it will show that $400 million of that was market losses, and most of it after he left town. Yes, prior to that he covered up the fact that his CFO distorted their results, a felony, but it's different than running off with $400 million."

Holden said, "Yeah, right. He didn't steal any money, he just had the resources to get enough plastic surgery to change him from looking like an NFL defensive tackle into Cary Grant, build a multimillion-dollar house in Antigua, and pay off half the government officials down there for over ten years."

Katie leaned back from the screen, her face going blank. Holden thought maybe he had her off balance, so he decided to push forward. He said, "And you? I send you to Antigua to bring Rudiger, or Conklin, back, then the two of you collude to orchestrate some hijinks at a JPMorgan Chase branch in southern Manhattan. After that you disappear with enough money to afford zillions of dollars in doctors for your father and a humongous beachfront property in Cape Verde."

"You can't prove anything about any money. Let's just say I had a sugar daddy that bought me a house and helped out my father. You've got nothing there."

Holden was starting to get angry now. He gritted his teeth. "You flew to Cape Verde on a phony Angela Conklin passport. That's passport fraud, 10 years minimum, 15 maximum."

"You can't prove that, either. You can only prove that *somebody* left the U.S. under that passport."

Holden said, "When we found you in Morocco, the two of you were flying around on phony U.S. passports as James Scott Rockford and Elizabeth Davenport."

Katie leaned forward again and smirked at him. "Maybe so. But if you were confident enough that your snatch-and-grab in Morocco would've held up in front of a judge, you'd have brought us straight back to the U.S. instead of dumping us in the UK so the Brits could extradite us the regular way. In that case are you so sure a judge won't throw out those passports as evidence you obtained from us in an illegal seizure?" She paused a moment, then said, "I think you've got nothing there, either, Charlie. So am I really stretching it?"

Holden started to tap his foot under his desk. He realized it might show that his body was moving on the screen and forced himself to stop. He said, "Alright, I think we've had enough back-and-forth to understand each other's positions. I say we both sleep on it and talk again tomorrow. But nothing's going anyplace without you two getting your Suspect D on tape. Agreed?"

"Agreed," Katie said, "on talking tomorrow. I'll phone you."

The screen went dark. Holden looked up at the computer tech. "Did you find out where they are?"

The tech said, "They used some kind of security software. The signal was coming from different Internet locations, switching off every 45 seconds or so. It started out in the UK, then France, then Germany, then the U.S. and so on."

Holden felt his energy drain off. "How's that possible?"

The tech shrugged. "Some of that software is even available retail. You can buy one of them for your PC called Identity Cloaker online for 79 euros. I have no idea where they are."

Holden slouched sideways in his chair. *Damn.*

———

Back in their Geneva hotel room, Rudiger shut down the laptop on the coffee table in front of Katie. He'd watched her from out of range of the camera. There were a few times during the call that he wanted to laugh or urge her on, but he made sure not to react so he wouldn't distract her. "You did great," he said. "You gave him some things to think about, really spun him a few times. What do you think?"

She let out a long breath, seeming relieved. "I think we may have something, but Holden's not easy to read."

"I agree, but you clearly had him back on his heels when you were pushing back on all the charges he thinks he has against us."

Katie nodded. "Yes, and it was interesting that he didn't talk about any money other than the $400 million. I don't think he knows anything about the $40 million that you took from Myron's

David Lender

estate, and he clearly doesn't know how much we got from the safe deposit box, or its origin."

Rudiger said, "Were you bluffing about the illegal seizure making the fake U.S. passports inadmissible as evidence?"

"Posturing. But what I said could be true: if he was worried about the snatch-and-grab not getting past a judge, he has to be worried about a judge throwing out any evidence it turned up."

"So it looks like from a legal standpoint we've got a shot," Rudiger said.

"We'll see when I call him tomorrow."

Rudiger had a good feeling about it, but still decided to start thinking about a backup plan.

———

The next afternoon Katie and Rudiger were sitting on the balcony of their suite in the Hotel d'Angleterre having tea. She'd always been a coffee drinker, but she loved the aroma of the Earl Grey tea that Rudiger drank, so now it was a staple at their breakfast and in the early afternoon. She looked over at Lake Geneva, off a half mile in the distance, then at Rudiger. They both took her breath away.

Katie stepped away from the table on the balcony into their suite, turned to him and said, "Time for me to call Holden."

Once in the living room, she punched the numbers into one of the prepaid cell phones to call Holden's office. She had to hold for a minute or so, and then Holden picked up.

Katie said, "So where are we?"

Holden said, "Aren't we gonna do this on Skype?"

"Why bother, you can't find us anyhow."

There was a pause. Holden said, "You playing with me?"

218

"Last call, a little. Just letting you know we're a step ahead of you. But back to business. Are you in?"

"We have a go, in principle."

Katie said, "What does 'in principle' mean? Subject to running it up your flagpole?"

"It's a go. Let me worry about the details. I just need to work them out."

"We still need full immunity," Katie said, making sure she sounded firm.

"Yeah, on condition you and Conklin agree to cooperate and help us bring in Suspect D."

"You're not messing with me are you, Charlie? Because if you are, we'll figure it out and we'll disappear."

"I just need a few days to work it out, get things in place with the Swiss, get your immunity document worked out with the AG. Now it's time for you to let us know the identities of everyone, your Suspect D and your witnesses Mr. B and Sources Y and Z. But in principle, it's a go."

Katie could hardly believe it. She might actually be going home. To what, she wasn't sure, but she didn't care; it was home. "What's the timing and how do we do it?"

Holden said, "Two or three days. All I need is Suspect D's cell phone number to rig it up so we can listen in and record it when you go in to talk to him."

Katie listened, waiting.

Holden said, "When I'm set up at our end, you send Suspect D our complaint to soften him up, then you and Conklin, Rudiger, whatever you call him, meet with Suspect D and sweat him. You've done this lots of times before. I don't need to tell you what to say to get him to talk."

Katie said, "When do I see our immunity?"

"As soon as it's signed by the AG."

"Signed? I don't get to see a draft?"

"Don't be presumptuous. The Attorney General of the United States of America doesn't give out drafts of immunities for people to comment on. It's my job to make sure they say what they need to in order to get the deal done. And trust me, he doesn't give out very many of them. The AG's signature is binding. You'll have it before you go in to see Suspect D. Now tell me everyone's real names, or this thing stops dead right here."

Katie filled in the blanks for him. Ducasse and his father, Bemelman, the American Ladies.

Her hands were trembling when she put the phone down.

―――

Holden hung up the phone and looked at Johnston and Shepherds. He felt good about the call. He'd gotten the names, and felt like he'd snuffed out any objections from Katie in his last comments. For once he might've shut the little wise-ass up. He saw Johnston scowling.

"You got a problem?" Holden said to Johnston.

Johnston said, "Are you sure you want to do that?"

"Yeah. If that's what it takes to get this done."

"Full immunity?"

Holden leaned forward and put his elbows on his desk, stared down Johnston. "It'll say full immunity if they reciprocate by bringing in the Ducasses."

Johnston hesitated, then said, his voice strained, "And what does that mean?"

"The full power of the legal authority of the Attorney General of the United States of America will be behind a document that'll say they receive full immunity from prosecution for the stipulated charges as long as they help us arrest and prosecute the Ducasses. Only we won't be arresting and prosecuting the Ducasses."

Johnston froze. After a moment he said, "Why not?"

"Because I'm sending you and Shepherds to Geneva tonight. Tomorrow you're gonna talk to the attorney general of Geneva, who I had two conversations with today, and then you're gonna meet with Philippe Ducasse."

Johnston looked at Shepherds, then Holden, confused.

"Let me explain to you how this stuff works in the real world," Holden said.

CHAPTER 10

That night Katie and Rudiger figured they had a few days of breathing space to relax and enjoy Geneva, because the next few days after that promised to be both intense and unpredictable. They dispensed with cocktails in their suite that evening, agreeing to get dressed up and go out for cocktails and dinner. Rudiger said, "I have a plan for the evening. I'll surprise you."

Katie felt like it was a special evening as she got into the shower. When she finished showering and started putting on her makeup and jewelry, she stood in front of the sink in her bra and panties. She let Rudiger admire her as he walked past her and stepped into the shower, feeling his gaze on her. She remembered their first few wild evenings in New York, the Bergdorf Goodman lingerie he'd bought for her. *Give him a little thrill,* she thought. Anticipation of what was to come.

Katie was still dressing in the bedroom when Rudiger said, "I'll wait for you in the living room." He wore a gray salt-and-pepper suit with a white shirt and one of his Hermès ties, a new design. Simple elegance.

Katie put on a red silk Ralph Lauren Collection dress, an opera-length strand of pearls and carried a matching red Yves Saint Laurent clutch. She stepped into the living room and waited for Rudiger to react. She saw his eyes smile at her.

He said under his breath, "My God."

Katie felt anticipation dancing in her chest, said, "Did you say something? I couldn't hear you." She stood erect, wanting him to continue to admire her, aching for more from him.

"You're beautiful." She felt a flush of tears coming to her eyes as he extended his hand to her and she walked over, took his. Then he held out his arm and she hooked hers in his and they walked to the door. "I guess I should say something corny like 'Your chariot awaits.' I hope you don't mind we're taking a cab to dinner, then the theater."

Katie didn't think the chariot comment would have been corny at all.

She pressed herself to him, felt her breast against his arm, looked up at him. "I'm just a simple girl from Brooklyn. Why would I mind a cab?"

After dinner and the show, they returned to their suite at the hotel. Sitting on the sofa with a nightcap, Katie said, "There are all kinds of clichés about the way to a man's heart. The stomach, other places, you know. But with most women, it's through their families. Sometimes by befriending the grandmother. In my case, it was through my daddy."

Rudiger said, "I wasn't trying to do anything. I loved the guy. Besides, you and I hit it off right away anyhow. When we first got to know each other in New York, I knew you liked me, and I liked you."

"That came out wrong when I said it. I meant that Daddy helped bring us together, in our hearts. The other night when you talked about keeping house together, I thought about it and I can't ever remember feeling this way about anybody."

Rudiger took a moment, then said, "Me, too. Like we always were."

"So you feel the same way, too?"

"Yeah."

Katie felt her emotions stir. "You can't say it?"

"What?"

"That you love me." Katie smirked. "You can't say it, can you? Do you?"

Rudiger didn't respond.

Katie said, "See, you can't say it."

Rudiger said, "Haven't I shown you? Isn't that more significant? Why else would I have followed you to Cape Verde in the first place? Stuck with you after you pissed away my 30 million bucks, then escaped with you from the UK instead of running off on my own. I'm here now, aren't I?"

"Then say it."

"I'm not some guy who responds when you say 'Jump, froggy, jump.' I don't do anything on command." He leaned over and kissed her. He put his hands on her, those magical hands. He stroked her face, gave her goose bumps. She gave in to it, feeling like a high school girl with a new boyfriend. He stood, took her hand and walked her into the bedroom. They lay down on the bed.

"Oh, Rudiger," she whispered to him as he kissed her. Her entire body tingled like it was electrified.

He turned off the light beside the bed.

"Turn it back on, please," she said. "I like a little light. I want to see you." He turned the three-way on to the lowest level, then stroked her face, kissed her.

After they made love Rudiger propped himself up on one elbow. He said, "There's never been anyone like you for me. I don't see how there ever could be."

Katie smiled.

Rudiger said, "I love you."

Katie felt the words like an explosion of joy in her heart. "I love you, too," she said, believing it had always been so, and always would be.

———

Katie called Holden each day to see where he stood. Two days later he said he was ready. Holden insisted on doing the next call on Skype, so Katie set it up at their end in Geneva. At 4:00 p.m. Geneva time (10:00 a.m. in NYC), Katie was sitting on the sofa facing the laptop on the coffee table. Rudiger watched her, wondering if she was at all nervous, knowing how excited she was becoming about the prospect of going home. She talked about taking him back to her old Cobble Hill neighborhood in Brooklyn. She'd gone on, smiling and laughing, about some of the local restaurants that had been there since her father was a kid, local shops like Staubitz Market Meats she'd been going to with her mom since she could walk.

At one point he told himself to keep her from getting too enthusiastic in case the deal with Holden to get them back to the States broke down. But it was too much fun watching and listening to her to be a killjoy.

The screen clicked on and Rudiger reached out to start adjusting the keypad to switch Internet locations. From out of range of the camera he could see Holden's face, beaming.

"We're ready to go," Holden said, smiling and all buddy-buddy. "The AG of Geneva has the Geneva head of police fully briefed. The Geneva police will have plainclothes cops crawling all over Ducasse's street for whenever you set up the meeting at his office. Our techs have Ducasse's and his father's phones infiltrated so we can use them as listening devices to record all conversations." He paused, gave her another big smile. "That's it. So what's your game plan?"

Katie said, "Where's our immunity letter?"

"Done, signed by AG Martin and ready to send along with the final complaint, signed by me as soon as we're on board together."

Katie said, "We're ready to go at our end."

"That's great, but I don't see any 'we.'"

"What do you mean?"

"I've been talking to and seeing only you, Katie. Let me see Conklin, just to confirm this whole thing is real."

Rudiger felt an ominous tremor. If he stepped in front of the camera and this didn't work out, Holden would have much more than the old grainy photographs of him that Katie said his office had. Katie hesitated. Rudiger decided it was all or nothing; he switched to a different Internet address, then slid over next to her on the sofa.

"Hello there, old friend," Rudiger said into the camera on the laptop.

Holden said, "Long time never see," still doing his Mr. Friendly Old Pal routine.

Rudiger said, "Satisfied?"

"Yeah." They talked for another minute or two, Rudiger switching Internet addresses every so often. Katie and Rudiger walked Holden through their short game plan for the call to Ducasse and their rough script for the meeting with him in his office.

Holden said, "Okay. I'm sending out the immunity letter and the final complaint right now." A moment later Rudiger heard the ping of an email arriving in Katie's inbox. Holden said, "Good luck. Let us know when you schedule the meeting." He signed off and the screen went blank.

Rudiger stood up. He watched with anticipation as Katie pulled up Holden's email and read through the immunity letter. She started smiling near the end of it.

Rudiger said, "Everything okay?"

Katie leaned back in the sofa. "I asked for the moon, and I got it. Full immunity for you regarding anything related to your old hedge fund, a blanket immunity for anything related to any securities violations, flight from prosecution, passport fraud, a full IRS immunity for any funds you decide to bring back to the U.S. with you, the works. The same for me."

Rudiger got an uncomfortable sensation. "Anything suspicious about it?"

Katie laughed. "No. Like I said, I got everything I asked for, maybe even a little more."

If it seems too good to be true . . . Rudiger decided he wasn't going to say anything to Katie, didn't want to give her any nagging doubts because she'd need to be on her game over the next day or two. That was when he decided he needed to get more serious about a backup plan.

Katie said, "Do you want to call Ducasse or should I?"

Rudiger smiled. "I'd love to do it. You want to flip a coin?"

Katie walked to him and kissed him. "No, you go ahead. A little gift to you."

Rudiger sat on the sofa and picked up one of the prepaid cell phones. Since Holden's techs had already infiltrated Ducasse's cell phone, he dialed Ducasse's office number. He didn't want Holden hearing the conversation.

Rudiger identified himself as Walter Conklin and asked to speak to Ducasse. He picked right up.

"Philippe, this is Walter Conklin, the man you were introduced to as John Rudiger."

Ducasse paused, said, "Angela's ex-husband. So the two of you are back together?" He sounded more confused than hostile.

"No. In fact the woman you know as Angela Conklin, my ex-wife, is really Katie Dolan, a lawyer with the U.S. Attorney's Office based in New York. I'm working with her in helping to arrest securities frauds in exchange for a light sentence for the securities law violations regarding my old hedge fund. I'm sure you're aware of them. Katie and I are both undercover in a U.S. government sting operation. The $30 million Katie invested in your Fund V was the property of the U.S. government, bait you took. In a few moments I'm gonna be emailing you a complaint that Charles Holden, U.S. Attorney in New York, is ready to file against your firm, you and your father, for violation of U.S. securities laws. In short, it says that you're running a Ponzi scheme in your private equity funds." Rudiger paused, waiting for a reaction from Ducasse. He heard him clear his throat.

"What do you want?" Ducasse said, his voice now icy.

"After you've digested the complaint and reviewed it with your lawyer, Katie and I will come over and meet with you as soon as possible to discuss how we might make this go easy on you in exchange for your cooperation. You'll see the charges are pretty comprehensive and the evidence against you very damning."

Ducasse said, "I see," sounding wary.

"We can meet either with or without your lawyer. We don't care. But the discussion may go in a direction you may not want your lawyer to hear."

"What?" Ducasse said, now sounding surprised.

"Like I said, we'll leave it up to you, but things may take a surprising direction toward a creative solution to your situation that might make your lawyer squeamish." He paused. "And you and I both know you're not a squeamish guy when it comes to stepping over the line of legality, especially when it comes to making money."

Rudiger heard Ducasse's nervous chuckle and knew he'd raised his curiosity.

Rudiger said, "I suggest you arrange to have $35 million in liquid funds available for immediate wire transfer. How does a meeting tomorrow at 3:00 p.m. at your office sound?"

"I'll see you then."

After Rudiger hung up, Katie said, "What was all that about, the stuff about making his lawyer squeamish and the $35 million?"

"You always need a backup plan"

"What's going on?"

"I want him to think he can buy his way out of it."

"Get him on tape offering to bribe us?"

"Something like that."

———

Ducasse hung up from the call with Rudiger, sitting for at least a minute at his desk before his breathing returned to normal. At the beginning of the call he'd felt as if someone had knocked the wind out of him, scrambled his mind into a jumble. As the call progressed, he was able to take in air, start putting his thoughts together again.

At the moment he didn't know whether to accept what Rudiger had said at face value. Maybe the whole thing about the U.S. Attorney's Office wasn't true, and he and Angela had concocted some new scam. After all, Rudiger had been explicit about him having $35 million ready for wire transfer.

His internal radar had gone to full alert when Melinda Chase, resting with her head on her elbow in her bed after they had sex, had told him that Angela Conklin had called her for a meeting about a week earlier. They were to have met in the lobby of the Hotel d'Angleterre, and then Angela mysteriously canceled at the last minute.

Whatever Rudiger and Angela—Katie or whatever her real name was—were up to, he knew of one sure way to put a stop to it.

He took an envelope from his desk drawer, stood up and walked to the full-length mirror in his office, then buttoned his double-breasted jacket and smoothed the wrinkles out of it. He raised his chin, straightened his tie, adjusted his pocket square and the rose in his lapel, and then walked out of the office.

He walked to Place du Bourg-de-Four to a pay phone. He dialed.

"Yeah," Strasser said after the second ring.

"It's Ducasse. I need to see you. Are you available now?"

"Yeah."

"Meet me at our café."

When Strasser sat down at Ducasse's table, Ducasse said, "I've another job for you."

"Excellent," Strasser said, sounding enthusiastic.

"It's a man and a woman, the man of paramount importance. Photos and cash are in this envelope." He handed it to Strasser. "The photos aren't perfect. They're from our security cameras at our office, but I believe they'll suffice."

"How do I find them?"

"They're staying at the Hotel d'Angleterre, I'm not sure under what names."

"I'll get started right away."

"Yes, do. Getting the job done by early tomorrow afternoon is essential."

Strasser paused before saying, "That'll cost you a 50% premium."

"Very well," Ducasse said. "I'll have the additional funds at your hotel in an hour." He stood up, wishing he could be there to watch.

———

It was 8:00 p.m. that night when Rudiger said to Katie, "We're out of gin."

"Nothing in the minibar?" Katie said from the bedroom.

"No. I'm going out for some. There's a liquor store two blocks down."

"You sure you want to? We've got a big day tomorrow."

"I'll see you in 15 minutes," Rudiger said and left the suite. He walked out of the Hotel d'Angleterre lobby and turned up Quai du Mont-Blanc. As he did so he detected a man following him out of the corner of his eye. It must've been one of Krause's PIs keeping tabs on him.

Good.

He walked two blocks and didn't find the liquor store, now wondering if he had passed it without noticing. He stopped in the middle of the block, thinking. Maybe it was on the next avenue, Rue Philippe-Plantamour, that ran parallel to Quai du Mont-Blanc. He saw an alley across the street that connected with Rue Philippe-Plantamour. He crossed the street toward it.

As he entered the alley he glanced back to see the man was still following him, now stepping off the curb to cross Quai du Mont-Blanc in his direction. He kept walking but got a twist of unease. He pulled out his iPhone and called Krause.

Two rings, then a third.

"Krause here."

"It's Rudiger. I'm out on the street. You got a man on me?"

"Where are you?"

"In an alley across Quai du Mont-Blanc, heading toward Rue Philippe-Plantamour."

"Run."

Rudiger started sprinting. About halfway down the alley he saw the opening to a side alley that ran 90 degrees to the right. In the instant he reached the side alley, he heard the sound of a bullet ricochet and saw a chunk of the brick wall disintegrate above his head.

He got a blast of adrenaline and ran down the side alley, glancing over his shoulder and seeing the man crouched in firing position, a gun in his hand.

He sprinted down the alley, seeing near the end that it intersected with another alley that ran perpendicular to it. He got to the intersection and turned right, heading back toward Quai du Mont-Blanc. He felt a flash of panic after the turn and pulled up to a stop.

A dead end.

He turned around and looked behind him. Another dead end in the opposite direction. It was either take the alley back toward the shooter or stay here and make a stand.

Decide.

Even in this light, the shooter must've seen which way he'd turned. Whatever happened, at least Rudiger had the element of surprise. He trotted back to the intersection of the alleys, hearing the footsteps of the man approaching at a full run. Rudiger planted his feet, got into a half crouch, balled his hands into fists and raised both forearms.

He waited, channeling his former self as a 270-pound defensive end, poised for mayhem. The hole in the line open, the halfback running for it, Rudiger stepping in front of him, crouched and ready to flatten him.

Rudiger's pulse pounded in his temples.

The shooter's footsteps were only a few yards away.

Rudiger tensed, still waiting.

The shooter hurtled around the corner and Rudiger burst out of his crouch, threw his left arm out to block the shooter's gun hand and slammed his right forearm upward, clotheslining the man in the neck.

He heard the crack of cartilage as his forearm slammed into the man's windpipe. The shooter went over backward with the force of Rudiger's blow, Rudiger on top of him, both hands around the wrist of the shooter's gun hand.

He heard the man coughing and gagging as Rudiger got to his feet and dragged the man by his gun hand to the wall, braced the man's arm against it and then stomped on his wrist. He heard the snap of the man's arm breaking, the gun clanking to the concrete below and the man's scream of pain.

Rudiger let go of the man's arm and fished for the gun. In the moments it took to do that, the man was out from underneath him and dancing on the balls of his feet in a karate stance, his right arm dangling at his side helplessly.

Rudiger sprang for him, but the man danced aside, spun and threw a leg kick to Rudiger's ribs that had him seeing stars and sent him to the ground. He rolled to the side as the man threw another kick.

Rudiger stuck his left arm up to block the blow. He took it on the forearm, grunted in pain but didn't think he'd broken the bone. He glanced again on the ground to his left, couldn't see the gun, so he stood in a crouch and moved toward the man, both arms out, ready to grab him or ward off another blow.

The man's next kick went wide, and Rudiger did his lineman's spin move, then lunged forward to slam his shoulder into the man's hip, grabbing the hand of the man's broken arm at the same time. He yanked on it.

The man let out a howl of pain, then an animal roar as he threw a karate punch at Rudiger with his good hand. Rudiger took the blow off his shoulder, then turned and kicked the man's legs out from beneath him, putting him on his back in the alley.

At that moment Rudiger saw a gleam of light off the metal of the gun. He dove for it, picking it up as the man righted himself and came toward him. Rudiger turned and fired a round into his chest. The man fell backward into a sitting position, his mouth hanging open. Then he let out another roar and came straight at Rudiger again.

Rudiger put another round in his chest that sent him over backward onto the ground.

Rudiger stood up and walked over to look down at him.

The man's eyes were glazed but open, staring up at nothing. Then they focused on Rudiger and his mouth went into a sneer.

Rudiger raised the gun and put another round in the man's forehead.

Then he pulled out his handkerchief, wiped his prints off the gun, dropped it and ran out of the alley.

———

The next morning Ducasse was seated at the far end of the conference table on the first floor of his offices, his lawyer, Rupert Stillman, to his right. He didn't want to wait at the head of the table with his back to the door. He wanted to see these men, Shepherds and Johnston, minions of the U.S. Attorney for the Southern District of New York, Charles Holden, as they entered the room. It was out of the question to violate the sanctity of his office by inviting them there.

The past 24 hours had been astonishing. The call he'd received from Conklin, or Rudiger, the previous day had been disconcerting. Then, after he'd set Strasser on Rudiger, the voicemail he'd played back this morning from Rudiger was stunning. He had said, "Your boy failed. The cops will find him in an alley with a headache. See you at 3:00 tomorrow."

Then Holden's call on his cell phone this morning at 6:00 a.m. to set up this meeting.

And the complaint from the U.S. Attorney's Office that Rudiger had sent over immediately after his call the day before was downright petrifying. Stillman had assured him the appropriate course of action was to meet with Holden's men this morning, hear what message of Holden's they had to deliver, and then decide if it was worth getting concerned.

Concerned.

The complaint summarized his operation down to the detailed profile of his investors, including Bemelman's testimony on how Bemelman screened and channeled most of them to him. It contained a complete list of the transactions he'd fabricated over the years that had produced their extraordinary, and fictitious, investment returns.

Concerned, indeed. That complaint chilled him to the center of his bones. He was ready to grab his passport and run to his villa in Italy, stay buried there under an alias for the rest of his life.

The two men arrived, clothed in wrinkled suits, one drab gray, the other a mundane navy blue. White shirts with button cuffs, one in a rep tie, the other in a muted foulard. The one who introduced himself as Johnston had a puckered collar, probably a poly-cotton blend. *Pedestrian toadies.* Yet despite their unremarkable appearance, both carried themselves with an air of self-importance.

They seated themselves to Ducasse's left, across from Stillman, the one called Shepherds closest to Ducasse. He was glad that neither of them smiled, because he wouldn't have been able to bring himself to do so in response.

His agreement with Stillman was that Stillman would do most of the talking.

Shepherds said, "I presume you've read the complaint?"

Stillman said, "Yes."

Shepherds said, "In summary, it details 11 felony counts, violations of the U.S. securities laws. We have nexus due to the fact that 35 of your investors in Funds I through IV are U.S. citizens. The complaint hasn't been sent to a grand jury yet, so technically it's an 'information.' Sometimes we forego the process of going to the grand jury if we reach a plea bargain before the formal complaint is filed and charges are pressed."

The man paused. Stillman said, "I understand."

Out of his peripheral vision, Ducasse could see Johnston staring at him. He shifted his gaze to meet the man's. The man held his. After a few moments Ducasse looked away at Shepherds, yet he could still feel Johnston's gaze on him. Ducasse's neck began to feel prickly where it met his collar. He sensed perspiration on his forehead. He told himself to breathe evenly.

Shepherds continued. "We have not yet informed the Swiss authorities, or filed with them any preliminary papers regarding extradition."

Stillman nodded.

"Our purpose here today is to assure you of the gravity of the charges and discuss how the matter might be resolved without presenting them to a grand jury and formally filing them."

Ducasse glanced at Stillman. Their agreement was no deal today, even if something that looked attractive presented itself. They would just listen, then decide later how to proceed.

Stillman didn't respond to Shepherds. He sat waiting.

Ducasse took in a deep breath.

Shepherds said, "We know you're acquainted with an American woman, Caitlin Dolan, posing as Angela Conklin, who invested $30 million in your Fund V. Caitlin Dolan is a lawyer formerly with the U.S. Attorney's Office in New York who is now a wanted felon in the U.S."

Ducasse thrust his head back as he felt a bolt of shock. *Formerly? Wanted felon?*

"We also know you've met a man, Walter Conklin, another felon wanted in the U.S., under the alias of John Rudiger."

Where is this going? Are they both professional con artists? Is that what they were about with that phony propylene deal?

Shepherds went on. "Dolan and Conklin approached U.S. Attorney Charles Holden in New York about bartering their help in bringing about your arrest and prosecution in exchange for immunity from prosecution in the U.S. for both of them. They believe we cut a deal to do just that. I can assure you we haven't. We provided them with the complaint they sent you so that they could follow it up by meeting with you to discuss the terms of your cooperation with us. They intend to represent that Dolan is still with the U.S. Attorney's Office working undercover, and that Conklin is cooperating with us in various sting operations to apprehend financial frauds in exchange for leniency in sentencing for his crimes. I can assure you that none of that is true, either. Do you understand?"

Stillman said, "Yes."

Shepherds looked Ducasse in the eye. "Mr. Ducasse?"

Ducasse nodded. The realization was coming to him that this wasn't going to proceed as he first assumed. He was beginning to feel lightheaded.

Shepherds said, "The U.S. Attorney's Office is interested in apprehending these two felons and extraditing them back to the United States. I'm authorized by Charles Holden to offer you this deal: cooperate with us in apprehending Dolan and Conklin, and if we are successful in doing so, we will bury the complaint we sent you, never to file it with a grand jury to result in formal charges against you in the United States, and never to have it surface again. Further, we will neither show it to nor discuss it in any manner with the Swiss authorities."

Ducasse had to force himself from exhaling his relief in a whoosh. He sank back into his chair, seeming to lose control of his muscles.

He spoke for the first time. "What are you asking me to do?"

Shepherds looked directly at him again. "Wait in your office for them to arrive for your scheduled 3:00 p.m. meeting today and we will do the rest."

Stillman said, "The rest?"

"The Swiss authorities have been informed that Dolan and Conklin are likely here in Geneva already. They will apprehend them as they attempt to enter your offices and will be extradited to the United States."

No one spoke for a few moments. Then Stillman said, "When will we get this in writing?"

Shepherds said, "You won't."

Stillman said, "Then how can we be certain we really have a deal?"

"You can't."

Stillman wrinkled his brow as if in pain and said, "But surely you can't expect—"

"Rupert, stop, please," Ducasse cut in. He looked at Shepherds. "I accept your proposal."

———

Holden woke up at 6:00 a.m. without his alarm that morning. Shepherds and Johnston were supposed to call him at the office at the open of business New York time to report back on the meeting with Ducasse. By 7:00 a.m. he got tired of sitting around wondering and preempted them, phoning their hotel from his apartment. Shepherds answered and put him on speakerphone.

"So how'd it go?" Holden said.

"Just as we planned," Shepherds said. "Ducasse will play ball. As if we left him a choice. His meeting with Conklin and Dolan is set for 3:00 p.m. Geneva time today. The Geneva police will pick them up as they arrive at Ducasse's office."

"Great," Holden said. "Any issues?"

Holden heard one of them clear his throat, then Johnston say, "Only the issue of the immunity letter."

"And that's a nonissue. Johnston, you're a smart lawyer, right? I took you guys through this before."

"But Conklin and Dolan have a binding immunity letter from the AG of the United States."

Holden exhaled, impatient. "If, and only if, they help us arrest and prosecute the Ducasses. And like I told you before, *we* won't be arresting and prosecuting the Ducasses. The Swiss will. It's our loophole to neuter their immunity letter."

"Yes," Johnston said, "but the Ducasses have defrauded U.S. investors. It's an actionable offense for us. We can't just walk away from that."

"We can and we will," Holden said. "The Ducasses are peanuts compared with bringing in Conklin and Dolan."

"They've orchestrated a multibillion-dollar Ponzi scheme."

Holden raised his voice. "And if we wanted to prosecute them, we wouldn't get a shot at them until they got out of jail in Switzerland. Maybe you guys will still be around in 20 years, but I'll be on the beach someplace."

Johnston wouldn't let it go. "We can turn them over to the Swiss, show them everything we have."

"Not on your life!" Holden shouted. "That's one step away from pursuing them ourselves. If we took everything Conklin and Dolan gave us and handed it to the Swiss, they'd be prosecuting the Ducasses as our proxy. It would make it too easy for Conklin and Dolan to convince a U.S. judge that they fulfilled their end of the deal on the AG's immunity letter. The judge lets them walk—with full immunity—we lose our splashy bust, and we look like idiots on top of it."

Holden paused, ready to slam Johnston if he went on. When all he heard was silence on the line, he said, "I appreciate your youthful zeal, but AG Martin would have my ass if we even flirted with anything that would allow Conklin and Dolan to rely on his immunity letter. We're gonna do this my way." He paused again, waiting until he heard a few more moments of silence at the other end. Then he said, "Great job today, guys. We're almost there," and hung up.

At 2:30 p.m. Geneva time, Rudiger decided Katie and he should have another cup of tea. He thought it might help calm Katie down. She showed few outward signs of tension, and she wasn't a pacer or fidgeter, but she was alternately doing both. She'd cross from the living room of their suite into the bedroom, preoccupied, walk onto the balcony to glance off at the view, her mind probably not even taking it in. She'd packed her bag hours earlier, and now periodically reopened it to check for things, even walking back into the bathroom to make sure she'd collected all her toiletries.

Rudiger made two cups of tea and put both of them on the table on the balcony.

"Join me for a last cup of tea on the balcony?"

Katie smiled at him and crossed the room. They sat beside each other at the table, looking out over Geneva, Old Town speckled with sun on the hill, the lake off in the distance, green extending seemingly forever beyond it.

"We have plenty of time," Rudiger said.

Katie looked at her cell phone. "Not really."

"We're going to be late for this meeting," Rudiger said. "On purpose."

"Any particular reason?"

"I always try to be late to meetings like this. Let Ducasse stew a little, let Holden worry that something's gone wrong. Puts everybody off balance, gives us the advantage."

"However slim," Katie said. She smirked at him.

"Alright, there's another reason, too. Remember Krause, whose PI firm I hired to check up on Bemelman and watch our backs? I asked Krause to put some of his people on the ground out there, eyes and ears to make sure we aren't walking into something. Particularly not another goon with a gun like the one Ducasse sicced on me last night."

He saw Katie cringe and decided he wouldn't bring up the subject of his encounter last night again. He said, "I'm okay, really," and smiled. "Just some bruises."

After a moment she said, "I think it was back in London I told you, 'Remind me never to underestimate you.'"

Rudiger reached for Katie's hand, sipped his tea. They sat like that for a while longer, and then he said, "I told you last night I packed a blond wig and a fake mustache for me, and our cosmetic contact lenses."

"I touched up my dark hair in case I need to remove my wig for a getaway disguise," Katie said.

Rudiger looked over at her and smiled, squeezed her hand. "Good. We're ready, then."

As he said it he was aware of the butterflies in his stomach.

———

Ducasse stood in his office, comfortable in its enveloping familiarity and security. He looked out the windows, standing in front of them between the chairs that faced his desk. It was one of the rare times he had the motorized window shades pulled up and the mahogany shutters open to allow the day to illuminate his cave.

He held the prepaid cell phone he'd received an hour earlier by messenger, a mysterious note enclosed in the envelope from Holden that said, 'It is essential that you keep this with you. I will call you once the show starts. Holden.' Its bulk felt awkward in his hand, but less so than if he put it in his coat pocket, where it would cause an unsightly bulge and press into his side in his form-fitting custom suit.

He kept watching Rue Beauregard below, expecting to see a taxi or limo drive down the one-way street from the right and stop in front of his building, anxious to get this meeting over with. He checked his watch again.

3:15 p.m. *They're late.*

He looked to the left down the street, checking for the Geneva police. He knew they must be there, but couldn't see anyone milling around. Activity was usual for midafternoon. He glanced to the right again, now saw a van blocking the middle of the street, congestion behind it, then both rear doors open on a taxi a few cars back. A tall man with brown hair and a slight-framed woman with midlength strawberry-blonde hair got out of the taxi, both dressed in conservative business suits. They walked down Rue Beauregard, then joined together on the sidewalk, heading toward Ducasse's building.

His pulse picked up. They were half a block away, no one following them, still heading toward his building.

Where are the police?

Ducasse saw two men climb out of a parked car, then block the sidewalk in front of the couple. Another six men emerged from three more parked cars and jogged down the sidewalk from behind. The men encircled the couple, spoke to them for a few moments and then piled them into one of the parked cars. The other men walked back up the street and climbed back into their cars. The drivers of the last two cars placed portable revolving police lights on their roofs and pulled out into the street with sirens wailing.

Ducasse's heart was thumping as all four unmarked police cars drove off in a convoy. He began to laugh, and then tears flushed into his eyes and his knees started to buckle. He stepped to the side and leaned on one of the chairs.

Oh my God, it's over.

The prepaid cell phone in his hand rang, startling him. He stood up straight and put the phone to his ear.

"I need you to listen carefully and do exactly what I tell you to do," the voice said. It was Rudiger, or Conklin, or whatever bloody name the man was using today. "First check your cell phone for an email I sent you."

He pulled his phone from his coat pocket and looked at it.

"You see it?" Rudiger said. "It's from jrudiger@gmail.com."

Ducasse found it.

"It's a draft I forwarded to you. Do you see the list of people the final is addressed to? One is the guy who writes DealBook for the *New York Times*, another is one of the senior reporters for the *Wall Street Journal* and the last is the guy who writes the Lex column for the *Financial Times*. I knew all those guys in my former life, and still talk to them every couple of years. The email is only two pages long, concise for its sensational content. It also has about a ten-page attachment in a Word document. Don't let me stop you from reading, but it summarizes the complaint from the U.S. Attorney's Office, including the sworn affidavits of the witnesses. I have that email teed up in my iPhone right now, and all I need to do in order to destroy you completely is hit 'Send.' You want me to do that?"

"Don't be absurd. What do you want?"

"I want you to get your father and go downstairs immediately and get into the black SUV you'll see out front with the door open. Do it now. Don't think, don't stop, don't do anything else. I'm watching you through my eyes and ears on the street and if you try anything, I'm going to hit send. Go, now." The line cut off.

Ducasse ran from his office, his heart pounding again, retrieved Father and then rushed downstairs. He found the SUV with the door open. A man in a suit and tie ushered Father and him in, and then sat down by the left side door. Another man in a suit and tie was in the front passenger seat. The SUV drove off. The man next to him said, "Gentlemen, your cell phones please." Ducasse took Father's from him, pulled his from his pocket and handed them both to the man, who opened the backs and removed the batteries, then put them in his pocket. Ducasse realized he was still clutching the prepaid cell phone.

The man said, "You can keep that one if you want."

He saw another black SUV start to pull out from the curb, causing their driver to swerve around it, barely missing it, and then he heard the crunch of fenders behind him, spun his head and saw that another black SUV had crashed with the one they'd almost hit. He heard horns honking from the inevitable pileup of cars behind the crash. The driver of their SUV sped down the street, waited for a moment at a red light, then pulled out and ran it straight through the intersection, cars screeching to a halt, some swerving around them. Now he heard police sirens behind him. His hopes rose, thinking maybe the police would rescue Father and him.

The man next to him said, "Nothing to be alarmed about. Please continue to look straight ahead."

The SUV proceeded out of Old Town across the Pont du Mont-Blanc and on for a few more blocks, turned onto Rue de Lausanne, then entered the parking garage across the street from the Warwick Hotel. It drove all the way to the back of the garage and stopped next to a van marked with the name Dunkel Laundry Service Company.

The man next to him said, "Gentlemen, if you'll come with us, please." The man got out of the SUV, as did the other man in the front seat, and they ushered Father and him into the back of the van and closed the doors. He heard the SUV drive away. Two other men were inside the van wearing tan coveralls and caps with the name of the laundry on them. They put identical coveralls on Father, then him. The men put caps on their heads as well.

One of the men in coveralls seated them on the floor of the van. "Don't yell, don't make a scene or you'll regret it. Remember that "Send" button on Mr. Rudiger's cell phone," the man said directly to him. Ducasse's mind started racing, his knees feeling weak again. He looked at Father, who seemed resigned and calm.

The van started moving and a moment later he heard sounds of the city as it pulled out into the street.

Ducasse felt his heart sink.

——

Rudiger and Katie were seated on the sofa in the suite they'd rented at the Hotel du Rhone. He'd just finished explaining to Katie the arrangements he made with Michel, their StudioCanal producer in France, for his actors to perform the little charade on the street in front of Ducasse's building. And with Krause's PI firm for the snatch of Ducasse and his father.

"You could have told me," Katie said.

"I didn't want you to worry, thought it might throw you off," Rudiger said. He heard a knock on the door.

"That's them." Rudiger's pulse quickened.

He got up and opened the door. Four men in tan coveralls and hats walked in. The PI's men stripped the coveralls and hats from Ducasse and his father. They threw the coveralls and hats on a chair, then left the suite.

"Sit down," Rudiger said and pointed to chairs across the coffee table from where Katie sat. He scrutinized Ducasse; he had the look of a frightened animal, ready to attack out of panic. Rudiger sat down next to Katie and held up his iPhone. He said to Ducasse, "Remember, all I need to do is hit 'Send.' So keep yourself under control."

Ducasse's father reared back and said, "This is an outrage. Do you honestly think you can—"

"You should be quiet, old man," Rudiger said.

Ducasse said, "Yes, Father. Be quiet."

His father muttered something under his breath and then held his tongue.

Ducasse said, "What do you want?"

Rudiger stared him in the eye. "We'll do the talking."

Katie leaned forward and said, "Our original game plan was simply to get the $30 million, plus expenses, that you bilked me out of with your scam. Then things got a little more complicated. We ran into our old friend, Charlie Holden."

Rudiger said, "Rather, he ran into us."

Katie said, "But here we are again, and we were on the verge of bringing you down in exchange for getting ourselves off the hook. But it seems like Holden double-crossed us."

Ducasse said, "Call it what you want, but I have a deal with Holden, and nothing is going to happen to me, regardless of the little play your people performed on the street in front of my building today. You'll never get out of Switzerland without being apprehended. Then you're going back to the United States, and to jail."

Rudiger sat up straight. *This is it.* "Now shut up and listen. As Katie said earlier, we want our $30 million back. And like I said on the phone to you yesterday, round it up to $35 million. That's $3 million for our advisor in Morocco and $2 million for expenses."

Ducasse said, "I don't leave that kind of money lying around."

"Yes you do, and you're gonna get on the phone and call your banker and tell him to wire it to our bank." Rudiger pulled a slip of paper from his pocket and pushed it across the coffee table to Ducasse. "These are the wire instructions." Then he pulled another prepaid cell phone from his pocket and slid it over, too. "Make the call, now."

Ducasse didn't move, just glared at Rudiger.

"Okay, let's just explore this for a minute, shall we? Even if we get caught before we get out of Switzerland, I push this button and the entire story of what you characters have been doing for the last ten years goes to the *New York Times,* the *Wall Street Journal* and the *Financial Times.* Once that story breaks, even your Swiss authorities will have no alternative but to act. But even if they don't immediately, your business will be destroyed by scandal and your investors will scream for an investigation and for their money back. Eventually you'll get arrested, prosecuted and convicted." He turned to Ducasse's father. "You, old man, will die in jail, disgraced." He turned back to Ducasse. "And you, Mr. Fancy Pants, will spend the next 25 years in a Swiss jail sleeping in the same bunk with some 250-pound tattooed con who's gonna make you his bitch. And if you ever get out of the Swiss jail, you're gonna get extradited back to the U.S. and the same thing's gonna happen to you in a U.S. jail. Only the U.S. con who makes you his bitch is gonna pass you around to his friends when he needs them to do him a favor." He picked up his iPhone off the coffee table and held it facing Ducasse, a finger of his other hand poised. He allowed his anger to flow as he narrowed his eyes and said, "Now, am I gonna push this button or are you gonna wire the money?"

Rudiger saw Ducasse swallow hard and look down at the wire instructions on the coffee table.

Ducasse said, "What's keeping you from sending the email after I wire the money?"

"All we ever wanted from the outset was the money back, plus expenses."

Ducasse and Rudiger stared at each other.

Ducasse's father said, "Oh, for God's sake, wire the money."

Ducasse reached down, picked up the paper, then grabbed the cell phone and dialed. He gave his banker the wire instructions.

Rudiger let out a sigh as gradually as he could, not wanting Ducasse to notice it.

Then he started thinking about the next step, wondering if the Geneva police really might have a major manhunt in progress. He forced the thought away, focused on the moment. When Ducasse put the phone down, Rudiger said, "Okay. Now we wait for my banker to call me saying the wire transfer's arrived."

They waited for an hour. Ducasse's father had to go to the bathroom twice and Katie escorted him each time, leaving Rudiger and Ducasse staring at each other.

On his father's second trip to the bathroom, Ducasse said through taut lips, "They'll catch you. You're the ones who are going to jail."

Rudiger looked at the circles of perspiration under the arms of Ducasse's suit jacket. He laughed in his face and said, "That's a lot of bravado coming from a little man who's sweated through his suit. Did you piss in your pants, too?"

Finally, Rudiger's iPhone rang. He picked up the call, turned and nodded at Katie.

He put his iPhone back in the breast pocket of his suit jacket and when he removed his hand, a gun was in it. He waited for the fear and shock to show in Ducasse's eyes and then with one motion fired a sedative dart into his chest, then his father's. Both men slumped in their chairs.

Rudiger said, "That ought to hold them for 12 to 18 hours." He pulled out a handkerchief and wiped his prints from the gun, left it on the coffee table.

Katie and he walked into the bedroom. Rudiger pulled their contact lens cases from his pocket and put them on the bureau beneath the mirror. Katie removed her wig and put in her brown contacts. She helped Rudiger put on his blond wig, then he glued on his mustache and put in his blue contacts. They walked back into the living room of the suite and put on the coveralls and hats. As they left the room, Rudiger hung a DO NOT DISTURB card on the door handle. He said, "That should keep housekeeping away in the morning, so nobody should find them until after checkout time when somebody goes in to clean up."

When the elevator got downstairs, they stepped out and walked through the service entrance to where the laundry van was waiting. They climbed in back and the van drove them to the airport.

Rudiger exhaled, felt his tension start to bleed off. *Almost there.*

———

An hour later Charlie Holden clutched the phone in his office, getting an earful from Attorney General Martin.

"How the hell could they sneak out a second time?"

"The Geneva police picked up a French couple who matched Conklin's and Dolan's descriptions right outside Ducasse's office. We're sure they were plants to draw off the police, but they can't prove anything. It took a half hour at the station to figure out they had the wrong people. By then, we figure Conklin and Dolan were long gone. They still can't find Ducasse and his father."

"Great, just great," Martin said.

Holden already had a world-class headache gripping his temples. He decided he wasn't gonna subject himself to any more of this. He said, "I'll call you when I know anything more," and hung up. *What a mess.*

―――

Ducasse awakened before Father, his mouth tasting sour and his chest burning. He looked through the window to see midmorning sun on the hills of Old Town. *What happened?*

Then he remembered.

He looked down and saw the dart protruding from his chest. He pulled it out, then tried to stand to check on Father. He fell to the floor. After another five minutes he raised himself to his feet, using the chair to steady himself. He walked to Father, shook his shoulder, and he stirred.

"What happened?" Father said.

"Rudiger shot us with some form of tranquilizer dart."

"How long have we been out?"

"I'm not sure," Ducasse said, "but it appears a long time. It's now morning."

Father blinked and looked around the room.

"I'm going to phone the police," Ducasse said.

"That's not a good idea. Start with this U.S. Attorney in New York, Holden. He can explain everything to our Swiss police."

Why is Father so obtuse sometimes? "He already has. He set everything up with our police. They were part of the whole plan. Now that it's gone wrong, wouldn't you rather deal with our own people than the Americans?"

Father turned to him and said, "Don't be a fool. You told me yourself the deal was immunity for us in exchange for bringing in the man and the woman. And they obviously escaped."

Ducasse scowled. "They'll never get out of Switzerland."

"My, but you're certain of yourself for a man who's been masterfully outwitted and conned out of $35 million."

"They'll never see any of that money. How long do you think it will take to trace that wire transfer?"

Father sat up straight. "Do you honestly believe they haven't closed that bank account and shuttled the money to a half dozen other accounts around the world by now?" Now Father laughed in his face. "Haven't I taught you anything, you *neophyte*?"

"Oh please, old man," Ducasse said and looked around for the phone, found one on the bureau.

When he walked to it Father shouted, "Don't!"

Ducasse ignored him and dialed.

Father just glared at him, then out the window for the ten minutes it took the police to arrive. When they did they treated Father and him more like prisoners than victims, saying little and putting them in the backseat of separate squad cars. They drove straight to the Ducasses' offices. The place was abuzz with police activity, a half dozen squad cars outside, a group of reporters and camera crews standing in front of the building and a crowd of pedestrians milling around, watching.

"What's going on?" Ducasse said, raising his voice, mustering as much bravado as he could.

"Inside," was all that the patrolman said, then ushered Father and him past the throng of reporters that now encircled them shouting questions. "What do you have to say about the Ponzi scheme accusations?" "How much did you take?" "Do you know who the witness is who stepped forward?"

Ducasse pushed through the front door, feeling his heart slamming in his chest, his legs weak. Inside the vestibule, a tall man in a topcoat stood and said, "Philippe Ducasse, I am Captain Wilhelm Dolder of the Geneva police. We are freezing the bank accounts of Banque d'affaires Ducasse, yourself and your father immediately, and commencing an investigation of your books on suspicion of running a Ponzi scheme with your private equity funds. We have a confidential informant who is prepared to testify against you. I am hereby placing you in custody on suspicion of securities fraud."

Ducasse felt his stomach churning, then ran to the corner and vomited.

———

Rudiger and Katie had taken a private charter jet to Madrid, where they spent the night. They slept in the next morning and ordered a light breakfast from room service.

After breakfast Rudiger said, "I was gonna suggest we stay here a few days, relax and take in the city, but I miss Styles."

"Me, too, and even though he's comfortable with Flora, I'd hate to have him think we've abandoned him."

They changed IDs and planes and flew into Cape Verde. They arrived at the ClubHotel Riu Karamboa around midafternoon.

Katie's heart melted when they returned to their room and were reunited with an excited Styles. "Hello, little man," she said as he rolled onto his back for her to rub his belly. They ordered a rib eye steak from room service and took turns cutting pieces and feeding it to him. Later they took a run on the beach with Styles, Rudiger carrying the ball launcher and throwing balls ahead for him.

When they got back to the hotel, Rudiger showered while Katie dyed her hair back to her natural color. When she got out of the shower and walked onto the balcony, she smelled the aroma of Earl Grey tea and felt warm inside. Rudiger had a pot on the table.

Styles was curled up next to Rudiger's chair. She crouched down and stroked his head. "A big meal, a run and now it's time for a nap, eh?" When she stood up she noticed the business section of the *New York Times*, a section of the *Wall Street Journal* and the Lex column of the *Financial Times* open on the table.

"What's all this?"

"Our man Ducasse in the news."

"What?"

"The Swiss police have frozen the bank accounts of Banque d'affaires Ducasse, Ducasse and his father, and stepped in to supervise the operations and investigate the books. A witness tipped them off to a suspected Ponzi scheme Ducasse and his father were running."

Katie laughed, feeling it all the way down to her stomach. She sat down and said, "I hope he gets my package before they throw him in jail."

"Package?"

"From the hotel in Geneva I sent him back the *My Fair Lady* dress he gave me with a note that said, 'Thanks, but no thanks.' I thought I looked like Mary Poppins in the thing anyhow." Katie smiled, then felt a burst of anxiety. "Oh no."

"What's wrong?"

"So Bemelman went to the police? What's going to happen to him?"

Rudiger said, "I talked to him about it a few days ago, when I sent him Holden's final complaint against Ducasse. He told me he'd already decided that if the U.S. Attorney's Office didn't pursue a case against Ducasse, that he was going to the Geneva police with the affidavit he signed for us and Holden's complaint, and tell them everything he knew in order to wreck Ducasse. His lawyer told him that he stood a good chance of getting off with only probation and some community service work. He was ready to retire in another two years anyhow, and even if his bank fired him it wouldn't be able to take his pension from him."

Katie sighed, relieved. "Good for him."

Rudiger said, "And you'll love this." He grabbed the business section of the *New York Times*, open to DealBook, and handed it to Katie. "The *Times* reporter talked to Holden, who went into some spiel saying he was shocked by the allegations against the Ducasses. He said that if sufficient evidence supported the allegations, and if the Swiss authorities didn't do anything, the U.S. Attorney's Office would vigorously pursue the Ducasses' extradition and prosecution in the U.S. Holden pledged that if the Ducasses were convicted in Switzerland, he'd go after them when they were released from jail."

Katie laughed again. She said, "Charlie, grandstanding again. I almost feel bad about him being able to crow about a potential bust."

Over tea Rudiger said, "So what's next? Where do we go?"

"I remember our talk about going home to the States."

Rudiger gave her a sad smile. "It was nice to dream about it."

Katie smiled back. "Yes, it was. When I saw that immunity letter I was sure we could pull it off." She paused, reached over to squeeze his hand. "Almost."

"But our old friend Charlie Holden double-crossed us."

Katie nodded.

"Or tried to . . ." As Rudiger's voice trailed off, his gaze left hers and drifted out to the horizon.

After a moment Katie squeezed his hand again and said, "What?"

He didn't respond.

"Rudiger?"

He still didn't respond.

The wheels were turning. She felt a glow inside, knew there was still hope. When would she learn never to underestimate this man?

ABOUT THE AUTHOR

David Lender is a former investment banker who spent 25 years on Wall Street. After earning his MBA at Northwestern University's Kellogg School of Management, he went on to work in mergers and acquisitions for Merrill Lynch, Rothschild and Bank of America. His first three novels—*Trojan Horse, The Gravy Train* and *Bull Street*—turned him into an e-book sensation. He lives in northern New Jersey with his family and a pitbull named Styles. More background on David and his writing can be found at www.davidlender.net.